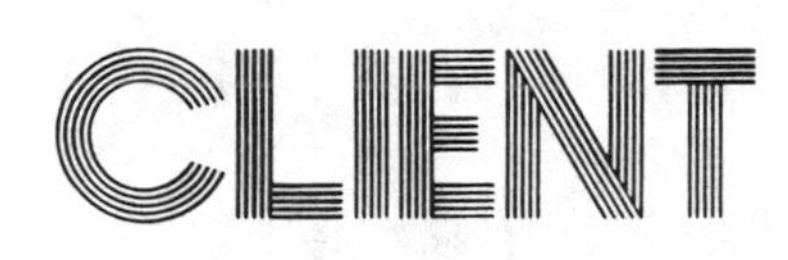
CLIENT

ALSO BY PARNELL HALL

DETECTIVE
MURDER
FAVOR
STRANGLER

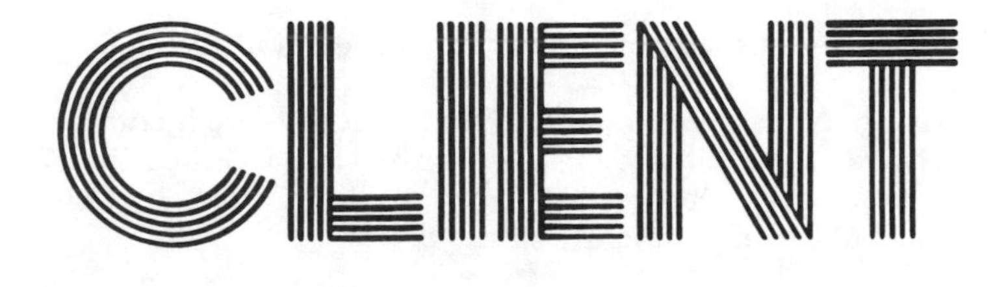

A NOVEL

BY

PARNELL HALL

DONALD I. FINE INC.

NEW YORK

Library of Congress Cataloging-in-Publication Data
Hall, Parnell.
Client / by Parnell Hall.
p. cm.
ISBN 1-55611-169-X (alk. paper)
I. Title.
PS3558.A37327C6 1990
813'.54—dc20 89-46025
CIP

Manufactured in the United States of America
10 9 8 7 6 5 4 3 2 1

Designed by Irving Perkins Associates

This novel is a work of fiction. Names, characters, places and incidents are either the product of the author's imagination or are used fictitiously. Any resemblance to actual events, locales, organizations or persons, living or dead, is entirely coincidental and beyond the intent of either the author or publisher.

For Jim and Franny

1

I have bad teeth.

I guess I was fated to have bad teeth. See, I'm on the far side of forty, which means I grew up before the age of enlightenment. When I was a boy, people didn't know what they know now. Even the high school coaches, people whose job it supposedly was to tune and mold our fine young bodies, knew no better. The basketball coach gave us gum to chew during the game, and soda pop after. And this was in the days before Trident and Diet Pepsi—the effect was like soaking our teeth in a concentrated solution of sugar-water.

Things weren't any better in terms of prevention. As I've said, public awareness was limited at best. Fluoride had arrived, but was still perceived by many to be a communist plot to pollute our water system. As a result, Crest toothpaste was fighting an uphill battle to convince the public that it was, indeed, "an effective decay-preventive dentifrice that can be of significant value when used in a conscientiously applied program of oral hygiene and regular professional care." That was a bit of a mouthful for anyone, with or without good teeth, and not everyone was buying it. Crest did better after they shortened the slogan to, "Look Ma, no cavities!" God how I hated that exuberant, smiling eight-year-old kid who grinned his pearly whites at me on the one snowy channel our secondhand black and white TV could pick up in those days. No cavities. I remember when I was twelve years old going to the dentist, and, "Look Ma, eighteen cavities."

Eighteen.

It took four visits to fix 'em all. And the fourth, wouldn't you know it, was my two front teeth, which miraculously, had never been affected before. So all my previous fillings had been silver, and I had four anxious weeks to fantasize what my impending sex life would be like with ugly metallic fillings forever messing up my endearing smile. Which didn't happen, of course. My front teeth were filled with porcelain, or something white, which didn't look all that bad, and though I was an awkward, confused, nervous adolescent and my sex life was no great shakes anyway, I didn't have my dentist to blame for it.

My dental problems continued into my twenties. I never had eighteen cavities again, but I sure had a good, steady string of 'em. I also gained wisdom teeth, if not wisdom, and the subsequent painful extractions, including one from a Spartan sadist who didn't believe in Novocaine. "Take aspirin," he counseled me, when I gurgled the word "codeine" through bloodied mouth after twenty minutes of cutting and slicing to retrieve broken off roots. I took, as I recall, the better part of a fifth of scotch, and never went to him again.

By the time I hit my thirties, all of my teeth that had not been extracted had been so extensively drilled and filled that it seemed to me if I got any more cavities, there wouldn't be anything left to hold the teeth together.

There wasn't.

It was in my thirties that I first became introduced to crowns. "Gonna need a crown," my dentist said, nodding his head judiciously, and quickly dispelled any thoughts of impending royalty by explaining what he meant was that there wasn't enough tooth left to hold a filling, and he had to file the sucker way down and put a cap over it. The cap was an artificial tooth. It was made of metal, sometimes with porcelain on top, in case it was near enough the front of the mouth to show. It didn't taste all that great, but what the hell, it was better than going straight to dentures, and as I reached the end of my thirties and one cap followed another, I came to the happy realization that soon all of my teeth would be metal, and there would be nothing left to go wrong.

Naive me.

Welcome to the wonderful world of periodontics.

A sudden excruciating ache in one of my long-since capped molars sent me rushing to my dentist, who immediately diagnosed an incredible abscess. Teeth, I learned, even capped teeth, have roots. And these roots, if not properly nurtured, can decay, erode, suffer bone loss, abscess, and seriously endanger the future of an otherwise perfectly fine capped tooth.

Needless to say, the abscess was but a symptom of the problem. All of my teeth were in this precarious position. What I needed, the periodontist told me, with what I thought was ill-disguised glee, was immediate and total oral surgery. Of course, there was no coercion used to impel me to do this. There was an alternative. The alternative was to do nothing and let all my teeth fall out.

I opted for the surgery. In doing so, I learned the reason for the periodontist's glee. The charge for the surgery was thirty-two hundred dollars.

This posed a bit of a problem. I am not particularly wealthy. In fact, I am not even solvent. I have a wife and kid to feed. And I live in New York City, where things are not particularly cheap.

And I'm self-employed. Stanley Hastings, Private Investigator. Don't take that the wrong way. I don't carry a gun or have car chases, or do any of that other stuff that immediately springs to mind when someone mentions P.I. But setting that aside, the fact is I'm self-employed. Which means I have to carry my own health insurance. And it's minimal. And dental isn't on it.

My thirty-two hundred dollar gum surgery required a bank loan. I'm paying my mouth off on time. And if that weren't bad enough, it turns out the surgery is just the first step. Then there's the maintenance. In order to keep my teeth from falling out, I have to go to the periodontist's every three months to have my gums retreaded at eighty-five bucks a whack by one of the bevy of attractive young hygienists kept for that purpose. I suppose I shouldn't complain. I'm sure in New York City there are places where I'd have to pay much more than eighty-five bucks to have a pretty girl hurt me.

Be that as it may, no matter what I do, the debt just seems to keep getting bigger and bigger, and my chances of ever paying it off smaller and smaller.

Which is why I didn't throw Marvin Nickleson out of my office.

2

"I have a problem."

Music to the ears of a private detective. But then, I'm not your average private detective. In fact, I'm hardly a private detective at all. I chase ambulances for the law firm of Rosenberg and Stone. All that entails doing is interviewing the accident victims who call in response to Richard Rosenberg's TV ads, signing them to retainers, and then photographing the scenes of their accidents.

But I wasn't ready to lay all that on Marvin Nickleson just yet. I contented myself with a noncommittal, "Oh?"

We were sitting in my office on West 47th Street. It was ten o'clock on a Monday morning. I'd stopped by my office to pick up my mail and check my answering machine before heading out on my morning rounds. I got out of the elevator and there he was, standing in front of my door. All five foot four of him. That's an approximation, by the way, and like most of my observations, probably inaccurate. Suffice it to say, he struck me as short. He was a slight little man with curly red hair, and a thin, stringy, red moustache. He wore round, steel-rimmed glasses. He was dressed in a suit and tie, as I was, but as mine was thrown together catch as catch can from an ever-thinning wardrobe, his was tailor-made and right fine.

I was surprised to see him waiting there. I was more surprised to find out he was waiting for me. I unlocked the door, let him in, and uncluttered a chair for him, since my office is not set up to receive clients, since I have none.

And there we sat. As far as I was concerned, my "Oh?" was as much of a contribution to the conversation as I was required to make. As I said, I'm not used to receiving clients, and if this man was gonna act like one, he was gonna have to carry the ball.

He did.

"It's my wife," he said.

I sighed. It appeared more was expected of me after all. After a moment's hesitation I ventured, "Yes?"

Apparently that was the right thing to say, because he immediately nodded in agreement. "Yes," he said. "And you're a private detective, right?"

I hesitated. There were so many ways to answer that question. See, I don't consider myself a *real* private detective. But I didn't feel like launching into a lengthy explanation. "Yes," I said.

Once more I'd made the correct response. He nodded his head up and down again. "That's why I'm here. I need to hire a private detective."

I figured I'd give it one more shot. "Why?"

I'd hit the right button. He nodded once, held up his hand and said, "All right. Here's the picture. My wife and I are separated. Not divorced. Just separated. Maybe it's my fault, maybe it's hers, I don't want to go into that, it's not important, the fact is we're separated."

He stopped, tugged at his moustache. "And I don't like it. I don't like being separated. I want my wife back. You know what I mean?"

I knew what he meant. I just didn't know what I was supposed to do about it. And the way things were going, I wasn't sure if he was going to tell me.

Monosyllables had been doing O.K. for me. I decided to be daring and go for two. "Why me?"

He jerked his thumb. "I work right down the street. I've had business in this building before. I've seen your name on the directory. Stanley Hastings, Private Detective. I never hired a private detective before, so I didn't know what to do. Then I remembered your sign."

I sighed. My sign. That rang a big bell. It was my sign that had lured my first potential client into my office. I'd turned him down. Subsequently, he'd lost his life and his genitalia. In what order, I couldn't tell you. Still, it was not a pleasant memory.

I decided to give up the hard-boiled, taciturn approach. "All right," I said. "What do you want?"

"I told you. I want my wife back." He tugged at his moustache again. "But that's not what you mean, is it? You mean, what do I want you to do. Well, you gotta forgive me. I've just never done this before. I told you, my wife and I are separated. I'm looking for a reconciliation. She isn't. She hangs up on me. She won't return my calls. She's gone back to using her maiden name.

"And . . ." He paused and tugged at his moustache again. I began to wonder if it was so scraggly because he'd gradually tugged out all the hairs. He looked down at the floor and then looked up. "I think she's seeing someone. And it kills me, and I want it stopped."

I shifted restlessly in my chair, an action he interpreted correctly. "No, no," he said. "I don't expect you to stop it. That's something I've got to do. I just want you to find out."

I figured I'd had enough, but I figured I ought to let him finish his pitch. "What, specifically, is it you want?"

"All right," he said. "Here's the dope. My wife's name is Monica. She's gone back to her maiden name, which is Dorlander. She lives in an apartment at 413 East 83rd Street. It's my apartment, I mean, my name's on the lease, but now you'll see Dorlander on the bell. When we separated, I was the one who moved out." He smiled, ironically. "Of course.

"Anyway, my wife's a lot younger than I am. She's twenty-seven. She works for Artiflex Cosmetics Company on Third Avenue. She's an executive there. One of those high-voltage, high-powered types. She makes close to sixty thousand a year. That's also part of the problem. I only make forty."

I said nothing. And for good reason. Working for Rosenberg and Stone, I make ten bucks an hour and thirty cents a mile. If I got forty hours a week, I'd be making twenty thousand a year, but the work isn't steady, and I average twenty to thirty hours, tops.

"All right," he said. "That's the picture. I think she's seeing someone. Maybe someone from the office, but maybe not. She may be seeing him during the day, she may be seeing him at night, I don't know. The thing is, as an executive, she has long lunch breaks and can more or less plan her afternoon hours.

"So here's the pitch. I don't think she's fooling around in the morning. If she is, well, she's too smart for me on the one hand, and too screwed up on the other, there's nothing I can do about it.

"But from lunchtime on . . ." Here he gave his moustache a final furious tug and looked me in the eye. "I want you to stake out her office, starting at one o'clock. Pick her up when she leaves for lunch and see where she goes. If she's seeing somebody from the office, you may strike paydirt in the afternoon. If not, you pick her up when she leaves work, tail her home, or wherever she goes. If she's home and there's nothing stirring by nine o'clock, you wipe it out, that's your eight-hour shift. If there's something shaking, you're into overtime.

"Now, as I told you, all I want you to do is identify the bum. I'll take care of him. But if they go to a motel, I want the whole schmear. License plate number, and the name they registered under. And whether they gave the right plate number on the register. If you can, a copy of the motel registration.

"I also want pictures."

I looked at him. "I thought you wanted a reconciliation, not a divorce."

"I do. I do. But I'm not going to get anywhere until I know who I'm dealing with. And I'm never going to get anywhere with her until I've got some hard evidence to confront her with. She'll just lie her way out of it. She's good at it, believe me. When you see her, you'll know.

"So, that's all I'm asking for. I want the evidence, and I want the pix. I'll take it from there."

"But you don't know for sure she's seeing anyone."

"That's true."

"And even if she is, this could take weeks."

"Right."

"And there's no guarantees."

"Of course. So what do you say?"

That was the point where I should have thrown Marvin Nickleson out of my office. Actually, that's an exaggeration. In fact, for me it's practically hyperbole. I am not a violent person by nature, and I would never actually throw anybody out of my office, even if I were physically capable of doing it. Show him the door would probably be a little more accurate.

And that's what I sincerely longed to do. Marvin Nickleson's case was straight out of a 40's grade B movie. It made me feel slimy just thinking about it. The whole thing reeked of sleaze.

But I have bad teeth.

And life is strange, and beggars can't be choosers, and sometimes you have to do things you don't really want to do. Which is why, in my mind, I'd already agreed to the employment.

I didn't jump at it, however. I hedged.

"Say I do this," I said. "There's just one thing."

"What's that?"

"I can't start today. I'd have to start tomorrow."

He frowned. "Why?"

"I have other cases pending. I have to clear the decks."

Which was true. If I took this case, I was gonna have to fit it in around my duties to Rosenberg and Stone, which wasn't going to be easy. I must say I had severe reservations.

So did Marvin Nickleson. That didn't suit his plans at all.

"I'd prefer you to start today," he said.

"I understand. I just can't do it."

He frowned and shook his head. "It has to be today," he said, and stood up.

I hated to see my potential client going south, but I stood my ground. "I'm sorry, but I can't do it," I said. "Perhaps you can find another detective who can."

I'd struck the right chord. He frowned, thought that over. By the time he hunted up another private detective and went through the same spiel, it would be too late to do anything today anyway.

He took a breath, blew it out again, and sat back down. "All right," he said. "Tomorrow."

"Fine," I said. "Now let's get some of the details cleared out of the way."

"Like what?"

"Well, for starters, how will I spot the young lady in question?"

He frowned. "Of course. How stupid of me. I told you, I'm new at this game." He reached into his jacket pocket. "I forgot to give you the snapshot. Here it is."

He pulled it out and laid it on the desk.

I picked it up and looked at it, and my estimation of Marvin Nickleson shot up considerably.

It was a closeup of Monica Dorlander Nickleson's face. It was only a Polaroid, but blown up it could have passed for a portfolio picture. Marvin Nickleson's estranged wife was gorgeous. Jet black hair pulled straight back from a lean yet soft-featured face. High arched eyebrows, gently rounded nose, lips full yet not too full. A face carefully made up to show not a trace of makeup. The type of face you'd expect to see on the cover of a fashion magazine.

I wasn't sure how a real private detective would react. Whistle? Say, "That's some dame." I mean, this was the husband after all, and the estranged one at that. Under the circumstances, any comment could seem unfeeling and crass.

I merely nodded and said, "This will do fine."

Apparently he'd expected comment. He cocked his head and said, "You can see why I want her back."

"That I can. O.K., that takes care of spotting her coming out of her office building. Now, your apartment house. What kind of building is it and how do I get in?"

"You don't."

"Oh?"

He shook his head. "You couldn't get in anyway. It's a modern high-rise. Security is tight. All visitors are stopped in the lobby. So you don't go in. You stake it out outside."

"Then how can I tell who's calling on her?"

"You can't. But it doesn't matter."

"Oh?"

"Yeah. See, I don't have to worry about that. The security works both ways. If she's seeing someone, she won't have him come to her apartment. Cause they'd stop the guy in the lobby before they'd let him up. I wouldn't need to hire a private detective. I could prove she was seeing someone just by slapping a subpoena on the doorman."

I nodded. "I can see you've thought this over."

"Hey. It's my wife. So you don't worry about who comes to see her there. You just stake out the building to see where she goes."

"Yeah. All right. What about your address. Phone number. Where do I reach you?"

He frowned. "That's a problem."

"Oh?"

"Yeah. I'm staying in a rented room in Riverdale."

"What's the number?"

"That's just it. There's no phone."

"Can I call you at work?"

He looked horrified. "God, no. This is my wife we're talking about. We've been married four years. Most of the guys at work know her. Some of them are closer to her than they are me, you get the picture?"

"Yeah. Where's work?"

He looked at me. "You won't go there?"

"No. I won't got there."

"You could really fuck me up, you know. You come to my office, the fat's in the fire, you know what I mean?"

"Hey," I said. "You hire me, I'm on your side. I just want to know who I'm dealing with."

He looked at me a moment. His moustache twitched. "Of course," he said. "Work is Croft, Wheelhouse and Green. Sixth Avenue and 56th Street. It's an ad agency. I do layouts for 'em."

"Layouts?"

"Sketches for ad copy, or storyboards for TV commercials."

That rang a bell. Back in my youth, shortly after the dawn of time, when I was butting my head against a stone wall trying to make it as an actor, on one of those rare occasions when I had actually managed to scare up an audition, it had turned out to be for a TV ad and I had had to read off a storyboard, which consisted of a series of drawings of little TV screens with what was supposed to appear on them, with the copy written underneath. Mine depicted a man and a wife with a fishing pole huddled on a riverbank in a driving rainstorm, expressing surprise and delight that the elusive fish that they had been trying to catch could be purchased fully cooked and ready to eat for under ten bucks at a chain of seafood restaurants. While, naturally, I didn't get the part, as far as I know the commercial never aired anyway. Sour grapes and small consolations.

So this was one of the guys who drew those things. I had a fleeting thought. If I solved this case for Marvin Nickleson, maybe he'd be grateful enough to get me some auditions.

Very fleeting.

"O.K.," I said. "So that's the place I don't go to. And I can't go see you and I can't call you. So how do we keep in touch?"

"Well," he said. "I'll have to call you."

"How? I'll be out on the road."

"I'll call you at night after you knock off."

I shook my head. "No good."

"Why not?"

"I only knock off at nine if nothing's happening. Otherwise, I'm still on the job."

"So? Then I'll get no answer."

"No, you'll get my wife. I don't want you calling my wife."

Marvin Nickleson nodded. Apparently, he understood about wives. "So I'll call you in the morning."

"I won't be here."

"Where will you be?"

Where I'd be would be out working for Rosenberg and Stone. But that was none of his damn business.

"I don't hang out here. I just come by to pick up my mail."

"Like today?"

"Yeah. Like today."

"O.K. I'll call you when you pick up your mail. This when you come by? Ten o'clock?"

I shook my head. "No. Earlier."

"When."

"Nine o'clock."

"O.K. I'll call you at nine o'clock."

I sighed. This was getting to be a real pain in the ass. "O.K.," I said. "I'll be here at nine o'clock. You call me then. If I haven't heard from you nine-fifteen, I'm gone."

"Fine. So whaddya say?"

I wanted to say no. It was fine for him. From my point of view, it sucked. If I took this draggy, distasteful job, I'd be committed to being in my office every morning at nine o'clock. Which some days would be fine, but some days would be a royal pain in the ass, seeing as how I would have to juggle all my duties to Rosenberg and Stone into my morning hours, unless I wanted the Marvin Nickleson case to dork me out of my steady employment.

Yeah, it was a drag, but then again what wasn't? And time, fate, my lack of ambition, my lack of acting and writing talent, my sign in the lobby downstairs, and my bad teeth, had all conspired against me, and in one cosmic vin-dit, as Kurt Vonnegut would say, had suddenly thrust me into making an irrevocable decision, which I was sure I would instantly regret, that of taking on my first real paying client.

So I sighed, took a breath, and said the words I'd secretly been longing to say for quite some time.

"All right. Two hundred bucks a day plus expenses."

3

I must say I had severe reservations.

Which happens to me a lot. I'm basically insecure, and I always have doubts, even in the best of circumstances. And these circumstances were far from the best. Once Marvin Nickleson had laid ten twenty dollar bills on the desk, given his moustache a final tug and nodded his way out the door, I had time to stop and think things over. Frankly, I didn't like what I thought. While Marvin Nickleson was there, I could talk to him and take his story at face value. Which was natural for me, cause I'm pretty gullible and I believe what people tell me.

But the minute he was gone, the whole thing seemed totally unreal. Come on, here's a poor fucking graphic artist who wants his wife back, so he hires a private detective at two hundred bucks a day to get the goods on her so he can affect a reconciliation? Could that possibly be true? Not likely. Not with the guy wanting pictures. No, pictures smacked of adding fuel to the fire in a particularly messy divorce.

But that wasn't my problem, was it? It wasn't up to me

if the Nickleson marriage survived or failed. I'd been hired to do a job, that was how I had to look at it. And if I did the job, if I did as the client requested, the result would be on his head, not mine. Wouldn't it?

I leaned back in my chair, closed my eyes, and rubbed my head. Christ, now that Marvin Nickleson was gone, the whole thing seemed totally unreal. As if it had never happened. As if I'd just imagined it.

I exhaled and opened my eyes. There on my desk was the stack of twenty dollar bills. That was real enough. I'd wanted it, I'd accepted it, and now I had to earn it.

Next to it lay the picture of Monica Dorlander. I picked it up and looked at it again. Bright, intelligent, ambitious. A lean and hungry look. This was the woman whose life I was going to destroy.

Stop it, I told myself. Asshole. You can't look at it that way.

A comic impulse seized me. I turned the picture upside down.

"Can I look at it this way?" I said aloud. My Groucho impression was poor, but then I'm a failed actor anyway.

That got me in a better mood. I turned the picture back rightside up. I fixed it with an eagle eye. Dorlander, your ass is mine. Think you're stepping out on Marvin Nickleson, you got another think coming. Not with Stanley Gumshoe Hastings on the job.

The sound of my beeper brought me back to reality.

Tomorrow. That was tomorrow. I still had today to get through.

I shut off the beeper and called Rosenberg and Stone.

Wendy/Janet, Richard Rosenberg's two-headed monster, answered the phone. Wendy and Janet were switchboard girls with identical voices, which made it impossible to ever know who you were dealing with. The only way to tell was by specifically asking, which, I had discovered, tended to piss them both off immensely. So I never did and I never knew.

"Agent 005," I said.

"Stanley," came the voice of Wendy/Janet. "I have a new case for you."

She gave it to me. A broken leg in Far Rockaway scheduled for four o'clock that afternoon. That was fine for today, since I'd stalled Marvin Nickleson, but wouldn't have done for tomorrow.

As if she read my mind, Wendy/Janet said, "And I have another sign-up for you for tomorrow."

"Then it better be in the morning. I'm tied up in the afternoon. I have to be back in Manhattan by one."

"Oh? No one told me."

"I just found out myself.

"Oh. Well, it's lucky. The appointment's for twelve."

"Where?"

"Coney Island."

I squeezed my eyes shut, then opened them again. "I can't do it."

"Why not?"

"I told you. I have to be back in Manhattan by one. I can't do a job way out in Coney Island at noon and be back in Manhattan by one."

"Well, you have to. The client has no phone."

"Then give it to someone else."

"No one's free. Rick's got a case in New Jersey, and Mike's got one in Queens."

"Don't either of *those* clients have phones?"

"Why?"

I took a breath and shook my head. Good lord, what was I doing? The Marvin Nickleson case had me so rattled I wasn't thinking straight. Why was I trying to argue with Wendy/Janet? I knew from experience that was futile. See, aside from their voices, the only other thing Wendy and Janet had in common was their intelligence. Or lack of it. If the two of them had a combined I.Q. of over one hundred I'd have missed my guess. And here I was trying to reason with one of them, which didn't say much for *my* intelligence.

"Never mind, I'll talk to Richard," I said, and hung up the phone.

I sighed. Yeah, like it or not, I was going to have to deal with Richard Rosenberg. Which, under the circumstances, shouldn't have been that bad. After all, I'd done him a real favor a few months back, during the Rosenberg and Stone murders. Besides helping him clear the matter up, I'd been instrumental in keeping the name Rosenberg and Stone out of the papers. Adverse publicity could have just about shut down Richard's business. As it was, Rosenberg and Stone was thriving. So by all rights, Richard should have been grateful.

But Richard is Richard. And while I grudgingly admit I admire Richard Rosenberg, I am well aware munificence is not one of his virtues. I hadn't gotten a bonus. I hadn't gotten a raise. I *had* gotten a word of thanks, which I'm sure Richard felt adequately repaid the debt, and I couldn't imagine his gratitude extending over a period of several months.

No, it wasn't going to be easy. Even though I wasn't asking for time off. Even though I wasn't turning down cases. Even though all I really wanted was the flexibility to plan my own schedule, I knew damn well what Richard's response would be.

Richard would chew me up and spit me out again.

He didn't.

Richard Rosenberg was in a blue funk.

It totally blew my mind. I'd never seen Richard depressed before. As far as I knew, the man only had one mood: hyperactive. He always reminded me of one of those miniature dogs that are so purebred and high-strung that they can't hold still and are always bouncing off the walls and yapping all over the place and nipping at your heels.

Not today.

Richard was slumped down in his desk chair when I walked in. Richard was a little guy, not much taller than Marvin Nickleson, actually, and he was slight of build, but one never really thought of him as small. Because Richard had a real showman's flair, and tended to dominate any group he was in.

But not today. Richard looked small and frustrated and unhappy.

"You wanted to see me?" Richard said. Even his high-pitched nasal bark seemed flat.

"Yeah. About my schedule."

Richard grimaced and waved me to a chair.

I sat.

Richard sighed. "You know," he said gloomily, "life's a funny thing. You're born. You live. You die. That's it."

Good lord. There was only one explanation. Richard had just been diagnosed with an incurable disease.

My mind was racing: Jesus Christ. So young. What was he? Not much more than thirty. What was it? Cancer? At his age? Or, Jesus, Richard was a bachelor and I knew nothing about his personal life and sexual preferences—could it be AIDS? Shit. The Nickleson case was off now. Tough luck, Marvin, but what can I do? I can't ask for time off from this man now. Shit. There goes my two hundred bucks a day. My chance to pay off my bleeding gums. Asshole. That's right, think of yourself. Poor Richard.

I wet my lips. "What's wrong?"

He looked up at me. "Wrong?"

"Yeah," I said. "What is it? Are you sick? Is something wrong?"

Richard drew himself up somewhat. "Sick? Why should I be sick?"

I blinked. Because if you're not sick I just wasted a lot of false sympathy and got upset for nothing, was the thought that sprang to mind.

So what the hell was wrong? It had to be business, though I didn't see how it could. I'd been pulling down my steady share of cases lately, and Richard at last count had two other investigators working and two more training, so how could business be bad?

It came in a flash. If Richard was getting the cases, business could only be bad if he was *losing* them.

The thought was staggering. Richard was so confident,

self-assured and aggressive, a Rosenberg loss was practically an oxymoron.

"So how's business?" I said. "You getting settlements?"

Richard snorted. "Settlements? I got nothing but settlements. I got settlements pouring in."

His eyes flicked momentarily as he recognized a dangerous subject—perhaps I was working up to asking for a raise.

"Not that we don't need it," he put in quickly. "My overhead is tremendous."

I nodded without enthusiasm. The ten bucks an hour and thirty cents a mile Richard paid me was top salary. His other investigators were making no more than that, and his trainees even less. And his office staff consisted of an underpaid Wendy/Janet, and an endless succession of college dropouts hired as paralegals at minimum wage. Though, I suppose to a man as tight as Richard Rosenberg that seemed like a tremendous overhead.

I wasn't any closer to finding out the reason for Richard's bad mood, and I realized Richard wasn't going to tell me. I pressed on to the business at hand.

"Well," I said, "the reason I came in here is I need to arrange my work hours."

"How so?"

"I need to shift my case load into the morning hours and free up the afternoons."

"Just tell the girls at the switchboard."

I blinked again. No explosion? No arguments? No protestations?

The phone rang.

Richard picked it up and said, "Yeah. . . . O.K., put him on." Then, "Rosenberg. . . . What case? . . . Felcher? I have a lot of cases, refresh my memory. . . . E-Z Wash Laundromat. Soapy water on floor, slip and fall, broken leg. Right. . . . Uh-huh. . . . I'll get back to you."

Richard hung up the phone and sighed.

"Insurance adjuster?" I said.

"Uh-huh."

"Giving you a hard time?"

"Giving me a settlement."

"Oh?"

"I'll have to offer it to the client. They'll take it, of course. Case closed." He shook his head. "And I'll have to recommend that they take it. It's the math, you see. It's not the most I could get—a jury would give me slightly more—but then there's the time, the court costs, the nuisance value. It's the percentages. I know them, the insurance adjusters know them. They're not lawyers, these guys. They're all mathematicians. It's all computerized. Just plug the numbers into a formula and out pops a figure. More standardized and routine every day."

Richard sighed and rubbed his forehead. "There's more to life than just money. You gotta remember that."

I stared. This coming from him. This to a ten buck an hour wage-slave.

"I have not been in court for three months." Richard stuck his finger in the air for emphasis. "Three months. The cases come in, the summonses go out, the offers come back and we settle."

Richard sighed and shook his head.

And the cause for his distress became clear. As a former actor, I recognized the syndrome. Richard the showman was out of work. Just like an actor, he was between jobs, a performer with no place to perform.

I would have liked to have been sympathetic, but quite frankly, I couldn't. Not considering my present situation. Not with money so tight I'd taken on the distasteful Marvin Nickleson case. Gee Richard, that's tough. Poor little rich boy. Nothing going for him but money. How sad.

But it did make *my* life easier. I left Richard sulking

and went out to lay his tacit approval of my work schedule on Wendy/Janet.

Which wasn't easy. First I had to sell them on the concept: me. In Manhattan. At one o'clock.

I had to conduct an impromptu math lesson on the formula, $D = rt$ (distance equals rate times time). It went something like this: a man is in Coney Island at 12:55. He must be in Manhattan by 1:00. So time equals five minutes. Manhattan is approximately twenty miles away, so distance equals twenty. If he had an hour to drive twenty miles, he could average twenty miles an hour to get there. But he only has five minutes. That's a twelfth of an hour. So the rate is twelve times twenty, or two hundred and forty miles per hour. Now at that rate, don't you think it's possible he might get a speeding ticket?

Out of the whole lesson, I doubt if Wendy and Janet got anything more than the sarcasm. If that. At best, they both wrote down that I was off work at one. How they would interpret that was anybody's guess. And Wendy, whom I take to be the more astute of the two, if such a term is applicable, did understand the concept of having one of the other investigators change one of his other appointments so that he could handle the Coney Island one.

I thanked them, picked up my car, which I'd left at a meter on 14th Street, and drove out to Far Rockaway.

Driving out there, I played the game I always play when I do sign-ups: how bad is it going to be? You see, a lot of Richard's clients aren't particularly affluent, and some of the neighborhoods they live in are pretty bad. And when I go walking into one of those neighborhoods in my suit and tie, people tend to think I'm a cop. Or a suicidal lunatic. I have a horror of walking into a crack den, which I sometimes do, and being shot for a cop, or mugged for an easy mark, which hasn't happened yet, knock on wood. But cowards die many deaths, and I've imagined the scenario many times. And on the way to an assignment I always speculate and fantasize and try to recall what I know, and generally drive myself nuts.

The client's name was Paul Jeffries. Now that's a neutral name, could be white or black. The address was Beach Channel Drive, that was the main drag, running all the way down the island. There were good and bad sections, like anywhere. I hadn't been to Far Rockaway much, it being way the hell out there, so I really didn't know.

The apartment number was a clue: 12-H. So it wasn't a slum. It was either a high-rise apartment building or a low-income housing project.

Experience prompted the fervent wish: please don't let it be a project.

It was, but not that bad. No lock on the outside door, but at least the glass hadn't been smashed. Both the odd and even floor elevators seemed to be working. The odd came first so I took it, even though I was going to 12, prompted by long experience—in a project, if an elevator shows up, you get in.

I took it up to 13, walked down a flight and found 12-H. The door was opened by a woman with white hair, cold, crisp, efficient and severe, in the starchy white of the medical profession.

"Yes?" she demanded.

"Paul Jeffries?" I said.

"Who are you?"

"Mr. Hastings from the lawyer's office."

"Which office?"

"Rosenberg and Stone."

She nodded grudgingly. "Yes. That's who he called. All right. Come in."

I did. She closed and locked the door behind me, then

turned to lecture me as if I were a truant schoolboy.

"All right. You can see him. But make it short and try not to tire him."

"What's he got?"

"Cancer."

"Of what?"

"Lungs, liver, colon, stomach. Just about everything."

"Is he conscious?"

"Yes. But he's very weak. Don't tire him."

"He'll have to sign some forms."

She threw up her hands. "Yes, yes, it's so important, isn't it?" she snapped. "Just try not to kill him."

I took a breath. Yeah, some cases are easier than others. I nodded assent.

She gave me a disapproving look, then led me to the bedroom. One last steely-eyed glare, and she stepped aside and let me in.

Paul Jeffries lay flat on his back in the bed. A white sheet was drawn up over him. Thin, stringy arms lay down his sides, pinning the sheet to his chest. He was a white man, tall, ancient, horribly emaciated. A thin hawk nose pointed to the sky. His mouth was opened in a perpetual *O.* His eyes were opened too, and his brow was furrowed, as if fiercely concentrating on something. If so, it was probably on breathing, which apparently was a Herculean task.

Sometimes I hate my job. Actually, often I hate my job, but sometimes more than others.

I moved up close to the bed. "Mr. Jeffries?"

The head didn't turn, but the eyes flicked momentarily in my direction. The lips moved with some effort, formed the word, "Yes."

"I'm Mr. Hastings from the lawyer's office. You called us about your accident. I don't want to tire you, but can you tell me what happened to you?"

One finger of the emaciated hand raised to point. Lips moved, and I leaned close to catch the words.

"Broke leg."

"Where?"

"City bus."

"You fell on a city bus. Fine. Was that getting on, getting off, or on the bus itself?"

"On. Bus moved . . . before sat down."

"Where?"

"Here. Bus stop. Outside."

"I see," I said. "You got on a bus outside here at the bus stop. The driver moved before you could sit down. You fell and broke your leg. Did an ambulance come and take you to the hospital?"

"Yes."

Better than I could have hoped. I could get the rest of the information from the hospital and the nurse. I had the guy's name and address. Just a bit more personal data, and I'd have the guy sign the retainers—probably have to guide his hand—and I'd be done.

"How old are you?" I asked.

"Ninety-five."

"Married or single?"

"Widower."

"Any children?"

"Dead."

"Grandchildren?"

"No."

"Brothers, sisters, relatives?"

"No."

"Who's your next of kin."

"No one."

"How about a friend?" I had to phrase this delicately. "Someone I can contact if I can't reach you."

His head shook slightly. "No."

"No one?"

"Outlived them all."

Hell. Just when I thought I had it knocked. I felt like a prick, but it was my job, so I had to do it.

"Mr. Jeffries," I said. "We are going to file suit in your behalf to get you money for this accident. It takes time to sue the City. In the event the case should drag on, and if you were to die in the interim, who should the money go to?"

His lips moved, but I didn't catch the words. I leaned closer.

"I'm sorry. What did you say?"

His lips moved again, and that time I made it out.

"Who cares?"

I blinked, and the whole thing hit me. I suddenly felt very lightheaded, very strange, the way you feel when someone says something that snaps your thought process around.

Exactly, Mr. Jeffries. Who cares? As sympathetic as I'd been feeling for Mr. Jeffries, I realized I'd been treating the sign-up entirely from my point of view, as something that had to be done, as something to get around. But Jesus Christ.

Here was a ninety-five year old man, with no relatives, no friends, no one in the world, a man with weeks to live at the outside, a man whose every breath meant pain.

And this man wanted to sue the City.

Not for the money. Not for any friend or relative. Not even for the satisfaction of winning, since he couldn't possibly survive long enough for that. And yet he wanted to do it. And *was* doing it, even though it cost him strength and caused him pain.

It all seemed connected somehow in my mind. Paul Jeffries on his deathbed wanting to sue the City. And

Richard Rosenberg, for all his money, wanting to fight in court.

And then there was me, a man of lesser goals, a man who just wanted to pay his teeth off and get out from under, but who, in order to try to do so, had been willing to take on the Marvin Nickleson case.

It seemed to me it must be all tied together somehow. It seemed to me it must all mean something, something about man's indomitable spirit, and relentless will to survive. Something about how man must struggle and strive no matter what, and that the struggle itself is that which we call life, that which makes a man alive.

Or maybe not. I'm saying it badly, and that wasn't really how I felt, and put like that it sounds rather trite.

But I had the feeling there must be something profound in all that somewhere, if only I were perceptive enough to see it, and articulate enough to say it.

5

Alice was on the computer when I got home. No surprise there. Alice was always on the computer these days. The machine in question was an NCR, hard drive, two floppie, IBM compatible. If you know what all that means you're one-up on me. All I know is the damn thing cost about as much as my teeth.

The computer was supposed to help me with my work. With my *real* work, that is, which is writing. My detective work is just what we in the arts call a job-job. Something you do to pay the bills. Writing is my career.

I use the word "career" loosely, in the manner of those in the arts. What it means, loosely, is "that which one would preferably be doing if this were an ideal world." Seeing as how this isn't quite a perfect world yet, I spend most of my time with broken arms and legs.

In all the time we'd had the computer, three months, I'd only used it once. Of course, I'd only had one job, a trade magazine article I'd gotten through a friend of a friend. That was a plum of an assignment, fifteen hundred dollars for three thousand words on the impact on society of recycling cans and bottles. Here I had to step lightly—in our neighborhood, the impact is largely having the trash bags ripped open and the garbage strewn on the street by bums looking for five cent deposit bottles. Since the article was supposed to advocate recycling, this wouldn't do for a theme.

At any rate, I got the assignment, and Alice insisted I do it on the word processor. After all, that's what we got it for, wasn't it?

I didn't want to do it. Frankly, it terrified me. I know I'm just an old fogy, but when I hit a typewriter key, I expect to see a letter appear on a piece of paper. I don't want to see it appear magically on some TV screen, flickering elusively and tantalizingly inches away, and always seeming to say, "You can't pick me up, can you?"

But we must all bend with the times. Alice clicked on the power, entered WordPerfect, and ushered me into the space age.

It wasn't that bad. After all, the keyboard is just a typewriter. A typewriter with a lot of extra keys I don't understand, but still a typewriter. And if I ignored all those distractions and just typed, I could do O.K.

Better than O.K.

First off, no carriage return. No need to judge when you're getting to the edge of the page, with or without a margin bell. No margin release. Just keep typing and the words jump down to the next line.

Far out.

And if you screw up, as I often do, no problem. No Correcto type. No liquid paper. Just backspace and try again. And if you leave out a word, hey, just insert it. Everything else shifts over.

After the first page I was typing like a fiend, fingers

flying over the keyboard. Hey, people are going to be recycling all over the place and I'm going to be cashing a fifteen hundred dollar check.

I was done in no time. Ten pages in three and a half hours. A new world's record. I'd made a lot of typos, but who cares. I had SpellCheck, the one extra function Alice had managed to teach me. I pressed "Control, F2," and when the machine asked, I told it to check the whole document. And like lightning, the machine whizzed through my whole article, highlighting each misspelled word and offering me a list of alternatives, which a touch of a single key could insert instead. In twenty minutes I'd corrected the whole thing and was done.

Unbelievable.

I pressed "Exit," and it asked me if I wanted to save the document. I pressed "Y" for "yes," and "Enter."

And the whole thing disappeared.

Poof. Gone. Vanished.

My whole recycling article. My work. My creation.

My fifteen hundred dollars.

Gone.

Unnamed.

Untitled.

Unsaved.

Gone.

And nothing would bring it back.

And Alice had taken Tommie out shopping for the day so I could work undisturbed.

And I had a deadline. And, of course, I had waited till the last minute to beat it.

When Alice and Tommie returned three hours later, I was back at the good old-fashioned typewriter, laboriously and feverishly attempting to recreate my masterpiece.

Not to fear. Alice switched on the computer, did something magical, and my original text reappeared.

But the damage had been done. To my psyche, I mean. And it would be some time before I would try that infernal machine again.

Not that I'm apt to get a chance to. As I say, Alice is always on the computer. And not just in WordPerfect, either. Alice is a master of all phases of the computer. She gets into the Direct Operating System (DOS), and makes it do all kinds of things. And once she gets in, she won't get out. She's a computer junkie. She types on impervious to me or Tommie or the outside world. I refer to this fixation as "hoggin' DOS," which, by pronouncing the "o" in "hoggin' " like the "a" in "ha," makes it a play on words for her favorite brand of ice cream. Despite such feeble puns as this, our marriage endures.

At any rate, I can't fault Alice's obsession with the computer. You see, she used to be a computer programmer for IBM. She gave it up when we had Tommie. Years later, after Tommie was successfully launched in kindergarten, she had gone back to IBM and reapplied for her old job. But it was no good. Time and technology had passed her by. The computers that five short years ago had seemed so sophisticated and modern were Stone Age implements now. Alice was not offered her old job back. Instead, IBM furnished her with a list of courses, which, if successfully completed, would make her eligible to apply for a position only two notches lower on the hierarchical ladder from the one that she had previously held. Alice, in a rare display of self-control, had restrained herself from telling IBM what it could do with its courses. But the whole thing had been a bitter pill to swallow, and while I still kid Alice about her computer obsession, as is my fashion, I always step lightly. And I have no illusions about whom the machine was really for.

"That's wonderful," Alice said, when I finally got her

off the screen long enough to tell her about Marvin Nickleson.

Predictably, her reaction was the opposite of what I'd predicted. I figured she'd see the job as sleazy and demeaning.

"Wonderful?" I said. "How is it wonderful?"

"Well, it's more money, for one thing."

"That's its only redeeming feature."

Alice looked at me. "Are you kidding? Hey, it's a real job. It's real detective work."

"In the lowest sense. It's spying on someone's wife."

"Yeah, but not for a divorce. So he can get her back."

"Yeah, well that's just what he says."

"Why should he lie?"

"How the hell should I know?"

"Then why assume it?"

There are some things in life you always forget, no matter how obvious they are, how simple they are, or how many times you resolve to remember. The thing I always forget is, I should never, ever try to argue with my wife.

"Look," I said. "I'm going to do it. I'm just not happy about it."

"You worry too much. Look on the bright side."

"What bright side?"

"See?" Alice said. "Your whole problem is your attitude. This case comes along and all you do is think of the negatives. Look at it this way. It's a goof. It's a lark."

"It's sleazy."

"It's only sleazy if you think sleazy. Don't think sleazy. Think glamorous. Tell yourself you're Jack Nicholson in *Chinatown.*"

"As I recall, Roman Polanski sliced his nostril open with a knife."

"You're incorrigible. You're a perfect pessimist."

"Algernon. *'The Importance of Being Earnest,'* Act One."

Alice frowned. "What?"

"That's a line from a play."

Alice shook it away. She was not to be tripped up that easily. "Now, the way you have to look at this," she said, "is it's a marvelous opportunity to broaden your field of experience. Make new contacts. Get referrals. Before you know it, you'll be making two hundred dollars a day every day."

That stopped me. That was the right note. Despite myself, my mind couldn't help leaping onto the obvious path, to the math I'd already done in my head. Two hundred a day. A thousand a week. Fifty-two thousand a year.

Yeah, that was the pot of gold at the end of the rainbow, all right.

6

But I still had to earn it.

The next morning I got up, showered, shaved, put on my suit and tie, dropped Tommie off at the East Side Day School, and drove out to Hollis, Queens to keep a nine o'clock appointment with Cynthia Woll, who had been a passenger in her boyfriend's car when that young gentleman had attempted to drive it through a light pole. The boyfriend had already been arrested for DWI, and Cynthia was about to compound his troubles by suing him for her broken leg, which, it occurred to me, might put a strain on their relationship. But that wasn't my problem. I signed her up quick like a bunny, and hotfooted it down to East New York where Mary Wilson had fallen on a subway platform and broken her hip. I signed her up like wildfire and discovered to my regret that the subway platform in question was right there on Pennsylvania Avenue, which meant I had to take the "Location of Accident" pictures as part of the sign-up. That was unlucky. If she'd fallen in Manhattan, or even somewhere else in Brooklyn, I could have just listed the subway address on the fact sheet, marked it "Pictures Required," and the pix would have been farmed out later as a separate photo assignment. But no, there it was within the arbitrary one-mile radius of the sign-up, which Richard had decreed was the cutoff point.

I drove down there, bought a subway token for a train I would not ride, went down in the station and found a crack in the platform just where Mary Wilson had said there would be one. That was a blessing—in a lot of subway station accidents you can't find a damn thing. I shot a whole roll of film and attracted a crowd of school kids who must have been playing hooky, but who weren't old enough to make me particularly nervous. I got some good shots, the kids were gratifyingly awed at the presence of a private detective, and it was only eleven-thirty when I got out of there. My assignments were all finished, and I was gonna have no trouble getting back to Manhattan by one, and I was feeling pretty good until my beeper went off as I got into my car.

I called Rosenberg and Stone and, sure enough, Wendy/Janet had another sign-up for me.

Now. Right away. With a client with no phone.

I was pissed. "I told you. I have to be in Manhattan by one. Why don't you give it to someone else?"

"Because it's on Mother Gaston and you're right there."

I blinked. Son of a bitch. Score one for Wendy/Janet. Whichever of them it was deserved credit for actually looking at the work schedule before parceling out the work. Mother Gaston was only blocks away.

I couldn't fly in the face of that logic. Not the logic of Wendy/Janet. After all, god knows when I'd ever see it again. I hopped in the car and drove over there.

And nearly had a nervous breakdown. The client, one Jackson Sinclair, was one of those crotchety old farts who won't be hurried. It was his accident and he was going to tell it his way. "You just listen, young man, I'm telling you."

He certainly was. And he certainly did. And by the time I finally snapped a picture of his broken arm, sustained, praise the lord, in a slip and fall in a Kentucky Fried Chicken in the Bronx—"Location of Accident" pictures to be taken at a later time—it was twelve-fifteen and I was going slightly bonkers.

I took the Interboro, sped up to the Grand Central, got on the L.I.E., hit only one minor traffic jam (small miracle), went through the Midtown Tunnel, and sped up Third Avenue to 51st Street.

Which presented me with a huge problem. You can't park in midtown. Parking anywhere in New York City is bad, but midtown is impossible. Uptown where I live it's, "NO PARKING, 8:00–11:00, MON, WED, FRI." Further down it's, "NO PARKING, 7:00–7:00, EXCEPT SUN." Midtown it's, "NO PARKING UNDER PENALTY OF DEATH."

I'd planned to allow myself enough time to leave my car uptown before starting my stakeout. No time for that now. In desperation, I resorted to one of those forbidden luxuries afforded only by the idle rich—an East Side midtown parking garage.

As I pulled in, I wrestled with a moral dilemma. It was my fault I'd taken on the extra assignment from Rosenberg and Stone, it was my fault I was late getting to my assignment here, and it was my fault I didn't have enough time to ditch my car elsewhere—in light of that, could I put the parking fee on my expense account? The conclusion I came to was, damn right I could. I might need my car, and I should have it handy. Not that big a moral dilemma.

But the point is, I was rather frazzled. But I do know this. It was seven minutes to one by the dashboard clock when I pulled into the garage. Even with getting my ticket, and giving the keys to the attendant, and getting out of there and walking half a block, I *know* I got to Monica Dorlander's office building by one o'clock.

But I couldn't swear to it, cause I don't have a watch. Well, actually I do, I have a two-dollar digital I got by taking my son Tommie to Yankee Stadium on Watch Day. But it broke. Not the watch itself—you could smash that with a hammer and it'd still keep going—but the plastic band broke, they always do, and when that happens you can't wear the damn thing. So I couldn't *swear* I got to the office building by one o'clock.

And that's what was driving me crazy.

Because Monica Dorlander didn't come out.

I stood there with the photograph in my hand, just to be sure, and waited and waited and waited, and she didn't come out.

It wasn't my fault. Marvin Nickleson had said one o'clock, and I was *there* at one o'clock, I'm sure of it. Maybe she went out earlier. Or maybe she had a busy day today and ordered in. Or maybe she was sick and didn't come to work at all, how the hell should I know? All I knew was, here I was on my first day of my first job of my first case, and the fucking woman didn't show up, and damn it, it wasn't fair.

By two o'clock I was driving myself crazy. By now I was watching both directions, to spot her going out in case she was having a late lunch, and to spot her coming back in case she'd had an early one.

By three o'clock I was beginning to feel like a total incompetent, which wasn't fair. I mean, was any of it my fault? No. Could I help it if she didn't show up? Maybe not, but it didn't make me feel any better. Here I was, the worst private detective that ever lived. A bungling amateur, who couldn't spot the subject with an address and a photograph. I mean, I'm so poor at faces anyway she probably walked right by me with her hair in a slightly different style and I didn't even notice. Why did I take this job? I must have been out of my mind, oh god I think I have to take a piss.

Not to mention the weather. It was January. It was cold in New York. I was working the day watch at a—

Stop it. You're not Jack Webb. You're an unsuccessful writer working at a job for which you are ill-suited. An unsuccessful actor, playing a private detective. A foolish, bungling, incompetent—

Did I say incompetent or incontinent? Why the hell are there no public bathrooms in New York City?

She showed up at three-thirty. By that time I was so hassled if her hair had been slightly different I think I *would* have missed her. But it wasn't. It was exactly like her picture. And bad as I am at faces, hers was one I wouldn't forget.

The picture was only a head shot. Up till now I'd had to imagine the body that went with it. And here I'd been uncommonly accurate. Slim, sleek, stylish—I could get all that even through her winter coat. But there was one aspect I hadn't thought of: tall. Long and lean. Monica Dorlander was a good 5′10″, 5′11″. In high heels that made her taller than I.

I blinked. I blinked again. It hadn't occurred to me she would be tall. I couldn't help imagining her next to Marvin Nickleson. What a pair. The long-legged greyhound and the scrappy Scottish terrier. I had a flash of the two of them in bed. Christ, it must be like climbing a mountain, Marvin. I chided myself for such unworthy thoughts. This is your client's wife here. A little respect, please.

Monica Dorlander was on her way in, not out. At three-thirty in the afternoon. In my book, that's a hell of a lunch. I remembered Marvin Nickleson saying she was a company executive. It occurred to me that with that type of lunch break, she must be a rather high ranking one. Either that or was fucking the boss. Damn. Another ignoble thought.

Monica Dorlander walked through the lobby and to a bank of elevators on the side that I could see plainly as she got in. The minute the doors closed after her, I turned, sprinted across the street to a restaurant, made out like a customer, and availed myself of the bathroom. I fooled no one, and incurred nasty looks from a waitress and the maitre d' on my way out. Tough luck for them. The deed was done. I felt the wicked thrill of reckless abandon. Daring daylight raid: desperado pees in restaurant, escapes without eating.

The thrill lasted until I got back across the street. It was replaced by my usual paranoia. I'd blown it. I'd lost her. She'd probably left work during the five minutes it'd taken me to dash across the street and relieve myself. I'd failed and failed utterly. And how could I justify charging Marvin Nickleson two hundred dollars for a day's work when I hadn't done the work? I'd lost Monica Dorlander, I'd blown the case, I was washed up as a private detective.

Two thoughts occurred to me at about that time. One was that I was not really cut out for this kind of work. That wasn't really a new thought. The other was that I was being a total paranoid jerk, that nobody takes a three hour lunch break, comes back to the office, and dashes right out again. No, big executive or not, three hour lunch or not, Monica Dorlander must serve some kind of function at her company, which she would now be carrying out. She'd had her fun and now she was fulfilling her duties. She'd be out around five o'clock.

I'd just had time to think this when she came out the front door.

I blinked. Blinked again. Yeah, that was her. No need to check the photograph. There's no mistaking Monica Dorlander.

I followed her up Third Avenue. One nice thing. She was easy to follow, being that tall. I followed her up five blocks, across Third Avenue and into another office building.

Decision time, which for indecisive me is always a moment of panic. Do I get in the elevator with her and find out where she goes, or say the hell with it and wait for her in the lobby?

The hell with it sounded good. It usually does. In decision making, I find the hell with it an extremely persuasive argument.

Having made that snap decision and allowed Monica Dorlander to venture up alone, I had time to reflect on my judgment. Not bad. Marvin Nickleson wasn't interested in her business contacts. If this was strictly business, she'd come out alone. If she was meeting someone, she'd come out with him. So I couldn't lose. Hey, so far I was doing great.

I pulled out my notebook and wrote down the address of the office building so I could include it in my report. It occurred to me my report would seem more official if I put down a few times in it. Since I didn't have a watch, I asked a passing stranger, and instead of telling me to go fuck myself, he told me it was ten to four. Some days you get lucky.

I realized I should have started keeping notes earlier. On the back of the previous page I wrote, "3:30—subject arrives office building." I then wrote, "3:40—subject exits office building." That gave me a nice little schedule: 3:30 in, 3:40 out, 3:50 into other office.

Too nice a schedule. I immediately had doubts. Ten minute intervals? Obviously approximations. Maybe I should fudge them somehow. "In—3:31, out—3:39, enters other office—3:52." Idiot. What the hell does it matter? What difference does it make? Shit, I better buy a watch.

I stuck the notebook back in my pocket and resumed my surveillance. I figured I knew the drill. She'd be out in a few minutes and I'd tail her back to her office building.

She wasn't and I didn't. In fact, she was in there so long I began to wonder if the building had another way out. Not that I could see. Not unless there was some back entrance you got to by going through the basement. And if Monica Dorlander had used that, it meant she'd spotted me. And she hadn't spotted me. Had she? No, of course not. So where the hell was she?

She was out at 5:05 by the upside down Timex of a guy leaning against the side of the building eating a hot dog. She walked out in the street and tried to hail a cab. Third Avenue is one-way uptown. I immediately walked downtown and tried to hail a cab, so if one came along I'd get it first. You can't be a gentleman in this business.

It being rush hour, cabs were hard to get, but after a few minutes one came by and I flagged it. The cab pulled into the curb and I got in. The cabbie, a sour middle-aged man whose license identified him as Adam Kaplan, grunted, "Where to?"

"Right here," I told him.

He frowned and squinted at me. "Huh?"

"Start your meter," I said. "I'm waiting for someone."

He scowled, shook his head. Under his breath he said, "Shit."

"What's the matter?"

"Waiting time," he grumbled. "You make no money on waiting time."

"Yeah," I said. "But you make a big tip for being so courteous about it."

He looked back at me again. "What?"

I decided to make his day. After all, no matter how I played it, when we pulled out, he was bound to notice no one else had gotten in the cab.

"All right," I said. "If you can do your best not to stare—you see that tall woman over there on the corner?"

He turned, stared, and turned back. "That one?" he said, pointing his finger.

"That's the one," I told him. "Try not to point at her again. That's who we're waiting for. But she doesn't know it. And if she still doesn't know it when we get where we're going, you've earned your big tip."

He thought that over. "You followin' her?"

"You got it."

"What are you, detective?"

I pulled out my I.D. and flipped it open for him. "That's right."

He looked at it. "Son of a bitch," he said. He clapped his hands, rubbed them together. "Son of a bitch."

It was one of the few fringe benefits of the job. I had, indeed, made his day.

When Monica Dorlander hailed a cab a few minutes later, Mr. Kaplan pulled out after her with enthusiasm. It was a big disappointment to him when she got out at 83rd Street.

I wasn't too happy about it either. All right, she'd gone home, confirming the fact that she was indeed Monica Dorlander and not some tall fashion model who just happened to look very like Monica Dorlander. But even a person as paranoid as I had to admit that that hadn't even been remotely possible. The woman I was following was the woman in the picture. So her going home didn't help me a bit.

And as I stood there on the sidewalk, looking across 83rd Street at her apartment building, through the front doors of which I could see the security man Marvin Nickleson had described hanging out in the lobby, the reality of the situation began to dawn on me. It was five-thirty. I was on duty till nine. In all probability Monica Dorlander wouldn't come out again. And I was destined to stand here freezing on the sidewalk looking at the front of her building for three and a half hours.

Not quite. She was out at ten to eight. I was across the street doing my impression of a popsicle. We hailed our respective cabs again and took off. This time I drew a driver who didn't give a damn where he was going or why. His attitude seemed to be that life was a drag, and this was his lot in it. His lot in this case turned out to be to drive us about twenty blocks downtown and stop in front of a restaurant, which didn't seem to thrill him. But I perked up immensely.

This was it. Pay dirt. Monica Dorlander was meeting someone for dinner.

I paid off the surly cabbie, walked up to the restaurant, and made out as if I were studying the menu in the window. Monica Dorlander had already gone in, and over the top of the menu I could see her handing her coat to the hatcheck girl and saying something to the maitre d'. The dining room was off to the left and then straight back, and I could see about half of it through the window. I hoped the table she was heading for would be in view so I wouldn't have to go inside.

There was a well-dressed young man sitting alone nursing a drink at a table near the wall, and I figured he was my man.

I figured wrong. Simultaneously, a waitress arrived and slid a plate of food in front of him, and the maitre d' seated Monica Dorlander at an empty table on the other side of the room.

O.K. Next theory. She's meeting someone, and he's not here yet.

When Monica Dorlander accepted a menu and proceeded to order, that theory began to look slightly shaky too. By the time the waiter arrived with her salad I began to have severe doubts.

I also began to get very hungry. I recalled Gene Hackman in the movie *The French Connection,* standing in the cold outside the posh restaurant watching the bad guys eat a sumptuous meal. Of course, that was a movie. Between takes, Gene Hackman could go into his trailer, get warm, and eat any damn thing he liked. But even forgetting that, within the context of the movie he was a cop, he knew what he was doing, and the guys he was tailing were crooks. On the other hand, I was a fool, I didn't know what I was doing, and the woman I was following was just a poor cosmetics executive who wasn't meeting anybody or doing anything else helpful, but was merely dining alone.

All alone.

And as course followed course, and I morosely stood on the sidewalk eating a hot dog à la Gene Hackman, the realization slowly dawned on me that the fact that Monica Dorlander had dined at a table in view of the window hadn't been such good fortune after all. Because if she hadn't, I'd have had to go inside and get a table to keep her in sight, and right now I'd be eating the same leisurely meal she was, compliments of Marvin Nickleson.

By the time Monica Dorlander had finished her coffee, paid the check, and taken a cab back to her apartment building, I was somewhat less than happy.

7

Marvin Nickleson wasn't too pleased either.

"She dined alone?" he said skeptically.

It was nine in the morning and he'd called me at the office, just as he'd said he would. I'd given him a rundown of the previous days events, which left him less than thrilled.

"I find that hard to believe," he said.

"Oh?"

"I know my wife. She's not the type of person to dine alone."

"Well, she did."

"Yeah. She did. And that makes me wonder."

"Wonder what?"

"If she was wise."

"What are you saying?"

"You know what I'm saying. What you're telling me doesn't sound right. It's too good to be true. It sounds like she's acting a part—the separated, but still faithful wife, dining alone. I mean, come on. There's only one reason why she'd do that. And that's if you fucked up and she spotted you."

"She didn't spot me."

"Oh yeah? How can you be sure?"

"I'm sure," I said, but my mind couldn't help leaping to Mr. Kaplan pointing, and then following too closely up Third Avenue. Perhaps defensively, I counterattacked. "She didn't spot me. If she was wise, it came from the other end."

"What?"

"You said you have friends in common. You must have been thinking about hiring a private detective for some time. Maybe you discussed it with someone. Even asked someone for a recommendation."

"I didn't do that."

"You *think* you didn't do that. Maybe you just asked someone if they'd ever used a detective agency. You didn't mention your wife or tell 'em anything about it, but the guy can put two and two together."

"No. It didn't happen. If she was wise, it's cause you fucked up."

I took a breath and blew it out again. I'm basically nonaggressive, but I was getting really fed up. "If that's what you want to think, fine. It's my fault. I fucked up. So I assume I'm fired, is that right?"

"I didn't say that."

"No, you didn't. You're just pissing and moaning cause you didn't get what you want. I told you this would take time. I told you there's no guarantees. I've been on the job one day. And if your wife's seein' someone, she didn't see him yesterday and that's just tough.

"And we're still talkin' 'if'—you don't *know* she's seeing someone, so don't blame me if she doesn't."

"I'm not blaming you."

"You sure could have fooled me. Now you want me on the job, or not?"

"I want you on the job."

"Then you owe me money. Incidentally, your wife's dinner ran over nine o'clock, so you owe me overtime."

"O.K. Bill me at time and a half."

"Bill you? What do you mean, bill you? I can't even reach you."

"Right. I'll have to get the money to you."

"Do that. Throw in an hour of overtime, plus fifty-seven eighty in expenses."

"How much?"

"Fifty-seven eighty."

"What for?"

"Taxis. Garages. You want an itemized statement?"

"Christ, no."

"Then you'll have to take my word for it. Fifty-seven eighty."

"All right."

"So when do I get it?"

"How long you going to be in your office?"

I had an appointment in the Bronx. "I have to leave in fifteen minutes."

"That's no good. O.K. Tell you what. I'll come by tomorrow at nine o'clock. Get my report in person. Keep on the job, I'll see you then."

He hung up the phone.

I hung up mine too. Shit. Having a client was not all it was cracked up to be. At least, having Marvin Nickleson wasn't. Now I'd have to wait a whole day to get my money. And to get it, I'd have to listen to him bitch and moan and watch him tug his moustache.

And I doubted if I'd have anything to report. Because, I figured, in all probability Monica Dorlander wasn't seeing anyone at all. In my book, she hadn't left Marvin Nickleson for another man. She'd left to get away from *him.*

I grabbed my briefcase, went out and picked up my car at the municipal lot on 54th Street, the only affordable short-term parking in midtown. Even it was up to a buck a half-hour. I hustled back quick like a bunny, but even so I missed the five minute grace period and had to pay for two half-hours, two bucks for forty minutes. I got a receipt. Hey, Marvin Nickleson, this one's for you.

I signed up the client in the Bronx and another one in Queens, didn't get beeped at all, and was back in Manhattan before noon. I would have had time to ditch the car and take a subway downtown, but screw that. I might need my car. Let Marvin Nickleson spring for another garage.

I stuck the car in the garage, had lunch, and toyed briefly with the idea of getting a receipt for Marvin. I rejected the notion, and strolled out at ten to one to take up my position on Third Avenue.

Where nothing happened. Nothing. And I thought yesterday was bad. Yesterday was a dream compared to this. I stood on the sidewalk, hands in my pockets, blowing out frosty air, and jumping up and down trying to keep warm, and nothing happened at all.

Except my beeper went off like crazy. It was as if Wendy/Janet were trying to make up for not beeping me all morning. They beeped me again and again. Four times, on four separate occasions, for four separate sign-ups.

There was a pay phone on the corner and it worked, so I had no problem calling in. And it wasn't more than fifty feet from the entrance to the building, so I could keep my eye on who went in and out.

But I had to write the assignments down in my notebook. And I had to get the addresses and phone numbers right, which requires concentration, particularly when dealing with Wendy/Janet. So, vigilant as I was trying to be, I couldn't help feeling I might have missed something. Particularly since the last beep was right around five o'clock.

I was careful during that one. I swear I kept my eyes on the door the whole time, even while I wrote down the numbers. Because the woman hadn't shown up all day long, it was time for her to leave work, and I was damned if I was going to miss her going home.

And I didn't. I'm sure I didn't. I got off the phone as fast as I could and I hustled back down to the doorway and I waited for Monica Dorlander to come out.

And she didn't. The whole world came out of that building, but not Monica Dorlander. And as the minutes ticked by, and as the stream of people leaving work trickled down to a precious few, I began to have severe doubts again. Could I possibly have missed her?

Five-thirty brought a fresh flood of departing business types, Monica Dorlander not among them.

Five-thirty-five that rush was over.

Five-forty. No one.

Hell. Was she working overtime? Had she not gone in today? Was she at a sales meeting somewhere else?

Or had I missed her during the goddamn phone call?

I hurried back to the pay phone. There was a woman using it, but I figured she couldn't talk long. Not in this cold.

She did. Five-forty-five. Five-fifty. Jesus.

The woman finally hung up.

I grabbed the phone, dialed 411, asked for a listing for Artiflex Cosmetics. I got the number, wrote it in my notebook, still watching the door to the building. I dropped a quarter in and dialed.

The phone rang five times. Shit. They're closed. Then there was a click and a rather harried voice said, "Artiflex Cosmetics."

"Monica Dorlander," I said.

"Gone for the day."

I hung up the phone, stepped out in the street, and hailed a cab.

I was in a foul mood riding up Third Avenue. Gone for the day? Of course she was. I'd missed her. Or had I? Gone for the day. What did that mean? That she'd been at work and left, or that she hadn't been in all day? Shit. Why couldn't the woman have said, "She just left," and then I'd know. Gone for the day.

I paid off the cab and took up my position in front of Monica Dorlander's apartment building.

And wondered what the hell I was doing there. Before I didn't know if Monica Dorlander was at work. Now I didn't know if she was at home. Yesterday I'd tailed her here. Today I was just here. Watching an empty nest?

It was too much. Nothing was going right. My first job, and everything was falling apart on me. It seemed as if events were conspiring against me to convince me that I was indeed incompetent. I needed some small reassurance. Some crumb.

I went to the pay phone on the corner and called 411.

"Could I have a listing for Marvin Nickleson—N-I-C-K-L-E-S-O-N—on East 83rd Street?"

A pause, then: "I have no listing on East 83rd Street. I have a Marvin Nickleson on East 14th Street."

"No. East 83rd."

"I have no listing at that address."

"How about M. Nickleson?"

"No sir."

"How about Monica Dorlander, same address?"

"I have an M. Dorlander on East 83rd."

"Would that be 413 East 83rd?"

"That's right."

"That's it. Let me have it."

"One moment please."

There as a pause, then a recorded voice came on giving the number. As I wrote it down it occurred to me that while Marvin Nickleson might want a reconciliation, his wife was busily washing that man right out of her hair. She'd already dropped him from the phone listing. In fact, it wouldn't have surprised me to find out she'd disconnected the old phone, and the number I'd just copied was a brand new listing.

I took a quarter out of my pocket.

And I hesitated. To call or not to call.

Hell. It was cold. I was anxious. What the hell.

I dropped the quarter in and punched in the number.

Two rings. Three rings. Shit. No one home. Four rings. Then, click, "This is Monica Dorlander. I'm not in right now, but—"

I hung up the phone. Great. I missed her at work. She didn't go home. I'm watching an empty nest.

I was cold, hungry, and pissed off. I would have loved to have hunted up a deli and had a cup of hot coffee and maybe a bowl of hot soup. But then she'd come home and I'd miss her. Worse, she'd come home, change her clothes, and dash out again and I'd miss her. I wouldn't know where she'd gone. I wouldn't even *know* she'd gone.

I couldn't risk it.

There was a Sabretts stand on the corner. Dinner for one, compliments of Marvin Nickleson. I wondered what the vendor would say if I asked him for a receipt. I ate the hot dog, washed it down with a can of soda. It was so cold I was afraid the can would cleave to my hand. It didn't.

I threw it in a trash can on the corner, a bonanza for some lucky bum who'd happened to catch my article on recycling.

I walked back the half-block to the entrance to Monica Dorlander's apartment building, which I had been watching all the time. I stood across the street and watched some more.

And nothing happened. A big fat zero. People went in, and people went out, but none of them were Monica Dorlander and I couldn't have cared less.

A police car pulled by slowly. It seemed to me the cop in the passenger seat was eyeing me suspiciously. Of course, it always seems that way to me, no matter what I'm doing. I have a built-in automatic guilt response to cops, perhaps as a residual effect of growing up in the sixties.

The car did not stop. The light did not flash on. The cop did not stick his head out the window and demand to know what I was doing. The car pulled on slowly down the street and turned the corner.

I breathed a sigh of relief. Then wondered if the car was just going around the block to see if I was still standing there when they went by again. I realized that wasn't even a remote possibility. More like a superparanoid delusion.

I acted on it anyway. I walked slowly back to the corner. I kept an eye on the building entrance as I went. I needn't have bothered. No one went in or out.

The police car didn't come back either. There was no reason that it should. I didn't look like a mugger or a rapist.

I went to the pay phone on the corner, picked up the receiver and dropped in a quarter. I pulled my notebook out of my pocket and called Monica Dorlander's number.

Same old shit. Two rings. Three rings. Four rings. Click.

And a voice said, "Hello."

I hung up fast.

Son of a bitch. A voice. Not a recording. A real voice. A real person.

Monica Dorlander was home.

It wasn't fair. I think I've said that before. Probably many times. But that was how I felt. That was the operative phrase to describe this damn case I'd gotten myself roped into. It simply wasn't fair.

I'd been watching the building. Even through my sumptuous repast of hot dog and diet soda, I had been vigilant. From the time I'd called Monica Dorlander and gotten a recording to the time I'd called Monica Dorlander and gotten her actual voice, I had been watching the front door, and I could almost swear she hadn't gone in and here she was home.

The operative word, of course, was almost. The tiny seed of doubt. Could I have missed her? Could *anyone* have missed her? All six feet of her? Not likely. So what happened?

There were several logical explanations. She was in the shower the first time I called so the answering machine picked up. Or she was one of those people who likes to listen to see who's calling before she decides if she wants to answer the phone. But then why would she have picked up the second time? Or maybe the first time the phone rang she'd been visiting a neighbor's apartment. That started a train of unsettling thoughts. Shit. What if the man she was seeing lived in her building? Not an altogether impossible occurrence. In that event, I'd never find out who he was. Not unless they were stupid enough to leave together. Which, if she were being discreet, Monica Dorlander would never do. Because in that event, as Marvin Nickleson had pointed out, he'd be able to get all the information he needed just by pumping the doorman. So if she was seeing someone in the building I was shit out of luck.

Damn. Minutes ago I'd been upset because Monica Dorlander wasn't home. Now I was upset because Monica Dorlander *was* home.

There she was, and here I was. And here I was destined to stay, freezing my balls off until nine o'clock tonight.

Unless, of course, she went out. Which she didn't. And by eight o'clock I figured she probably wouldn't.

I went to the pay phone, called my wife, and told her nothing was happening and I'd probably be home soon. She was glad to hear it because she was running out of sanitary napkins and wanted me to pick some up on the way. I assured her I would, hung up, and resumed my vigil.

And of course nothing happened. When nine o'clock rolled around, I packed it in and took a cab back downtown to pick up my car. Not to mention a receipt for Marvin Nickleson.

I drove uptown, found a parking spot on West End Avenue, and walked over to the Suprette on Broadway to pick up some groceries and ice cream.

And sanitary napkins.

Damn.

Pardon me, but am I the only husband who hates buying sanitary napkins? I mean, it would be different if I could walk in the store, grab a box of the damn things, plunk them on the counter, and hand the salesgirl the money.

But it's not that easy.

I walked into the store, found the right aisle, looked at the display, and, as usual, my eyes began to glaze over.

You see, there's not just sanitary napkins. There's all kinds and all brands. And there's only one kind that's the right kind, and I'm damned if I know what it is. All I can ever determine is, the right kind is the one I didn't buy.

You see, there's maxi-pads, and there's mini-pads. And there's super maxi-pads, and super mini-pads. And ultra-thin maxi-pads. And ultra-thin mini-pads. And small maxi-pads, and large mini-pads. And vice versa.

And there's different brands. And different brands have the same or similar designations. Only they mean different things. Ultra-super-mini-pads.

I stood there staring at the vast array of boxes, wondering which one is it? Or which one did I buy last time? If I could remember that, I would at least have a clue—I would know that *that* one was wrong.

Because they're always wrong. Because as I stand there staring at the boxes, the one thing I know for sure is, whichever box I finally happen to choose, when I get it home, Alice will look at it and say in a totally flat voice, "Oh. You bought ———."

And if I say, "Well, what kind should I have bought?" she won't answer me. She'll just smile slightly, and say, "Oh. It's all right." Because if the truth be known, the fact is there's so many damn styles and brands, she doesn't know either.

The thing is, I know this is going to happen. And as I stand there, looking through the boxes, all of this goes through my head. And it all just makes me more frustrated, embarrassed, and indecisive.

Indecisive. That's the key. Worse than Hamlet. To buy, or not to buy? Ultra-thin, or not ultra-thin?

And the worst thing about it is, the longer I stand there vacillating, the greater the chance some clerk is going to come up to me and say, "May I help you, sir?"

At which point I just want to vanish into the floor.

So I want to make a quick choice. But it isn't easy. Even if I make a stab at the size and brand, there are other considerations. For instance, there's scented and unscented. Here I have a clue. I know Alice wants unscented. After ten long years of marriage I have hammered that one out. But it's not that easy. As so often happens, here I am, standing in the store, staring at a box that I have narrowed down to be the most likely feminine napkin my wife might want. But it doesn't say anything on it. It doesn't say scented. And it doesn't say unscented. And no other box of that brand says scented or unscented, either. So which is it? Which concept is this the negative of? In other words, if I were to find the opposite box in this style and brand, which this store, of course, does not carry, would *that* box say on it scented or unscented? After long years of trial and error, I still have no idea.

Am I alone in this? If not, I'd sure like to know. I'd like to know if other husbands feel the relief I feel when the elusive box has been finally selected and purchased, and, if not totally appreciated, at least accepted into our house. The relief at knowing the crisis, at least for the time being, has been averted, and that I am once more off the hook and can relax and forget about the whole sordid experience.

Until next time. When the box runs out. And Alice, sweet Alice, is taken totally unawares by her own period, and I am sent out to do battle again.

Alice was hunched over the keyboard, typing furiously when I got home. I know she heard me come in, cause she said, "Hi," though she didn't glance up. I said, "Hi," to her back, went into the kitchen, set the bag of groceries on the table, and came back into our dining room/office.

Alice was still typing. She typed another few lines, then began pressing the function keys that fill me with such trepidation. Words and numbers flashed across the screen quicker than I could read them. One final key, pressed with a bit of a flourish, and Alice said, "There."

She looked up at me. "Hi. I got something for you."

"Oh?"

She riffled through the pages on the desk, pulled out one, looked at it, and handed it to me.

"What's this?" I said, taking it.

It was the sort of stupid thing people say to each other in conversation. I could tell by looking at it what it was. On the top of the piece of paper were the words, "STANLEY HASTINGS DETECTIVE AGENCY." They were large and printed in an elegant script. Underneath, in a more discreet standard type, were the address and phone number of my office. Underneath that was a double line.

Just because a thing is stupid doesn't mean you don't say it.

"What's this?" I said again.

"It's a letterhead. I got a new program. IBM Printshop. I made you a letterhead."

I frowned. "What do I need with a letterhead?"

"For your work. You got a job. You may get more."

"What?"

"This Nickleson guy—you have to bill him, don't you?"

"He's paying cash."

"Cash or check, he's paying. And he's gotta be billed."

"You don't understand. This is highly confidential. He doesn't want any record of this."

"No, but you do. You're doing work, and you have to be paid."

"I'm being paid."

"Not today."

"No. Tomorrow morning."

"Right. And you have to keep track. Yesterday you were into overtime, right?"

"Yes, but—"

"So he owes you for that. Plus for today. And you have expenses."

"Yes, but—"

"But what?"

"Marvin Nickleson wouldn't want—"

"Oh bullshit," Alice said, coming out of her chair. She snatched the paper out of my hand and crumpled it up. "If you don't want it, you don't have to have it. I try to do something nice for you . . ."

"And I appreciate it. I—"

"No you don't. You're so defensive. So negative. 'Marvin Nickleson wouldn't want.' Fuck Marvin Nickleson. You gotta give him bills. If he doesn't want 'em he can tear 'em up, burn 'em, flush 'em down the toilet. What difference does it make if your name's on a bill you show him? *He* knows you're working for him."

She was right. That's one of the big problems with my wife. She's often right.

"I'm sorry. You're right. I'll use them."

"You don't have to."

"No. I wasn't thinking. I need them."

"Don't humor me."

"I'm not humoring you."

"Yes you are. You don't *need* them. You just realize it won't hurt to use them."

I looked at her. "What's the matter?"

"What's the matter? What's the matter?" Alice took a breath. "It always happens. You get so caught up in what you're doing all you can see is your point of view. I got this program, and it occurred to me maybe I could do something with it. Letterhead. Fliers. Résumés. And this is nothing. You should see the stuff this thing can do. And maybe if I spread the word and put out signs, I could get some work out of this."

She snatched up the crumpled paper from the desk. "This thing for you is nothing. It was kind of a test run, so to speak. And what kind of a reception do I get? I can't even sell my own husband, who's getting it for free."

Despite myself, my eyes twinkled slightly.

She caught it. "No double entendre intended."

I put up my hands. "All right, all right," I said. "Hey, listen." I took her by the shoulders. "I'm very sorry, but you have a big problem. Your problem is you married a moron."

She smiled slightly at that. I pressed my advantage.

"And when you marry a moron, you have to pick carefully, or you're apt to be in trouble. If the moron you marry happens to be insensitive, unperceptive, and inarticulate, you are in *big* trouble. You have to make allowances. You know, like when you have friends over, you have to say, 'And this is the living room, please excuse my husband, the moron, sitting in the corner.' "

She giggled in spite of herself. Thank god. I hugged her, then played my trump card. "Want some chocolate ice cream?"

"You got chocolate ice cream?"

"Yeah."

"Where is it?"

I jerked my thumb. "Bag in the kitchen."

"You left it out? It'll melt."

She shot me a dirty look and stamped by me into the kitchen.

I followed, realizing I wasn't quite out of the doghouse yet.

Alice pulled the pint of ice cream out of the paper bag, squeezed it, and shook her head.

"Seems fine," I told her.

"Yeah sure," Alice said. She pulled off the top. Shook her head pityingly. "What else did you leave out?"

"Nothing that will melt."

"No. Just spoil," she said, pulling cottage cheese out of the bag. She gave me a look, stalked to the refrigerator, and put the cottage cheese inside. She stood up. sighed. "So tell me about it. She never went out, right?"

"Yeah."

"That's good."

"No, it isn't."

"Why not?"

"It doesn't help my client any."

"Why not?"

"It doesn't prove she's seeing some man."

"Does he *want* her to be seeing some man?"

"No. Of course not."

"Then he should be pleased."

Women's logic. God save me. But at least we were over the crisis and back on safe ground. I made a mental note to be sure to use Alice's letterhead to bill Marvin Nickleson, which, on refection, wasn't a bad idea, what with him being a day late in paying and me having so many expenses and all. And I made a mental vow to be as supportive as possible of Alice's work schemes, even though my gut reaction told me there wasn't any money in résumés and fliers and no one would really be interested, in view of which I made another vow to try not to be patronizing. And I thanked my lucky stars that on this particularly draggy day I'd managed to blunder through relatively unscathed, and was out of the doghouse at last.

Not quite.

Alice pulled a box out of the shopping bag and looked at it.

"Oh," she said. "You bought Maxi-thins."

Marvin Nickleson was pissed.

But not nearly as pissed as I was. He was pissed about the job I was doing, and I was pissed because he was pissed on the phone instead of being pissed in my office like he should have been.

It was 9:05 and I was pacing the floor impatiently when the phone rang. I hopped to the desk and scooped it up.

"Three-four-one-four," I said.

"Hastings? Marvin Nickleson."

My heart sank. "Where are you?"

"At work."

"What?"

"At the office."

"You're supposed to be at *my* office."

"I got a rush job. A big account. The boss is throwing a shit fit. I been here all night doing layout sketches. They want 'em yesterday, I'm nowhere near finished, and the boss is poppin' in every five minutes asking when they're gonna be done. If I start talking ad copy to you, you'll know what happened, just play along."

"Wait a minute. What—"

"I got no time for explanations. Did you get anything?"

"Not really. Look—"

"Shit. Call you back."

The phone went dead. I stared at it for a moment. Slammed it down.

And proceeded to get pissed.

On the desk in front of me was a stack of bills, nicely typed out on Alice's letterhead. One was for $37.50 for an hour of overtime on Tuesday. One was for $200 for Wednesday's surveillance. One was for $200 for today's surveillance. One was for $57.80 for Tuesday's expenses. One was for $44.25 for yesterday's expenses. On top was a master sheet adding up the total of those separate bills. Alice had typed them up on the computer and run them off for me last night.

And Marvin Nickleson wasn't going to see them. Because Marvin Nickleson wasn't in my office, Marvin Nickleson was in his office, working on ad copy.

By the time the phone rang ten minutes later I was thoroughly pissed.

"Three-four-one-four."

"Hastings?"

"Yeah."

"Sorry. The boss walked in. I gotta make this fast."

"Fine. Make it fast. Where's the money?"

"I got the money."

"Get it over here."

"I can't get away."

"Then I'll come there."

"Christ no! You wanna blow everything?"

"No. I just wanna be paid."

"I'll pay you. I'll pay you. Jesus Christ. Is it my fault this job came up? Don't worry. You'll get your money."

"When?"

I could hear him exhale. "How long you gonna be there?"

I exhaled myself. "I have an appointment at ten."

"That's no good. I got hours yet. Look, I'll have to meet you somewhere. We'll have to work it out."

"Where? When?"

"I don't know. I said, we'll have to work it out. Look, give me a rundown on what you got so far and let's figure out what we want to do."

What I wanted to do was slam down the phone and never talk to Marvin Nickleson again.

But I had those bills on my desk.

I took a breath. "What I got so far isn't much."

"Well, let's have it."

I gave him a rundown of the previous day's events.

That's when he got pissed.

"You called her office? You called her at *home*? Are you crazy? Are you out of your fucking mind?"

"Now look here—"

"Calling the office wasn't that bad. It was after hours. It could have been a business call. That won't bother her. But Jesus Christ. You called her at *home*? *Twice*?"

"Once was just the answering machine."

"Yeah. *My* answering machine. I know how it works. It counts the calls. Even the hang ups. She'll know someone called and hung up. Then she gets another call, *she* answers and you hang up. And you wonder why nothing's happening. She's not stupid. You expect her to go out after that? If she'd had a date, she'd have canceled it."

"Come on. I get disconnected calls all the time."

"Oh yeah? You estranged from your wife? You fooling around? You got something you want to hide? Christ. Why the hell'd you have to call her?"

"I had to find out if she was home."

"Bullshit. No you didn't. You were hired to watch the

apartment. What were you gonna do if she hadn't answered? Pack up and go home?"

I said nothing, but I was fuming. Marvin Nickleson was right. It was hard to take having Marvin Nickleson be right. I sat there seething with impotent fury.

"O.K.," he said. "It's a mess. Let's see what we can do about it."

That brought me back. "We're not doing anything about it until I get paid."

"Right, right. We have to work it out. This morning's out. So's this afternoon. I'll either be still working or I'll be asleep."

"I can't work unless I get paid."

"Yeah. All right. Look. Screw the office. Forget this afternoon. Do a half-day. Start at five. At the apartment house. Five to nine. I'll get the money to you there."

"When?"

"Whenever I can. I tell you, I'm in deep shit over here. This guy don't like the sketches, I'm back to square one."

"You're telling me you might not make it?"

"I'll make it. I just don't know when."

"What if she goes out?"

"You follow her."

"And I miss you."

"Can I help that? Jesus Christ, what do you want from me? If that happens, I'll be in your office tomorrow morning at nine. What more can I tell you?"

I didn't know.

I didn't like it, but I didn't know what I could do about it. I could refuse, but if I did, the job would be over, Marvin Nickleson would tell me to go fuck myself, and I wouldn't have a prayer of ever collecting the money he owed me. Even so, it was a big temptation to tell Marvin Nickleson to go fuck *himself,* money or no money.

But five hundred and umpteen dollars is a lot of money.

And in this vale of tears, we're all whores of one kind or another. Or to look at it another way, after Alice had been so kind as to have typed all those nice bills out, it sure would be a shame not to be able to use them.

I took a breath. I sighed. "O.K."

10

It could have been worse.

All right, so I lost a hundred dollars. The bill for two hundred dollars for today's surveillance would have to be torn up, and Alice would have to type out a new one for a hundred dollars for half a day's surveillance. But that didn't really bother me. Actually it was a blessing in disguise. Because Wendy/Janet had given me four sign-ups for today. And seeing as how they were spread out over three boroughs, there was no way I was going to get 'em all done in the morning. I'd have had to stall two of them until tomorrow. I didn't want to do that, cause if I did, it was a cinch Wendy/Janet would beep me with four more assignments for tomorrow, and the whole problem would escalate, and I'd wind up with a whole mess of sign-ups to knock off over the weekend.

And I wanted to keep my weekend free. Marvin Nickleson hadn't said anything about the weekend yet, but I had a sneaking suspicion he might consider Saturday and Sunday prime time for marital transgressions. In the event that he did, the son of a bitch was going to discover the weekend was also prime time for me. In other words, work on Saturday or Sunday equals time and a half from hour one. A base rate of three hundred bucks a day.

So I was happy to get the sign-ups taken care of. Besides, I figured, I wasn't really losing a hundred bucks either. The other way I'd have gotten two hundred bucks out of Marvin Nickleson, plus four hours for Richard Rosenberg equals forty bucks for a total of two hundred and forty. This way I was getting one hundred from Marvin Nickleson plus eight hours from Richard Rosenberg equals eighty for a total of a hundred and eighty. So my net loss was only sixty bucks, not a hundred.

Besides, four sign-ups fit very comfortably into an eight hour day. And I was able to spend the day touring around leisurely in my warm Toyota, instead of freezing my ass off on the sidewalk on Third Avenue, trying to spot the elusive Monica Dorlander going into or out of her office building.

I signed up a gentleman in Queens who'd slipped on the sidewalk, a woman in Brooklyn who'd fallen in a C-Town, a kid in the Bronx who'd been hit by a car, and a man in the Bronx who'd been mugged. All four were simple straightforward cases, even the mugging. The identity of the mugger, still unknown, was not my problem. My only concern was the broken lock that had allowed him access to our client's foyer.

In the course of the day's work I was beeped three times and given three more assignments for Friday morning. Which was kind of nice. I wouldn't have felt nearly so good about knocking off all my sign-ups today if tomorrow had been dead. For once things were working out. I finished all my assignments and was back in Manhattan in plenty of time to keep up my evening surveillance. I even had time to grab a slice of pizza on the way.

When I got to 83rd Street I discovered starting at five

o'clock had a fringe benefit. Parking regulations on Monica Dorlander's block were no parking from 8:00 A.M. to 6:00 P.M. The 6:00 P.M. part, of course, was a joke. By six o'clock on the East Side, there's not a parking space to be had. Which means people who want to park their cars on the street overnight park 'em at five o'clock, and then sit in them, fending off meter maids, until six o'clock rolls around.

Which was great. I pulled my car to a stop right across the street from Monica Dorlander's apartment building and sat in it with the motor running. And there wasn't anything suspicious about my doing it, because I was only one of a growing number of people doing exactly the same thing.

By five o'clock the block was already half full. By five-fifteen it was solid. By five-thirty, when Monica Dorlander pulled up in a taxicab and went into her building, there was no reason on god's green earth why she should have paid the least bit of attention to me.

I was glad to see her. After all, I hadn't seen her in two days. My only contact with her had been that time on the phone. I sure wasn't calling her again. So it was nice to know she'd come home.

I hoped she'd go out again. More than that, I hoped she'd go out soon. I mean, it was nice sitting in my warm car and all, but when six o'clock rolled around and parking became legal, everybody else would get out of their cars, and then I *would* look suspicious sitting in mine and I'd have to get out too.

And not only that, I wanted her to go out because I'd taken this rotten job and, distasteful as it might be, damn it, I wanted to do it.

She was out at five to six. With a suitcase. Hot damn! A suitcase.

I was so excited I was falling all over myself. Jesus

Christ, what did I do now? Should I follow her on foot or in the car? A suitcase means a trip. She's going someplace. She could be taking a plane or a train. A bus, even. If so, she'd take a taxi to get there. Should I hail one too? If she's heading for Port Authority, Grand Central or Penn Station, I should—there's no place to leave my car there. But if she's heading for the airport I should drive. Oh shit. What would a real detective do?

Monica Dorlander could have solved my problem for me by walking east, because 83rd Street's a one-way street west, and I'd have had to follow her on foot. But she went the other way. Decisions and revisions that a moment could reverse.

Fuck it. I killed the motor, banged the code alarm, and hopped out of the car. I crossed the street and tagged along behind her at what I assumed was a discreet distance.

She never looked back. She went a block and a half and turned into a parking garage.

Shit. Wrong again. I need my car. Should I get it, or should I hail a cab? What if I miss her? Nonsense, moron, they gotta get her car out. That'll take time won't it? Yeah, but how much? How the hell should I know? Decisions, revisions. Holy shit.

I turned and sprinted down the street, flashed across the avenue dodging traffic, and raced back to my car.

There was a parking ticket on the windshield. Are you kidding me? I was here at five to six. I grabbed it off, unlocked the door, flung the ticket on the passenger seat, and punched in the computer numbers on the code alarm. The red light went off. I started the car, gunned the motor, and pulled out from the spot.

I hadn't noticed, but the guys around me had wedged me in. There was no time to be subtle. I cut the wheel and pulled forward till the bumpers crunched, cut the other way and backed up.

The guy behind me had a code alarm too, one of the kind that goes off if you bang his bumper. I banged it and it did. The alarm was the kind that is a loud, steady whine that never shuts off. I hate them. Car alarms like that are always going off in my neighborhood, and nobody ever shuts them off, and they whine for hours and drive you nuts. My alarm shuts off after one minute and rearms itself, on the sound theory that by then the thief has either been frightened away or your car has been stolen. It only goes off if you try to get into the car too, not if you bang the bumper. I tend to think of people who have alarms such as mine as responsible citizens. I tend to think of people who have alarms such as the guy in back of me as assholes.

I banged his bumper four more times getting out. My head was coming off from the whine. My thoughts were getting jumbled. For a second I wasn't sure whether I was a car thief or an incompetent detective.

"Incompetent detective." I said it out loud, as I have a habit of doing sometimes, particularly when I'm hassled and anxious. And as so often happens when I find myself talking out loud to myself, it started a chain reaction in my head. I was on "Family Feud," and I had just blurted out the answer "Incompetent detective," and my family members were all clapping and shouting, "Good answer! Good answer!" and there was a loud ding, "Survey says!" and the number one panel flipped over reading, INCOMPETENT DETECTIVE–87 and the audience was clapping and the family was cheering, and Richard Dawson was saying, "The Number One Answer!" That's right, Richard Dawson, the original show, not the remake with what's-his-face—

A car horn brought me back to reality. I'd just lurched clear of the space right in front of a speeding taxi. The driver swerved around me, still leaning on the horn, and I could see him mouth the word, "Asshole!" I wondered if it was the Number One Answer. "We polled a recent studio audience and got their best response to this: What do you call a man who pulls out without looking?" "Jerk." Ding. "The Number Two Answer. One answer will beat it . . ."

I hurtled down the block, following the cab. It occurred to me it would be a good idea not to rear-end him. Still, I wanted to make the light. It was yellow as the cab whizzed through. I was glad the cabbie decided to go for it. I'd already decided to go for it, and if he'd hit the brakes we'd have been in trouble.

I flashed across the avenue, hit the brakes, and pulled to a stop alongside the parked cars. Up ahead I could see the driveway to the parking garage. I couldn't see Monica Dorlander, though. She was standing inside the entrance. Either that or she'd already left. Christ, was it possible? Could the car in front of the taxi stopped at the stoplight up ahead be hers? How the hell should I know? It was dark. All I could see were the damn taillights. Should I pull up ahead maybe, and get a better look? Of what, the garage or the car? Well, if she's not in the garage, you go after the car. What if she is in the garage, what if she's standing there, what do you do then? Slam on the brakes and back up? That's a great idea. Why don't you just paint a sign on your car, "Private Detective Surveillance Unit." Yeah, but I could get a little closer, maybe get a little better angle, spot her in the door.

A car nosed its way out of the garage entrance, straddled the sidewalk. The door opened and a man got out. He walked around toward the back of the car, out of sight. A few moments later he reappeared walking with Monica

Dorlander. She fumbled in her purse, handed him what I assumed was a dollar bill, and got into the car. He closed the door for her. I heard the sound of the engine starting again, and the car pulled out of the driveway. I pulled out and tagged along.

She went across town to Madison Avenue, up Madison to 97th, through Central Park to Broadway, down a block to 96th, and over to the West Side Highway. She got on the Highway heading north.

Traffic was still heavy on the Highway, so there was no chance of her spotting me. There was a chance of my losing her, however. I stuck right on her tail. There was no reason that should make her suspicious—in traffic like that, *someone* had to be behind her.

We were heading for the George Washington Bridge, so I figured we were going to Jersey. You guessed it. Wrong again. Just before the ramp she cut into the left-hand lane, went under the bridge, and on up the Henry Hudson.

We stopped at the tollbooth and paid a dollar to leave Manhattan, which always strikes me as a variation on the old joke: How do you make any money on Manhattan? Put a tent over it and charge everyone a buck to get out.

We continued on up the Henry Hudson, which turned into the Saw Mill River Parkway. I'm not sure exactly where that happens, and I doubt if anybody else is either. You're on one and then suddenly you're on the other and it's all the same road anyway and who cares?

By the time we hit the Hawthorne Circle and took the Taconic State Parkway north, I was damn glad I hadn't opted for that cab.

By that time I had also come to the cheery realization that since I was now driving around all over creation, I wouldn't be standing on the sidewalk in front of Monica Dorlander's apartment house when Marvin Nickleson showed up to give me the money.

Somehow that figured.

We'd been on the Taconic long enough so that I was beginning to wonder if we were going to Canada, when Monica Dorlander's brake lights went on, followed by her right-turn signal, and she took an exit marked, "ROUTE 55–POUGHKEEPSIE." I'd never been to Poughkeepsie before, but by then I was damn glad to be anywhere.

We didn't go to Poughkeepsie, however. We took Route 55 right through it, went onto a toll bridge over what I assumed was the Hudson River, and kept on going.

A few miles later, Monica Dorlander hung a left onto an unmarked road, and began winding her way up into the mountains. She made two or three more turns, always onto unmarked roads, and seeing as how we seemed to be the only cars on the road, I had to stay a good distance behind to keep her from spotting me. Which made it tricky, of course. If I lost her, I'd never find her again. In fact, it occurred to me I'd be lucky if I could even find my way back to Poughkeepsie.

Just when I'd begun to feel that Monica Dorlander wasn't going anywhere, that it was all a bad joke, that I was a man trapped in a shaggy dog story, I rounded a curve in the road just in time to see her slow down and hang a left into the Pine Hills Motel.

11

This was it. This was the real thing. This was what I'd been reading in detective stories all my life, and seeing in the movies too. The private detective tails the wayward wife to a motel.

I tried to remain calm. After all, I figured, real detectives don't start dancing up and down just because the quarry goes to a motel. I'm sure in divorce work such things are just routine. Moreover, Monica Dorlander hadn't gone to a motel *with* anyone. She'd just gone on an overnight trip and quite naturally checked into a motel alone. Still, after two days of absolute zero, two days in fact of barely seeing the woman at all, this had to be a major victory. And it was, after all, my first case.

I didn't want to blow it. I wasn't sure what standard procedure was in a situation like this, but I figured hanging a left into the motel after her probably wasn't it.

I pulled onto the side of the road a hundred yards short of the motel and killed the lights and motor. I got out of the car and, keeping in the shadows, walked down the side of the road to where I could size up the situation.

The Pine Hills Motel was a one-story, L-shaped affair with maybe a dozen units, the majority of these running back perpendicular to the road, the last few in the back jutting out parallel forming the L. The office, of course, was in the front by the road. Monica Dorlander's car was stopped next to it.

I went a little further down the road where I could get a better view of the door to the office, which was on the same side as the doors to the side units. I'd just gotten settled when the door opened and Monica Dorlander came out. I'd expected to see the manager too, but apparently he was content to let her find her own unit. She got in the car, started the motor, pulled up and turned into a parking space in front of one of the side units. It was hard to tell from that distance, but the best I could judge was that if the units were numbered consecutively starting at the office, hers would have been six or seven.

All right, what do I do now? Do I cross the road on foot and try to get a closer look at the unit number, or drive in the driveway, stop by the office, and try to verify it from there? The angle from the office would be bad, worse even than the angle I had now. But I'd be closer. Would I be close enough? Should I cross the road? The door to the office was on the side, but it had windows on the front. If the guy happened to be looking out them he'd see me. And if he saw me, that would be it. But why the hell would the guy be looking out the window? It's dark. There's a light on in the office. You know what that's like. The windows become mirrors. The guy'd have to put his face up to the window to look out. But what if he did? Schmuck. Just do it.

Why did the private detective cross the road? That was the first joke my son ever learned. Probably the first joke most kids learn. Of course in the joke it's chicken. Which in my case applies.

I crossed the road about fifty yards beyond the motel. There was no street light there, no headlights coming from cars. There was a half-moon, but you can't have everything.

Having crossed the road at this point, I now couldn't see the motel. It was hidden by pines and a hill. Truth in advertising. I could see the glow of the neon sign however. I walked back toward it.

I stopped in the shadow of the last pine before the clearing. From there I could see everything. Even the numbers on the doors. There were fourteen units, not twelve, ten back and four across. The numbers, as I'd assumed, started from the office and ran back and around. Monica Dorlander's car was in front of unit seven.

If cars were any indication, the motel was about half full. There was a car in front of unit eight.

There was no car in front of unit six.

I walked back down, crossed the road again, then walked in the shadows back past the motel to my car. I got in the car, gunned the motor, turned the lights on, turned into the motel and stopped in the driveway, just as Monica Dorlander had done. I got out of the car and pushed open the door to the motel office.

I was surprised. The motel, though small and simple, had seemed modern enough, an ugly blot of concrete and steel cut into the mountainside. The office was decidedly rustic. The walls were of cheap wood paneling. A gun rack with half a dozen rifles hung on one wall. In the corner was an old potbellied stove. Small logs were crackling in it, and I couldn't help wondering what the heating in the rest of the place was like. The manager's desk was not your modern hotel counter either, just a small beat-up wooden desk.

The manager sat behind it, watching a small, fuzzy, black and white TV. He was a man about my age, only stockier and, I supposed, more muscular, though it was hard to tell since he was wearing his coat, causing me more apprehensions about the heating in the place. The coat was the red-and-black-check affair that hunters use. A matching hat with ear flaps lay on the desk. He was a bull-necked man with a reddish face with what looked like two day's worth of dark stubble. Somehow the guy struck me as a parody of himself—the Woodsman. He was either the genuine article, or had gone to great pains to cultivate the image. I figured the only reason there wasn't a deer head on the wall over the desk was the guy was a lousy shot.

It was probably a combination of the two, but I think it was the man that surprised me more than the room. I guess subconsciously I'd been expecting Norman Bates.

He very reluctantly turned his eyes away from the TV and surveyed me with a look that told me he hadn't taken Motel Management 101.

"Yeah?" he grunted.

"I'd like a room," I said. I felt like a fool when I said it. Suddenly I had a flash I was in a Saturday Night Live sketch. I mean, what did the guy think I wanted? It was a motel. All they did was rent rooms.

I had a sudden flash of panic. Come on, snap out of it. Never mind the decor or the guy or how warm or cold it is. This is where you gotta shine. You gotta check Monica Dorlander's motel reservation, and you gotta get the right room.

The manager grunted again. "MasterCard, American Express or Visa?"

None of the above, since I didn't want a record of my stay.

"Cash" I said.

He snorted. "Two in a row. Don't see much cash these days."

Hot damn. Things were coming my way. Monica Dorlander had paid cash. That smacked of something furtive. I ought to know, cause I was doing it myself. Now for the clincher. Did she use her right name?

I wasn't going to use mine. I'd already made that decision. I'd sign the name Alan Parker in the register. Right under whatever alias *she'd* used. I couldn't photostat the register like Marvin Nickleson wanted me to, not without giving the show away, but I'd make a note of it and I could photostat it later, even if I had to get a court order to do it.

I've really got to stop reading murder mysteries. Either that or stop being a detective. Because detective fiction keeps raising these expectations that real life dashes away.

There was no motel register. The manager reached in the desk and pulled out a four-by-six registration *card* and slid it across the desk.

"Single room, sixty-two fifty plus tax, fill this out."

And he turned his attention back to "The Cosby Show."

I filled out Alan Parker's registration form. I decided Mr. Parker lived in Scarsdale. Where it said license plate number I made one up. I figured the manager wouldn't come outside to check it. He hadn't stuck his head out the door to check Monica Dorlander's.

I finished the form and slid it back to him. Now came the tricky part—getting the right room. After the bit with the motel register, my expectations weren't that high, and justifiably so.

He glanced at the card, took my money, and produced a key. "Unit twelve."

I frowned. "Look," I said. "I'm a gambler and I'm superstitious. Could you let me have unit seven?"

"Rented," he said.

I knew that, since Monica Dorlander had just rented it.

"Oh," I said. "Well, close to that. Six or eight."

This time he gave me a look. "Rented," he said.

He had a hard stare, and with him looking at me I felt like a poker player whose bluff has been called. I didn't know what to say next. I felt like any moment I'd start squirming and say, "Aw, gee, you got me, you're right, I'm not Alan Parker, I'm a private detective, and I'm tailing this woman, and I was trying to con you into giving me the room next door."

Fortunately he snorted, jerked open the desk drawer again, and looked inside. "I got units three, ten, twelve and thirteen. If you're superstitious, you don't want thirteen. Whaddya say?"

"Twelve will be fine."

He slid the key across the desk. "Checkout time's noon. The phones in the rooms are for local calls only. You want to call long distance, the pay phone's out front."

He snorted again and went back to his TV show.

I went outside and got in the car. As soon as I did, it occurred to me I should have taken unit three. Then I'd have been between her and the road, and if she wanted to go out, she'd have to drive past me. I considered going back in and asking for unit three. I rejected the notion. I'd probably aroused the Woodsman's suspicions enough already, and if he wasn't a total dunce he'd be bound to get wise.

I started the car and drove up to unit twelve. I didn't have a suitcase to lug in, since I hadn't planned on spending the night. I had my briefcase, so I took that. I didn't want to look funny checking in with no luggage. Not that anyone was looking.

I unlocked the door and found a light switch. About what I'd expected—bed, dresser, table, chair, TV—your standard motel furnishings. The only windows were in the front, except for a small frosted one in the bathroom in the back. So much for clandestine surveillance. Or for Peeping Toms, if you will.

I set the briefcase on the bed and pushed back the curtains on the front window. Not bad. Screw unit three. Considering I couldn't get an adjoining unit, I was right where I wanted to be. Unit twelve being on the other leg of the L meant I could look diagonally right across at the door of unit seven. As far as seeing who went in and out, it was just as good as being next door.

The drawback, of course, was if Monica Dorlander did have a visitor, I wouldn't be able to try to listen to the conversation through the wall. Though, it occurred to me, that probably wouldn't have worked anyway, unless I had a snooperscope, or whatever they call that type of electronic gizmo they slap on the wall to hear conversations next door. So not getting the adjoining unit probably didn't matter.

As if on cue, a baby began to cry next door. The walls were paper thin, I heard it plain as day, and if I'd gotten unit six or eight I could have heard Monica Dorlander snore. Somehow that figured.

All right, what did I do now? I looked around the room as if to get a clue.

I got one. The telephone, for local calls only. Pay phone in the front.

I made sure I took my motel key, went out, locked the door, and walked across the parking lot to the front. It was there all right, just where the Woodsman had said it would be, mounted in one of those little metal boxes like in New York. By New York I mean the City—I was still in New York State, but if you live in Manhattan, *that's* New York.

The country is different.

Real different.

There was a mound of snow around the phone stand

that a snowplow clearing the parking lot had pushed up against it. The snow had frozen over and turned to ice. Making a phone call was like climbing Mount Everest.

I draped the receiver over my arm, clung to the top of the call box for dear life, and punched in the number.

Alice answered on the fifth ring.

"Hello?"

"Hi. It's me."

"Oh, hi. Listen, I'm in the middle of something. Can you call back?"

"Not very well. I'm standing on a glacier."

"What?"

"I'm calling long distance from somewhere in the North Woods."

"Stanley?"

"Not really the woods. Actually, I'm at a motel with a young lady. But if you're busy, I'll call you back. What are you doing?"

"Huh?" Something on the computer. Stanley—"

"That figures."

"Damn it, what's going on? Where are you?"

"Best I can figure, somewhere northwest of Poughkeepsie. Monica Dorlander packed a suitcase and took off in a car. She drove up here and checked into a motel. She's in unit seven. I'm in unit twelve."

"Why didn't you get the adjoining unit?"

"You read too much detective fiction."

"What?"

"The adjoining unit was rented. Anyway, she's here, I'm watching her, and I won't be home tonight."

"I guess not. Wow. That's great. You followed her to a motel, just like in the movies."

"Not quite."

"Why do you say that?"

"Well, for one thing, she's alone."

"So?"

"I don't think Marvin Nickleson hired me to catch her masturbating."

"Don't be silly. She's meeting someone."

"That's the theory. But he's not here yet, and I'm just hanging around. Anyway, I just called to say I wouldn't be home."

"Yeah. Right. So what'd you say about a glacier?"

"The phones in the room are the old fashioned windup kind, only go about two hundred yards. I'm at a pay phone out front mounted on top of an iceberg."

"So I can't call you there?"

"Don't even try. I'll call you tomorrow."

"What about your other cases?"

Shit. I'd forgotten all about them. I had three of them too. I'd have to call Wendy/Janet and have her farm 'em out to the other investigators.

I was in the middle of thanking Alice for reminding me when the door opened halfway down the row and Monica Dorlander came out.

"Shit. She's going out. I gotta go."

I hung up the receiver. As soon as I did I realized I didn't want to hang up the receiver. Because that meant I was finished with my phone call, and then there was no earthly reason why I should stand freezing on top of a mountain of ice, so I'd have to start walking back to my room. Which meant walking straight into Monica Dorlander.

I snatched up the receiver again and pretended I was making another call. Wonderfully inconspicuous. A lone man perched on a mountain top in the wilderness making a phone call.

Monica Dorlander didn't seem to notice. She got in her car and pulled out.

All right. What do I do now? She didn't take her suitcase, so she's obviously coming back. But should I tail her to see where she goes? Of course I should—she didn't come up here for no reason, it's obviously got to be important. Good god, what are the pros and cons? I had to weigh the chance of her spotting me against the worth of the information I could learn by being on her tail.

Monica Dorlander drove past me, went out the driveway and turned left. Damn. Not back the way she came. A new direction.

That clinched it. I sprinted for my car. If the manager happened to be looking out the window he was gonna think I was weird, but I couldn't help that. I hopped in and gunned the motor. Switched on the lights and pulled out.

By the time I got out the driveway and hung a left there was no sign of her. Of course. I took off after her.

It was tough going in the ice and snow. I was driving too fast for existing conditions, and a couple of times I came close to going off the road. If I had, the game would have been over. Snowbanks along the side were deep. Getting the car out of one of them would probably require a wrecker. Whether one could be found in the woods at that time of night was beyond me.

So, I feared, was this fucking job.

I'd gone about two miles and just about given up hope when I saw taillights. Thank god. If it's her, of course. But somehow it had to be. We hadn't passed any side roads that I could see for anyone to have pulled out behind her. And I couldn't imagine her passing anyone, the road conditions being what they were.

I slowed to a saner speed and crept up on the car. I got close enough to verify the fact that it was hers, then dropped back to a safer distance.

We wound around down the mountain. I'd lose her taillights on the curves, but pick 'em right up again. There was nothing to worry about. No chance of her losing me.

Not unless during one of those momentary lapses when her taillights disappeared around a corner she suddenly pulled into a hidden driveway and killed the lights and motor.

I worried about her doing that.

She didn't. She just drove slowly and steadily down to where the mountain road gave way to more level terrain. About half a mile further on she came to an intersection and hung a right. Oddly enough, I was turning right too.

The road, though unmarked, seemed better traveled than the one we'd been on, more likely to exist on some highway map or other. It was wider and the snow was better cleared.

It was straighter too, which was good in that I could drop back further and still keep her in sight, and bad in that my headlights would be in her mirror the whole time.

In about two miles we started seeing signs of civilization. Houses. A store. A gas station.

In a flash of panic I looked at the gauge. Still a quarter of a tank, thank god. But I'd have to get gas sometime. Where? When? How the hell would I do it?

That's not important right now. She'll need to get gas too. Don't think about it. This is a town. She's here. She's meeting someone. This is it. Don't blow it.

More lights, more houses, and suddenly we're driving down a commercial strip.

Her right blinker went on.

I tensed. Eased up on gas. Slowed the car. Careful now. Don't get too close. Don't turn right on her tail. But don't pass her by either. Easy.

She slowed, pulled into the right-hand lane.

And turned into a McDonald's.

I drove on by and pulled into the driveway of a used car lot, which was of course closed that time of night. I turned around in the lot, pointed my car back out at the road, and looked over at the McDonald's next door.

I was pissed. I mean it's my first case, and I'm nervous about it, and I'm trying so hard, but nothing's going my way. I mean, why the hell would Monica Dorlander, long-legged, high-powered executive, get in the car and drive a hundred miles out into the middle of nowhere to go a McDonald's?

Well, probably because she was hungry.

I looked over at the McDonald's and, sure enough, there was Monica Dorlander's car waiting in line at the drive-up window. Yeah, she was hungry.

I suddenly realized I was hungry too. Since breakfast, I'd had one slice of pizza, and that was hours ago. But I couldn't get in line behind Monica Dorlander. She'd see me for sure. She wouldn't think anything about it, but then she'd see me at the motel. And Marvin Nickleson had already accused me of letting her spot me.

No I couldn't go to McDonald's.

But right across the street from the McDonald's was a Burger King. No surprise there. Where there's a McDonald's there's always a Burger King, or vice versa. Or if not an actual restaurant, at least there's a sign, indicating the rival restaurant is half a mile down the road.

In this case, there was an actual restaurant. Shit. How many cars were in line there? I couldn't tell. From where I was, it was on the other side. Should I risk it? Did I dare?

Fuck it, I'm starving.

I pulled out, crossed the road, drove around the back of the Burger King. I was in luck. Two cars ahead of me. I was third in line. She was fourth in hers. No sweat. Got it knocked.

But the guy at the microphone was taking his own sweet time. Christ, how much can you say about a hamburger? The guy could be writing a book. Shit. That's right. Burger King takes special orders. *Have it your way.* Christ, that's an old ad, you're dating yourself again. Screw that, the thing is, that means they aren't ready to go, they have to cook 'em up. Which wipes out my three car to four advantage. Should I risk it? Do I still have time? Or should I say the hell with it and back up? Can't, there's a car behind me. Oh Christ.

The guy finally shut up and drove around to the window. The next car moved up. This was my chance to make a break, to get out of line.

Screw it. I'm hungry.

The woman in the car ahead of me was fast. I pulled up to the microphone, ordered two bacon double-cheeseburgers, a large order of fries, and a vanilla shake. I pulled out in a hurry, as if it mattered how long it took me to get to the takeout window with two cars still ahead of me.

Bigmouth was still at the window, probably waiting for his double whopper with ketchup and onion, hold the pickle, hold the lettuce, hold it between your knees, Jack Nicholson rides again.

Right. Jack Nicholson. I was supposed to feel like Jack Nicholson in *Chinatown.* I don't remember, but I don't think he ate at Burger King.

Bigmouth got his order. So did the woman. Now me. Come on, come on, where is it? They're waiting on the shake. Screw the shake. No, here it is.

I paid the money, grabbed the bags and pulled out of the driveway, just as Monica Dorlander pulled out of hers.

We drove straight back to the motel. Slow, steady, uneventful. Thank god. I needed that.

I hung back when I saw the motel sign. I pulled over and gave her a minute or two to get inside. When I pulled into the parking lot, she'd parked her car and gone in.

I parked my car and went in too. I put the bag of burgers

down on the dresser and hung up my coat. Then I dragged the small table and chair over to the window. I got the bag and spread the burgers, fries and shake out on the table. I sat down, pushed the curtain aside so I could see the door to unit seven.

And remembered that I hadn't called Wendy/Janet.

Shit. I cast a baleful glance at the useless phone on the stand next to the bed. Then I put my coat back on, went out, and climbed the glacier.

I was in luck. Wendy was in and was obviously in the middle of something, probably with her boyfriend, because she didn't try to argue, she just agreed to switch my cases, took down the information, and got me off the phone as quickly as possible. Minor triumphs and small consolations.

I went back to my unit, sat down, pushed the curtain aside again, and proceeded to have dinner. Of course, by then the food was cold as ice, and it was all I could do to choke it down.

I must say I was pretty dispirited. While I ate, I tried to build myself up, did my best to convince myself that I was a real detective on an important stakeout, conducting a skillful, clandestine surveillance of the subject.

It didn't help knowing I'd almost had a nervous breakdown just going to Burger King.

12

He showed up at ten-thirty.

That's an approximation of course, since I still didn't have a watch, but I had the TV on for company, and it was right in the middle of an L.A. Law rerun. I was lucky it was a rerun, cause if it was a new show I might have gotten interested in it and missed him. Though probably not, since the guy did me the favor of showing up during the commercial, most likely the midshow one, hence the ten-thirty approximation.

I almost missed him anyway cause he came on foot. What I'd been watching for, of course, was a car to drive up. None did. But suddenly there was a man walking up to her door. Jesus Christ. Where did he come from? I hadn't seen him cross the lot, but then as I say, I hadn't been looking for him, I'd been looking for the lights of a car. Had he crossed the lot at all, or had he come walking down the row, perhaps from one of the other units? I didn't know.

And I couldn't see his face. He wore a long trench coat with the collar up, and a hat pulled down over his eyes.

Whether that was to conceal his identity or merely to protect him from the elements, I had no idea. At any rate, the coat was dark and the hat was a small-brimmed gray and white check affair, and that was all I could see.

The man knocked on the door of unit seven. Seconds later it opened and he went in.

Great. The ace detective strikes again. Monica Dorlander's lover just called on her, and I don't know who he is, where he came from, or what he looks like. The best I could log in my notebook was, an unidentified man of whom I had no description, materialized out of nowhere and entered her unit somewhere in the middle of a lawyer show.

So what the hell did I do now? Marvin Nickleson said he wanted pictures. How the hell was I gonna get pictures? I guess if I were a real detective, when Monica Dorlander went out to McDonald's I'd have picked the lock to her unit, and I'd be hiding in her closet right now with a flash camera waiting to hop out and say cheese.

No I wouldn't. I'm confusing real detectives with movie detectives again. A real detective wouldn't do that shit.

But what would he do?

I had no idea.

I took a deep breath and blew it out again, recited, "I'm calm, I'm calm, I'm perfectly calm," from *A Funny Thing Happened on the Way to the Forum.*

First calm thought: pictures will be a bonus, if you can get them at all. Your main job is to I.D. the man.

I popped open my briefcase, pulled out my Canon Snappy 50 and slung it around my neck. I hopped back to the window, raised the camera and focussed on the door to unit seven.

Second calm thought: shots from here will be worthless—you have no telephoto lens, and from this distance through a pane of glass with no flash, it simply cannot work. You have to go outside.

I didn't want to do it. I'd been dressed for work—Richard's work, that is—so I didn't have a heavy overcoat, just a light topcoat thin enough to fit comfortably over my suit. It was perfectly fine for walking to and from the car in New York City, but not for something like this. And of course I had no boots, just street shoes.

Schmuck. Literally getting cold feet? What you gonna do?

My suit jacket was draped over the back of the chair. I pulled it on. I grabbed my topcoat off the hanger and pulled it on too. I checked my pocket to make sure I had my motel key, and slipped out the door.

Cold? You don't know from cold. For starters, the temperature must have been close to zero. Plus a cooling breeze had come up and was whipping down the mountain at something just short of gale force. I don't know how they compute wind-chill factors, but it occurred to me that one way would be to stick a private detective outside and see how long it takes him to turn blue.

Now that I was outside, I figured I had two options: walk up to the unit and try to listen through the door, or find a hiding place from which to shoot pix of the guy when he came out.

I decided to go for both. Instead of cutting across the parking lot, I walked along the front of the units, trying to give the impression I was on my way to the office and the phone up front. I was staying under the shelter of the overhang of the roof in order to protect myself from the wind. On the one hand it was a hollow ruse, but on the other hand, no one seemed to be watching anyway.

I slowed in front of unit seven, stopped, and leaned my

ear toward the door. No good. With the wind whistling around me I couldn't hear a thing.

Two units farther down I stepped between two cars, walked out into the parking lot, and kept going till I was out of the light. I stopped, turned, and looked around for a place to hide. Nothing looked good. The cars parked in front of the units were bathed in light from the motel—no chance to crouch behind them. And the rest of the lot was wide open—no canister, no dumpster, no cars parked along the far side.

Still, that was where the shadows were, the shadows from the overhanging trees on the hill. I backed up into them, slowly, grudgingly, not wanting to get too far from the motel, but still wanting them to swallow me up, to make me invisible to anyone coming out the door.

My foot disappeared into a mound of snow. Shit. I'd backed all the way off the lot.

I pulled my foot out. My shoe was full of snow. I couldn't see taking it off and shaking it out, though.

Damn. What did I do now? I couldn't back up any further, and my head was still in the light.

I crouched down. Brilliant idea. Now I was totally in the shadows. I was also squatting in a horrendously uncomfortable position with a shoe full of snow.

I flopped forward onto my knees. I maneuvered my feet free and wiggled them, to try to get the circulation going. My left foot felt positively numb. My hands didn't feel too hot either—I had no gloves. I rubbed my hands together, stuck 'em in my pockets.

I knelt there looking at the door to unit seven wondering how long this guy was going to take, and what the fuck I was gonna do if the son of a bitch decided to spend the night.

He was out in less than five minutes. Talk about quickies. This guy could have been up for the Premature Ejaculator of the Year award.

If that's what he was there for. Somehow I didn't think so. Not with the long-limbed Monica Dorlander. It would take longer than that just to get her undressed.

At any rate, he was so quick I wasn't ready for him. The door opened and out he came, and I started and grabbed for my camera, only my hands were in my pockets and I had to get 'em untangled first, and when I did my fingers were still so numb I could hardly hold the damn thing, and by the time I got it up to my eye the guy was already walking away. I fired off three quick shots anyway, though in my heart of hearts I knew they wouldn't be any good. Not at that distance, not in the dark, and not without a flash. It was small consolation to know that even if I had been ready, even if I'd clicked it off just as he got out the door, it still wouldn't have done any good. Cause the guy had his hat on again, and as he walked away toward the front of the motel, and as I fired off the last of my futile pictures of his back, I realized I still hadn't seen the guy's face. Well, hell, pictures were a long shot anyway—no pun intended—the main thing is I.D. the guy.

I got to my feet, no easy task. Even in that short time my muscles had cramped up in the chilling cold. Getting up required putting my hands down in the snow. I eased to my feet, swayed unsteadily for a moment, brushed the snow off my hands.

The retreating figure hadn't seen me. He hadn't turned around or even broken stride. The door to unit seven was closed, so Monica Dorlander hadn't seen me either.

O.K. Go get him.

I kept in the shadows, lurched off toward the front of the motel. The guy had stepped out into the lot, was walking along the rear of the parked cars. He kept on going, past the office and out the driveway. At the bottom of the drive he turned right, walked on down the road. As soon as he turned the corner, I followed.

The light was on in the motel office. I hoped the Woodsman was watching "L.A. Law." Or any show, for that matter, that would keep him from looking out the window.

I hit the bottom of the drive and turned right. Shit. The guy was out of sight. There was no street light in that direction, just the dark void that had swallowed him up.

But he had to be there. There was no place he could go. So if he walked and I followed, eventually we'd come to the light and I'd spot him.

Unless he heard me and turned back. Chilling-Thought-Number-409. Log it in the notebook under 'paranoia' or 'prudence,' depending on your mood.

I gritted my teeth, forged ahead. I noticed I was limping slightly, favoring the snow-filled shoe. I wondered what the chance was of getting frostbite. "Private Detective Loses Toe: while conducting a routine surveillance of—"

Stop it. No routines. This is important. Get it done.

I limped on.

There came a metallic click from ahead of me in the distance. I instinctively ducked. Then a small light. But not the flash of light from a bullet. It was the light that comes from a small bulb. Then a metallic slamming sound and the light went out. Moments later, a motor roared to life. Then more lights, two red dragon's eyes gleaming at me. And two white lights shining on ahead.

Shit. The son of a bitch parked in the road. He was too far ahead for me to see the licence plate number or even the make of the car. He parked in the road and walked back, which means he must be as important as hell, and here he is getting away, Jesus fucking Christ.

I turned and sprinted for the motel. Or at least my version of a sprint. I must have looked something like a gimpy flamingo, hobbling on stiff legs, topcoat flopping in the breeze.

I negotiated the driveway, reached my car, fumbled for my keys. I hopped in, punched off the code alarm, started my car. I wheeled around, tore out of the parking lot, fishtailed coming out of the driveway, and sped off on what I knew would be a futile chase.

It was. By the time I got back to the main roads there was no sign of him, and countless directions he could have gone. Picking any of them would have been stupid—nothing to choose from. And even if I found a car, there would be no way of knowing if it were his.

I put my tail between my legs and slunk back to the motel.

Monica Dorlander's car was still there and her light was still on. Thank god. That would have been the ultimate humiliation, losing her in the process of losing him.

I parked the car and went back to my room.

The TV was still on, of course. I hadn't had time to switch it off when I went out. It must have been after eleven, cause the news was on. It was a local station, and they were covering a car wreck in Poughkeepsie. I watched for a few minutes. If you think New York City news is bad, try this sometime.

I flopped down at the table again, pushed the curtain aside. Nothing doing. The light was on, the door was closed, the car was there. All shipshape.

But the horse had left the barn. Monica Dorlander had had a caller. And it had been important enough that the guy had been discreet enough to leave his car parked on the road, not the sort of thing a person would choose to do in this weather. And I'd blown it. Muffed it. Fucked up utterly. Jesus Christ, I thought. How the hell was I going to get off charging Marvin Nickleson two hundred bucks a day, plus time and a half for overtime, plus gas, tolls, motel bills, etc., when I was giving service like that?

I sat there watching the door to Monica Dorlander's unit, feeling slightly lower than shit, while in the background the local news droned on.

Monica Dorlander must have been watching the local news too, cause when it was over the light in her unit went off.

Oh shit. What did I do now?

I was sorely tempted to stay up and sit there watching the door of the unit just in case, in the off chance something might happen and I could catch it, and redeem myself for blowing everything utterly so far.

Like hell.

I switched off the TV, hung my pants and jacket over the back of the chair, crawled into bed and went to sleep.

13

I dreamed someone stole my car.

It was one of those dreams where you wake up and you can't remember what you were dreaming. So I didn't know who, what, why, where, when, any of the circumstances. All I knew was, someone stole my car.

It was the middle of the night, it was dark, and for a few moments I didn't know where I was. Then I remembered. I was in a motel room on a mountaintop in the middle of god knows where, and if someone stole my car I was in a lot of troublc.

I got out of bed, staggered to the window, pushed the curtain aside. No. My car was there. It was also dark as hell, so it must still be the middle of the night. Mental-Note-to-buy-a-watch-Number-207.

I tumbled back into bed and went to sleep again. This time I dreamed someone was nailing me into a coffin, not an uncommon dream, I'm sure, but then I'm not that inventive. Certainly not a pleasant one. Here I was still alive, and these idiots didn't know it, and they were nailing the lid on the coffin, and I was yelling and screaming but no one could hear me, and they just kept hammering, bang, bang, bang.

I woke up and light was streaming through the cracks in the edge of the curtains and someone was pounding on my door. Jesus Christ, what the hell time is it, Mental-Note-to-buy-a-watch-Number-208.

I got out of bed and pulled on my pants. If it was Monica Dorlander wanting to know what the hell I was doing following her, I didn't want to be standing there in my underwear.

I opened the door. It wasn't Monica Dorlander. It was a uniformed cop of some type. I say of some type, because the uniforms I'm used to are New York City uniforms, and this sure wasn't that. And I wasn't really alert enough to focus in on what it was. All I knew was that he was a stocky young officer, probably ten years younger than I, and that he didn't look happy.

"Yes?" I said.

The officer fixed me with a cold stare. "Alan Parker?" he said.

Oh shit.

I am not at my best in the morning. Till I've had a cup of coffee I find it hard to focus on anything. And the last thing in the world I'd want to do would be answer questions for some cop.

And the first question was the hardest. Alan Parker? How the hell did I answer that? If I said yes, I'd have lied to the police and I'd be in a lot of trouble. And if I said no, the police would know I'd lied to the Woodsman and I'd be in a lot of trouble. Basically, I was in a lot of trouble.

I tried simple deflection. "What's this all about?"

It didn't work. The square jaw jutted out another inch. "Is your name Alan Parker?"

I took a breath. "I am registered as Alan Parker. This is my room."

His eyes narrowed. "Got any identification?"

Oh sweet Jesus. "Yeah," I said. I reached in my back pocket and pulled out my wallet. I flipped it open to my driver's license.

He looked at it. "Stanley Hastings. Gee, Mr. Parker, could you tell me what you're doing with Mr. Hasting's driver's license?"

"It's my driver's license."

"So you say."

"Take a look at the picture. It's a photo I.D."

"Yeah, but chop shops make 'em up for you. You steal Stanley Hasting's license, put your picture on it. It's done all the time."

"I'm Stanley Hastings. That's my license."

"And who is Alan Parker?"

"No one. I just signed the name."

"Why?"

"Because I didn't want a record of my stay."

"Why?"

I shrugged. I didn't really know the answer. Actually, there was no reason in the world why I couldn't have written Stanley Hastings in the register. What difference could it have possibly made? Who would have cared? I guess I was just seduced by TV.

But that wasn't what he was asking. He was asking what I was doing staying there under an assumed name. And I didn't want to tell him. So the shrug was as good an answer as any.

He glared at me for a moment, then grunted, "Put your shoes on."

"Why?"

"Because you're going outside. Now you can put your shoes on or not, it's entirely up to you, but if you don't, I bet your feet will be cold."

I put my shoes on. The guy took my jacket off the chair

and handed it to me. I realized he was doing it to see if I had anything heavy in the pocket. Ditto my topcoat. I put it on.

He jerked his thumb. "Out."

He stepped aside and I walked by him out the door.

And stopped dead.

The parking lot was a flurry of activity. There were cops everywhere. Some dressed in uniforms like him. Some in other uniforms I didn't recognize either. There were half a dozen extra cars parked, not in front of the units, but crisscross in the parking lot. The doors of several of the units were open, and there were people standing in them looking out.

The door to unit seven was open, but Monica Dorlander wasn't standing in it. Two cops were standing in front of it however. Somehow it seemed to be the focus of attention. As I watched, a third cop came out.

All in all, things did not look good.

My buddy prodded me in the back, which I took to be an invitation to start walking. I stepped out into the parking lot. He put his hand on my arm, probably as a helpful gesture to suggest our rate of speed. We marched out into the parking lot and up to one of the parked cars.

A young cop dressed in the same uniform as my buddy was standing next to it.

"Got a live one, Chuck," my buddy said. "Keep your eye on him."

Chuck, who couldn't have been that far out of his teens, snuffled once, said, "Right," put his hand on my arm, and fixed me with what he must have thought was a steely glare. The kid was young, inexperienced and nervous, but it didn't matter. I wasn't going anywhere.

My buddy left us and walked off toward the motel office. I looked and saw the Woodsman standing out in front of it talking to a couple of other officers. My buddy walked up to him and apparently said something, but his back was to me and it was too far away for me to hear. He turned back and looked over at me. The Woodsman looked at me too, and then nodded his head, and I could see him saying something to my buddy.

While this was going on a car pulled into the driveway. Or I should say started to pull into the driveway. It made the turn, started up the little incline toward the office, and stopped. Where the car stopped the sun was shining right off the windshield and I couldn't see the driver at all.

But I could see the license plate.

Now, I'm not patting myself on the back here. As I've said, I'm not that observant. At the moment I was still groggy with sleep, intimidated by cops, not really sure of what was going on and terrified I was about to find out. So for me to catch a license plate number under those circumstances would be a small miracle slightly on a par with the parting of the Red Sea.

But it was a New York State plate. And in recent years New York State did a smart thing. There were so many cars in the state the license numbers were getting too long to fit on the plates, so they substituted letters for numbers. That solved the problem, because there are twenty-six letters and only ten numbers. So whereas six numbers would only allow nine hundred and ninety-nine thousand nine hundred and ninety-nine plates, three letters and three numbers could accommodate all the cars in the state. So now all New York State license plates, except the personalized ones, consisted of groups of three letters and three numbers, separated by a picture of the Statue of Liberty.

In most cases, of course, the three letters were gibberish, but in some cases they formed words.

Now I know under those circumstances I could never have caught a license plate number. And in fact I didn't catch any numbers.

But the first half of the license plate of the car that pulled into the driveway was "POP."

Apparently POP changed his mind about registering at the motel. I can't say as I blamed him. I don't think I'd register at any motel where a dozen policemen were crawling about. At any rate, POP backed right out the drive, spun the wheel, and took off back the way he'd come.

I looked around at the officers in the lot. Aside from me, I don't think anybody noticed. Particularly my buddy, who was already on his way walking back.

He walked up to me, pointed his finger and said, "You're the guy." He looked at Chuck. "He's the guy."

"Is that right?" Chuck said.

They both looked at me.

I wasn't going to ask them what they meant by the guy. For one thing, I didn't want to give 'em the satisfaction. For another thing, I figured I already knew.

When I said nothing my buddy said, "You watch him. I'm gonna phone in."

"Right," Chuck said.

My buddy walked over to the police car, reached in the window and pulled out the microphone of a police radio. He pressed the button and said, "This is Davis, over."

The radio squawked something that I couldn't make out, and Davis said, "I got him. What you want me to do with him?" The radio squawked again. Davis said, "Roger, over and out."

Davis swung open the back door of the car and said, "Get in."

I never was big on resisting authority, no matter what form it happened to take. I got in the back of the car.

I was just beginning to wake up. It had occurred to me by that point that nobody seemed likely to offer me a cup of coffee, and I was gonna have to do without. So I was doing the best I could of brushing the cobwebs out of a severely befuddled mind, and trying to size up the current situation.

Which wasn't that hard to do. I mean what with there being so much police activity and all, and people standing around staring and cops going in and out of unit seven, it didn't take a genius to figure out my surveillance of Monica Dorlander had somehow taken a turn for the worse.

And when, while Davis was getting the police car turned around, a meat wagon pulled up and joined the cop cars in front of unit seven, I must say I began to have serious concerns for the state of Monica Dorlander's health.

They drove me down the mountain along a few twisty roads into a small town and pulled up in front of a police station. I knew it was a police station because the sign on the front door said, "CHIEF OF POLICE." Otherwise I wouldn't have had a clue. It was a small frame house just like all the other small frame houses in the town. The sign "CHIEF OF POLICE" was hanging from the front door on hooks, and it occurred to me maybe all the houses in town had hooks, and whoever was getting to be police chief that day, well they just gave him the sign.

Chuck and Davis got out, and Davis opened the back door. I took that as an invitation to get out and did. They put their hands on my arms and led me up to the police station.

Surprise. It was indeed a police station, not a private home. It was a large room, outfitted with files, desks, wanted posters, what have you, all the necessary accouterments. It even had a wooden rail with a gate dividing the room in two. This seemed excessive to me, seeing as how the room wasn't that big. Beyond the gate in the back of the room in the left-hand corner was a large desk. Seated at the desk was a large man. I figured he was the Chief of Police. I also figured he wanted to see me. On both counts I figured right.

His name was Chief Dan Creely, if the sign on his desk were to be believed. If the man himself were to be believed, the only plausible explanation could be that long ago he had seen Rod Steiger in *In the Heat of the Night* and never gotten over it. He was as I said a large man, with a beerbelly gut that spilled out over the belt of his low-slung pants. He had a round, jowled face, adorned with wire-rimmed glasses. He chewed gum incessantly with a bulldog jaw. He spoke in a high pitched whine that aspired to be Southern drawl but occasionally lapsed into Brooklyn twang.

This explained the wooden gate—Rod Steiger had had one too. It occurred to me all it would have taken to make the man truly happy, would have been to have an officer named Courtney, so he would have been able to say, "Courtney, could you *try* to get me long distance."

Chief Creely had one other distinguishing characteristic. He seemed to regard every person he met as a performer of fellatio. Whether this was a paranoid fear or merely wishful thinking on his part, I have no idea. At any rate, he so designated them. How he squared this with the Steiger image, I'm not entirely sure. Maybe he figured the movie came out before the MPAA rating codes went into effect, and with today's more relaxed standards that's how Steiger would have talked. At any rate, that's how he did.

When we came in, he shifted his bulk in his chair, pointed his finger at me and said to Davis, "This the cocksucker?"

I have to admit that doesn't happen to be one of my favorite terms of formal address. But as I said, I'm not big on standing up to authority. I decided to keep quiet and let them straighten it out.

"Yeah, that's him," Davis said.

Chief Creely grunted and got up from his chair, no small feat, big as he was. He wandered out through the gate, closed it, and parked his butt on the wooden rail.

He jerked his thumb at me, but spoke to Davis. "What's his name?"

Davis grinned, as far as I knew, a first for him. "Well, now, that seems to be the bone of contention. According to his driver's license it's Stanley Hastings. According to the motel register it's Alan Parker."

Chief Creely grinned back. "Is that right? So the cocksucker's got two names?"

"At least two. Far as we know."

"Wonder which one's his."

"Odds favor Stanley Hastings. His driver's license seems to be genuine. And that's the name on his other I.D."

Good for Davis. I hadn't even seen him looking.

"Which name does he answer to?"

"Neither. I asked him if he was Alan Parker, he told me something noncommittal like go fuck myself."

"In those words?"

"No. He was just loquaciously evasive."

Creely grinned. "You going to night school, Davis? Shit. Loquaciously evasive."

"That's what he was."

"Was he now?" Chief Creely said, still talking to Davis, but casting an eye over me. "You know something? I don't like loquaciously evasive cocksuckers. Loquaciously evasive cocksuckers give me a pain in the ass."

"I know that," Davis said.

Chief Creely turned his attention to me. "All right, you," he said. "I'm going to ask you some questions, and you're going to answer them. If you answer them short and sweet, we're going to have a good time. If you answer them by being loquaciously evasive, then I'm gonna chain you to the wall in the back room on a charge of talking too much. Then you can talk to the wall all you want till you get it out of your system and we'll try the whole thing again. How does that sound to you?"

"Fine," I said. Short and succinct.

Creely nodded to Davis. "Guy learns fast." He turned back to me. "All right. What's your name."

"Stanley Hastings."

"Is that right? Tell me, did you stay at the Pine Hills Motel last night?"

"Yes."

"What name did you sign in the register?"

"Alan Parker."

Chief Creely nodded. "Nothing evasive about that, Davis. You just have to know how to question these cock-suckers. All right, let's go for the biggie. Why did you sign the name Alan Parker if your name's Stanley Hastings."

"Because I didn't want there to be a record of my stay."

Creely pursed his lips and frowned. "I sense the onset of an attack of evasiveness. *Why* didn't you want a record of your stay?"

"Because I'm a private detective."

Chief Creely's eyes widened. You would have thought I'd told him I was from outer space.

He turned to Davis. "He's a private detective?" Creely said incredulously.

Davis shrugged his shoulders helplessly. "First I heard of it."

"Did you ask him?"

"Why the hell would I ask him that?"

Creely turned back to me. "Got some identification?"

I reached in my jacket pocket and pulled out my I.D. I

flipped it open and passed it over to Chief Creely. As I did, I suddenly realized Chief Creely was fulfilling his lifelong dream. We were doing the movie, and I was playing the Sidney Poitier part for him.

Chief Creely folded my I.D. and handed it back to me. "All right," he said. "You're a private detective. That simplifies things. Now, I'm going to ask you some questions and you better have the right answers. Before I do, let me help you out a little. Now Frank Ramsey—that's the owner of the motel, the guy who checked you in last night when you signed the name Alan Parker—he says you made a big deal about trying to get unit six or eight. It was only when they turned out to be rented you settled for unit twelve. Now with that to jog your memory, perhaps you could tell us what you were doing at that motel."

"I'm a private detective. I was hired to follow someone."

"Who?"

"You know who. The woman in unit seven." After a pause I added, "The dead woman."

Creely raised his eyebrows. "The *dead* woman. Did you hear that, Davis?"

"Yeah. I heard that."

"So," Creely said. "The dead woman. Now how did you know the woman was dead?"

"Give me a break," I said. "I get woken up by cops knocking on my door. The parking lot's full of police cars. I get hustled down here to answer questions, and when we leave there's a meat wagon pulling up to unit seven. If I didn't think the woman was dead, I'd be the dumbest private detective ever lived."

"That's entirely possible," Creely said. "It doesn't answer the question."

"*Is* she dead?" I said.

Creely chuckled. "Good ploy. Asking the question as if you didn't know the answer. But I'm afraid it's too little too late. You know damn well she's dead. Dead as a doorknob."

I must say that was a relief. Not that I wanted Monica Dorlander dead, but if she was, I wanted to know it.

See, by now my brain was starting to clear out, and I was starting to make some hard decisions, which it was necessary for me to do, seeing as how I'd gotten myself in a pretty precarious spot. And one of the decisions I'd made was, any information I had, these guys were welcome to it.

Now, I know that blows my image. A private detective's supposed to hold out on the cops, protect his client, and solve the case himself. But that's TV, where some writer has carefully constructed the plot, where if the client wasn't innocent to begin with there wouldn't be any story, so of course he is, and if the detective told the police what he knew the show would be over, so naturally he doesn't, and so on and so forth.

Real life's a little different. Here's how I figured: if Monica Dorlander was dead, my job was over. If she was dead, then Marvin Nickleson wasn't going to get her back, and there was nothing I could do for him. So it couldn't hurt for me to tell my story to the cops.

Unless of course Marvin Nickleson was the one who killed her. In that case it would hurt a lot. But in that case I didn't care. Because if he killed her, he was a rotten son of a bitch who deserved what he got. Now maybe that's an attitude unbefitting a private detective, but I never was any great shakes at it anyway, and the way my first case was turning out, it seemed unlikely I was ever gonna have a second.

And there was another thing. And that was my ace in the hole. If these guys were suspecting me of anything at all—which seemed entirely likely—well, what all of them seemed to have lost sight of was the fact that none of them had ever read me my rights. Which meant I could tell 'em anything I wanted, and nothing I said could ever be used against me. Not that there was any reason why it should. But then I wasn't familiar enough with the laws about obstructing justice and accessory to murder to be able to know for sure just what sort of trouble I might be in. So knowing I was legally safe to talk had to feel kind of good.

I frowned. "I see," I said. "Well, that simplifies things."

"How is that?" Creely said.

"I was hired to follow this woman. If she's dead, my job's over."

"Uh-huh," Creely said. "And who hired you?"

In for a penny, in for a pound. "Marvin Nickleson."

"Marvin Nickleson? And who is that?"

"Her husband. Her estranged husband, rather. They're separated but not divorced."

Creely nodded. "And that's where you come in. You were looking for evidence for the divorce."

"Actually, he was hoping for a reconciliation."

"Yeah, well he ain't gonna get it."

A police radio on a desk by the wall squawked.

Creely grunted, walked over there, plugged in a headset, slipped it on, and pushed the button on the mike. "Creely here. Talk to me." He listened for some time, said, "Got it. Keep me posted." He unplugged the headset, plopped it on the desk and strolled back over.

"Well now," he said. "Mr. Hastings, is it? We're identifying the woman. The dead woman. The one you were following for her husband."

"Oh?" I said.

"Yeah. And we got the same problem with her that we had with you. A coincidence I'm sure, but there you are."

"What do you mean?"

"With regard to her name, of course. Now your name is Hastings, but you registered under the name of Parker.

Now in her case, she registered as Judy Felson. Now we went through the contents of her purse. According to her I.D., her name's not Felson."

"Right," I said. "It's Dorlander."

He shook his head. "No."

"Oh," I said. "Then it's Nickleson."

"No, it's Steinmetz."

"What?!"

"That's right. Julie Steinmetz. Does that name mean anything to you?"

Nothing at all. Nothing except I'm totally fucked. Nothing except all my finespun rationalization had just flown out the window. Jesus Christ. It had never occurred to me the dead woman could be anyone other than Monica Dorlander. I knew she'd had one visitor last night, and one more potential visitor this morning, what with the car with the license plate POP. So why couldn't she have had a third? Actually, she must have had a third, since someone wound up dead. And if that third visitor was a woman, she could have just as well wound up dead as Monica Dorlander.

Except for the car. Monica Dorlander's car was still in front of the unit. So that would point to her being the corpse. Unless she took the dead woman's car instead and left hers there. But why should she do that?

How the hell should I know?

All I knew was, if Monica Dorlander wasn't dead, I'd already spilled my guts to the cops. Including giving them Marvin Nickleson's name. Which would probably lay me wide open for a lawsuit on the one hand, and fulfill my prophesy of being the world's dumbest detective on the other.

I blinked. "That's gotta be wrong. The dead woman is Monica Dorlander. She lives on East 83rd Street. She works at Artiflex Cosmetics on Third Avenue."

Creely squinted at me through his glasses. "Is that so?"

"Yeah, that's so," I said. "If there's any question about the matter of identity, maybe I'd better see the body."

"Oh yeah?" Creely said. "Hey, Davis, listen to this guy. Maybe he ought to see the body. Well for your information, the body's on its way to the morgue, and you're not. In point of fact, you're not going anywhere. Monica Dorlander, huh? You come in here with your two names, and then you start telling us fairy stories, and the next thing I know you're telling me how to do my job.

"Davis," he barked.

"Yes sir."

"I'm getting a little sick of this cocksucker. Take him in the back room and chain him to the pipe."

Davis took me in the back room and chained me to the pipe. Not the most pleasant thing in the world, but not the worst either. At least I knew the routine. The boys from Major Crimes in Atlantic City had done the same thing to me when I was down there. Apparently in law enforcement, holding cells are a luxury.

Davis chained me to the pipe with handcuffs, went out and closed the door, so as I wouldn't be able to hear the conversation in the next room.

Great.

I stood there and looked around. It seemed to be a small storeroom of some type. There were piles of cardboard boxes, a few battered files. But no furniture of any kind.

The pipe I was chained to was a metal pipe running from the floor to the ceiling. It might have been a water pipe of some kind. If so, I sure hoped it was the cold one. If the thing started heating up I was in a lot of trouble.

Since there was no chair I had two choices: I could stand up or sit on the floor. Sitting on the floor in my suit and topcoat would be rather undignified. I stood there, waiting to see if Davis would come back. He didn't.

As time stretched on, dignity became somewhat less of a priority. Fuck it. I'm exhausted. I'm sitting down.

Small problem. The pipe had a metal support piece attached to the wall about waist level. The handcuff around the pipe was above that. I could sit on the floor, but only with my right arm raised up in the air.

Since I didn't have a watch, I don't know how long this further indignity delayed my decision to sit. It could have been fifteen minutes. It could have been half an hour. Time's a funny thing when you're chained to the wall. At any rate, I finally gave in. I eased slowly down the wall, not wanting to rip my arm out of my socket. It was a big relief when my ass hit the floor. Thank god. My right arm was extended far enough for it to be a slight strain, but at least I wasn't hanging on it.

I sat there and pondered my fate. I could see a lot of things happening, most of them bad. My best-case scenario had Davis coming in and unlocking the handcuffs, Creely bawling me out and sending me home, me calling Marvin Nickleson and telling him there was no charge and I was washing my hands of the whole affair, and then me eating my expenses, cutting my losses, learning my lesson and vowing never to take on another client again.

My worst-case scenario had some nosy kid from a Boy Scout troop on a field trip to the local police station poking his head in the storeroom door and discovering the bleached bones of a private detective's skeleton chained to the wall.

It had been a long enough time that my worst-case scenario had begun to seem likely when, sudden reversal, my best-case scenario began to come true. The door opened and Davis came in and unlocked the handcuffs.

What a relief. Except my right arm was completely numb and moving it was agony. But under the circumstances, that seemed a small inconvenience. I screamed slightly when the arm dropped to my side, but that was about it. I flopped onto my knees, pushed up with my left hand, and struggled to my feet.

"Let's go," Davis said.

I went. No argument there. I didn't know where we were going, but I sure as hell wanted to be out of that storage closet.

Davis led me back to the front room. Chief Creely was there. So was Chuck. So was another cop, somewhere in between Chuck and Davis's age.

There was a woman with them. She was fortyish, plump, with glasses and rather frizzy dark hair.

Davis marched me up to them.

Creely turned to the woman. "All right. Take a good look. You ever seen him before?"

I gulped. Jesus Christ. They're identifying me already. For what?

The woman squinted at me through her glasses.

"Well, what about it? You ever seen him before?"

I didn't think so. I hadn't seen her before, as far as I knew. But then I'm terrible with faces. She was looking at me kind of funny.

"I'm not sure," she said. "The face is familiar, but I can't place it."

"Think. It's important."

"Well, I should hope so. Dragging me up here."

"Please, ma'am. Just look at him."

"I'm looking at him."

"Davis, we're just getting full face here. Show her the profile. Walk him around some."

Davis turned me back and forth, led me in a circle. As we walked back to them I saw her eyes widen through her glasses.

"That's it. That's it," she said. "That's the guy."

"What guy?" Creely said.

"I saw him in the street."

"Where?"

"Outside my office building. A couple of times. I wouldn't have thought anything of it, but I saw him again outside my apartment house."

My head was spinning. Office building? Apartment house? What the hell was she talking about? I assumed she was from the motel. I hadn't been to any office or apartment building up here. She must mean New York, and—

It slammed me in the face. My stomach suddenly felt hollow.

I looked at the woman. "Who are you?" I croaked.

She said nothing.

I turned to Creely. "Who is she?" I said, though in my heart of hearts I already knew the answer.

Creely snorted. "As if you didn't know. She's Monica Dorlander, of course."

My head was spinning. It was as if layer upon layer of reality were being stripped away. First Monica Dorlander was dead. Then Monica Dorlander wasn't dead. Then Monica Dorlander wasn't Monica Dorlander.

Chief Creely prodded me in the arm. "What about you? You ever seen this woman before?"

"No."

"Oh, is that right? Monica Dorlander. The woman you were following. The woman who spotted you following her. You've never seen her before?"

"That's not the woman I was following."

"Oh really? You told us she was."

"I was wrong."

"Is that right? Let me see if I've got this straight. You told us you were following Monica Dorlander. You staked out her home. You staked out her office. But you weren't following her."

I took a breath. "Let *me* get something straight." I turned to the woman. "Your name is Monica Dorlander?"

She said nothing.

I turned to Creely. "Could you tell her to answer me?"

"Go ahead and answer him."

"Your name's Monica Dorlander?" I repeated.

"Yes."

"You live on East 83rd Street?"

"Yes."

"You work at Artiflex Cosmetics on Third Avenue?"

"That's right."

I looked at Chief Creely and shrugged helplessly. "I've been had."

"So you say," he said. "All right ma'am. Let me ask you this. You ever been here before?"

"Here?"

"This neck of the woods."

"No."

"Ever stay at the Pine Hills Motel?"

"No."

"What about yesterday? Last night. Did you drive up here from New York and register at the Pine Hills Motel?"

"No I did not."

"You didn't register there under an assumed name?"

"An assumed name. Say, what is this?"

"You didn't register there under the name Judy Felson?"

"I most certainly did not."

"The name Judy Felson mean anything to you?"

"Not a thing."

Creely nodded. "I didn't think it would. Then let me ask you this. Do you know a Julie Steinmetz?"

She frowned. "I don't think so."

"You don't think so?"

"The name doesn't ring a bell."

"Too bad," Creely said. "I'm sorry, ma'am, but I'm going to have to ask you to do something slightly unpleasant. Davis?"

"Sir."

"Take Miss Dorlander down to the morgue. Have her look at the body."

The woman's face paled. Her jaw dropped open. "Body!"

"Yes, ma'am. I'm sorry, but we're going to have to see if you can identify the body."

"Body!" she said again. "You mean . . ." She stole a glance at me. "You mean . . . he *killed* someone?"

"Well now, ma'am—"

Her eyes were growing wider and wider. "And you let me stand here talking to him? You let him *question* me?"

She started backing away during this. Davis was right at her elbow.

"You let him see my *face*!" she said in horror.

Davis piloted her smoothly out the door.

Creely turned back to me. "That woman doesn't like you."

I took a breath. "You all but told her I was a murderer."

"Did I now? Now that's real unfortunate. I don't know where she got that impression.

"Now let's talk about you. Let's talk about the bullshit you've been spewing out ever since you walked in this door."

"It's not bullshit."

"Then what is it?"

"I told you. I've been had. Suckered. Played for a dope."

Creely chuckled. "Gee, how could anyone do that?" His face hardened. "Now look. I want some answers, and this time I want 'em straight. You don't know the woman who was just here?"

"No."

"You weren't following her?"

"No."

"Then who were you following?"

"Another woman."

"Who?"

"Probably the woman that's dead."

"Julie Steinmetz?"

"If that's her name."

"So why were you following her?"

"I thought she was Monica Dorlander."

"How could you make that mistake?"

"I didn't make that mistake."

Creely frowned. "What?"

"I didn't make a mistake. I followed the woman I was supposed to—"

I broke off, remembering something any competent detective would have remembered hours ago.

Creely said, "What is it?"

"Look, Chief," I said. "If I were to reach in my hip pocket real slow and take out my wallet, could you tell these guys not to shoot me?"

Creely glanced at Chuck and the other officer. "I could make the suggestion. If they disregard it, there's not much I can do."

"Great."

I reached in my back pocket and took out my wallet. I opened it, riffled through some papers, and pulled out the picture of Monica Dorlander. I handed it to Creely.

"Here you are."

"What's this?"

"That's a picture of the woman I was hired to follow. The woman I was told was Monica Dorlander."

Creely studied the picture. "Nice looker."

"I thought so too."

Creely turned to the two officers. "Either of you guys get a look at the body?"

They shook their heads.

"No, sir," Chuck said. "I think Davis did."

"Well, that don't help us much. He's on his way to the morgue." Creely turned back to me. "This is the woman you were supposed to follow?"

"That's right."

"She doesn't look anything like Monica Dorlander."

"I know that."

"Then why did you think she was?"

I took a breath. How many times did I have to say it? "I told you. I was set up."

"You were lied to?"

"Yes."

"You were told the woman in this picture was Monica Dorlander?"

"Yes."

"By whom?

I took another breath. "My client. Marvin Nickleson."

The door opened and another officer came in. They sure grew 'em young around here. I guess those with any gumption got the hell out.

He had a man with him. An elderly gentleman with a flowing mane of white hair.

"That him?" Creely said.

"Yeah, that's him," the officer said, leading him forward.

"All right," Creely said to the white haired man. "I want you to take a good look at this guy and tell me if you've ever seen him before?"

The man peered at me, frowned, shook his head.

"Never saw him before in my life," he said.

I looked at Creely. "Don't tell me," I said.

Creely grinned. "That's right, Mr. Hastings. Good guess. Allow me to present Mr. Marvin Nickleson."

"Your name's Marvin Nickleson?"

"Right."

"You work for Croft, Wheelhouse and Green?"

"Yes."

"As a graphics artist?"

"Yes."

"Let me take a guess. You live on East 14th Street?"

"Yes, I do."

Creely looked at me. "You know this man?"

"Never saw him before in my life."

"You know his name, address, and where he works, but you don't know anything about him?"

"I know his name because you just told me. I know where he works because I was told that's where he works. I know his address cause when I called information to get his phone number I was told they had no Marvin Nickleson on 83rd Street, but they had a Marvin Nickleson on East 14th Street. I didn't call that number cause I knew it wasn't him."

"It *is* him."

"Yes and no."

Creely closed his eyes. "Hold on a minute. You were going to call Marvin Nickleson?"

"No."

"Then why did you want his number?"

"I wanted to call Monica Dorlander."

"Why would you get Marvin Nickleson's number to call Monica Dorlander?"

"I thought it would be the same number."

"Why would it be the same number?"

"Because Monica Dorlander was his wife."

During this exchange Marvin Nickleson's eyes had been darting back and forth between Creely and me like a guy watching a tennis match. Now they widened and his mouth fell open.

Creely turned to him. "You know Monica Dorlander?"

Marvin Nickleson blinked. "Who?"

"Monica Dorlander. You know Monica Dorlander?"

"No."

"You're not married to Monica Dorlander?"

Marvin Nickleson looked utterly bewildered. "No."

"And you never *were* married to Monica Dorlander?"

"No."

"How about Julie Steinmetz?"

"Who?"

"Julie Steinmetz. You never heard of Julie Steinmetz? You're not married to Julie Steinmetz?"

"No."

"How about Judy Felson?"

"Who?"

"You never heard of Judy Felson?"

"No."

"You're not married to Judy Felson?"

"No."

Creely was still holding the picture I'd given him. "How

about this? You ever seen this woman before?"

Marvin Nickleson looked at Creely. Then at the picture. Then up at Creely again. "No," he said.

Creely rubbed his head. "Great." He turned to the officer who'd brought Marvin Nickleson in. "O.K. Run him down to the morgue. Introduce him to Monica Dorlander."

"Sir?"

"The woman with Davis. You'll find them down there. Put 'em together and ask 'em if they know each other. While you're down there, have him look at the body."

As with Monica Dorlander, the word body had a chilling effect on Marvin Nickleson. "Body. Whose body?"

Creely nodded. "Yeah. That's the question."

The officer led Marvin Nickleson out.

Creely turned to me. "I can't wait to hear your explanation for this."

"I was hired by a man who told me his name was Marvin Nickleson. He told me the woman in the picture was his wife, Monica Dorlander, and he hired me to follow her. Now you know as much as I do."

"Oh, yeah," Creely said. "What I don't know is why. Why would he do that?"

That was indeed the question.

I was saved from having to answer it by the arrival of two more cops, this time in a uniform I recognized. They were state police. The state cops were older than Creely's men, though not as old as Creely. They also had an air of authority about them—cold, hard, determined.

The stockier of the two pushed forward. "Chief Creely?"

"Yes."

"Sergeant Dickerson. State police. We understand you've apprehended a suspect."

Creely wheeled his belly around in the sergeant's direction, put his hands on his hips. "Oh you understand that, do you?"

"That's right. Is that him?"

"That depends what you mean by him."

"I'm referring to the man who stayed at the Pine Hills Motel as Alan Parker, but whose car is registered to Stanley Hastings."

"You ran the registration?"

"Yes, we did."

"Good. I'm glad to have the confirmation."

"So are we. Well, sir, we're here to take the suspect back for questioning."

Creely stuck out his jaw. "You're what?"

"We're here to bring in the suspect. Plus any evidence you may have gathered."

Creely's eyes narrowed. "Oh, is that right?"

Sergeant Dickerson smiled condescendingly. "Chief, this is a murder investigation."

"I know it's a murder investigation."

"Well, that's why we're here. To bring in the suspect."

"On whose authority?"

Dickerson smiled again. "Chief, this is a small town with a limited force. Under the circumstances, in a murder case the state police have the authority to lend assistance to the local officer—"

"Lend assistance?" Creely's gum was going like crazy. "That's a good one. Lend assistance. I know what that means. That's a euphemism for taking over the investigation."

Sergeant Dickerson frowned. "Chief, no one wants to step on your toes here, but we have this murder that has to be cleared up. You must be aware that the state police—"

"I'm aware that the state police poke their nose in anywhere they possibly can."

"Now look, Chief—"

"Authority."

"What?"

"I asked you what authority."

"And I told you."

"You told me bullshit. Lend assistance. Standard practice. Yeah, that's right. We're a small town. If I run into trouble in my investigation, I can request assistance from the state police and you guys can provide it. I don't recall my requesting any assistance, do you? Until I do, I'm in charge. This case is in my jurisdiction. This is my prisoner and you're not taking him nowhere. Now, you tell the cocksuckers back at headquarters this is my murder investigation and I'm in charge here. Now if they wanna voluntarily render assistance I haven't asked for, I want reports on everything they do, I want every officer responsive and responsible to me.

"And that goes for you too. You guys been poking around that motel, you give me everything you got."

Sergeant Dickerson's face had darkened during the beginning of the tirade, but by now he had composed himself and was back to his superior smirk. He gave the other officer a look. "Sure, Chief," he said. "If that's how you want it."

"Fine," Creely said. "You guys got anything for me?"

"Yes, we do," Dickerson said.

"Well, let's have it," Creely said.

Dickerson smiled that superior smile again. "Oh, sure, Chief. Now I wouldn't wanna tell you your business, but do you really want to discuss it in front of the suspect here?"

Creely gave me a look. For a second I thought he was going to say yes, just so he wouldn't have to concede Dickerson had scored a point. But he thought better of it.

"Nothnagel," he barked, and I finally learned Chuck's last name—with a mouthful like that no wonder Davis called him Chuck.

"Sir?" Chuck said.

Creely jerked his thumb. "Chain him up again."

Chuck took me in the back room and chained me to the pipe again. He went back out, doubtless to give Chief Creely moral support.

Leaving me alone with my thoughts.

And what great thoughts they were. Monica Dorlander wasn't Monica Dorlander, Marvin Nickleson wasn't Marvin Nickleson, the state police and the local police were fighting over who had the right to arrest me, and I was in the back room chained to a pipe, but aside from that I was doing great.

I came back to the question Creely had asked me before the state cops barged in: why? That was a biggie all right. I knew *what* had happened. An unknown man had hired me to follow an unknown woman and he'd used the names of real people for both himself and her. I knew why he'd used real names. He was afraid I might start backtracking him, and if so he wanted the information to check out. He'd given me the name Monica Dorlander because that was the name of a person who lived in the building of the woman he wanted me to follow. So in case I disregarded his instructions, as I in fact did, by calling information or talking to the doorman, in either instance Monica Dorlander would check out. And in his case he'd made up the convenient bogus story about moving to a rooming house with no phone, and given me a work address which on the one hand was genuine, but on the other hand I was not supposed to call. I hadn't, but if I had, just to check up on him, they would have confirmed they had a Marvin Nickleson working there. And since he'd forbidden me to call him at work, even if I called the company to confirm he actually worked there, I wouldn't be apt to ask to talk to him.

Yeah, that's why he'd used the names. But the big why, why he'd done it at all, that I had no idea.

The door opened. Chuck came in, unlocked the handcuffs and led me back out again.

The place was quiet. The state cops were gone. For a moment I thought the room was empty. Then I saw Chief Creely sitting at his desk. The reason I missed him was he wasn't sitting up straight. His chair was tipped back, and he was slumped down in it. He looked exhausted, drained, like a prizefighter in his corner between rounds.

If so, the sight of me was like the bell for round ten. Creely's muscles stiffened. The chair tipped forward. Creely put his hands on the arms and heaved himself out of it. He stood looking at me for a moment. Then he leaned forward and picked up something from his desk.

It was a plastic ziplock bag. I knew it well, because my father-in-law happens to manufacture them. Funny what thoughts flash through your mind at a time like that. Thinking about the bag, when what I was really looking at was the contents.

It was a gun.

Creely came around the desk and lumbered over to us. He held up the bag.

"Take a look at this," he said.

I looked.

It was a gun all right. It wasn't a revolver, so it must have been an automatic. There endeth my expertise with guns.

Creely looked at me. "You ever see this before?"

"No."

"Are you sure?"

"Absolutely. I'm scared to death of guns."

Creely snorted contemptuously. I couldn't tell if it was because he believed me, or because he didn't.

Creely handed the plastic bag to Chuck. "Here. Run this down to the lab in Newburgh. And when you turn it over to the cocksuckers, you make it clear the reports come directly to me. You got that? Not to the state police. Here. To me."

"Yes sir."

Chuck went out.

Creely turned to face me. "I'm going to give you one more chance. You *sure* you never seen that gun before?"

"Is that the murder weapon?"

Creely grimaced. "Jesus Christ. What is it with you, you keep asking me questions? I ask you a question, you don't answer, you ask me a question back. Who's in charge here? The state cops think they are. You think you are. Look here. I'm in charge. You're in deep shit. I ask the questions, you answer. You don't like it, we resume your love affair with the pipe in the back room.

"Now. I was being nice and giving you another chance. Perhaps I should say your last chance. So tell me. Have you ever seen that gun before?"

"No."

Creely nodded. "Fine. Glad to hear it. Now about your question. The one you thought was more important than mine. Was it the murder gun? Well now, that's what it's going to the lab to see. They'll fire some test bullets through it, and then they'll send over to the morgue, and if the cocksuckers over there haven't made a mess of the fatal bullet, they'll be able to tell."

"Fatal bullet?"

"Oh yeah. Best we can tell, she was shot once in the heart. There's no exit wound, so the bullet's still in the body. So if the medics don't fuck it up, we can get a match."

Creely cocked his head at me and chewed his gum. "I don't know why I'm the one giving out all the information here, but I'm just a nice guy so I'll tell you.

"Odds are it's the fatal gun. It's been recently fired. There's one bullet shy of a full load in the magazine. Plus we found a shell casing from an automatic on the motel room floor. We ought to be able to match up the mark from the firing pin on the shell casing, as well as matching the fatal bullet. Now that has yet to be done, but I would say it's safe to assume this was the murder weapon."

"Where'd you find it?"

Creely smiled. "Thank you."

"For what?"

"For asking. See, I knew with a guy as inquisitive as you, if we just talked long enough eventually you'd ask the right question. The one I've been waiting to answer."

Creely unwrapped a fresh stick of gum and popped it into his mouth. I figured he was doing it just to prolong the suspense. To make me ask him again.

I couldn't help myself. I did.

"Where did you find it?"

He chewed his gum. Shrugged. "State cops found it. Weren't going to let me have it, either. Sons of bitches. Gonna take the gun and you too. Cocksuckers."

Creely shook his head. Frowned. Then his face brightened. "Oh, but you asked me where. Funny you should ask." He cocked his head at me and his smile was rather smug. "It was in the glove compartment of your car."

17

Stanley Hastings's Interpretation of Dreams.

Despite the code alarm, my car has been broken into many times. It's not that hard to do. The lock itself is simple. You stick in a screwdriver, turn, and the door pops open.

Of course when that happens the code alarm goes off and the ignition cutoff switch kicks in, leaving the car thief with a loud wailing car that won't start. No car thief wants to hassle with that when he can walk a few blocks and find another car that *doesn't* have a code alarm. So though my car's been broken into many times, it's never been stolen.

But the lock *is* vulnerable. And after each successive break in it becomes more so—the casing a little looser, the hole slightly more enlarged. (I never repair it of course—it would be a waste of money, and what would be the point?) So by now it was so bad that, if even I, the most inept of detectives, whom a locked door usually stymies, should happen to lose my keys, I could probably get in.

And someone had. They'd picked the lock and popped

the door open. The alarm had gone off. They'd taken the murder gun and put it in the glove compartment. Then they'd locked and closed the door and walked off.

The alarm had woken me, slowly, groggily. And as I said, my alarm is the kind that goes for a minute and shuts off. I'd woken up, baffled, confused, with no conscious recollection of having heard an alarm.

But having dreamed someone stole my car.

All of that came to me in a flash, of course, the moment Creely told me about the gun in the glove compartment. The murderer had put it there after the crime. I also realized of all the spots the murderer could have chosen, that was probably the one I liked least. No wonder the state cops were so hot for my bod. The only wonder was how Creely had talked them out of it. The only explanation must have been that it really was his jurisdiction, and if he wanted to tell them to go roll a hoop, he could.

And he had. And on reflection, I couldn't blame him. After all, here it was, probably his first murder case. And with the gun in the glove compartment, he had to figure he had it all wrapped up. Under those circumstances, why the hell should he let someone else take the credit for it?

He stood there looking at me. He was grinning sardonically like a Cheshire cat, and chewing his gum like a contented cow.

I knew what he was doing. He had dropped his bombshell, and now he was watching me to see if I'd break.

In a way, he was getting his wish. I wasn't quite at the point where I was gonna confess to this murder, but on the other hand, my poker face isn't that good, and if that's what we'd been playing, I bet Creely would not have been reading me for a full house. More likely for someone not playing with a full deck.

I wanted to say something brave, jaunty, cocky—toss off

a flippant zinger like a TV detective would do. Or perhaps raise one eyebrow, cock my head at him, and drawl out something caustically ironic, like Jack Nicholson in *Chinatown.*

Only I didn't feel like Jack Nicholson in *Chinatown.* If the truth be known, I didn't feel like Sidney Poitier in *In the Heat of the Night,* either.

If anything, I felt like the title toon in *Who Framed Roger Rabbit?*

"The door was locked and the code alarm was on?"

"I explained that."

"Explain it again."

I sighed and rubbed my head. "The murderer broke into my car. That set off the code alarm. Then the murderer stuck the gun in the glove compartment, locked the car and got out of there."

"How'd he lock the door without a key?"

"Come on, Chief. You drive a car. You push the button down and hold the door handle up when you slam the door."

"Then how'd he reset the code alarm."

"It resets itself. Actually, it never turns off unless you punch the computer numbers in. The siren shuts off after one minute. But the alarm is still set, and if someone tries to get into the car it will go off again."

"It did go off again."

"Oh?"

"When the state police searched your car. That's how

we know the door was locked and the alarm was on." Greely chewed his gum. "Now, in the middle of the night, when you allege someone broke into your car."

"Yeah?"

"The alarm went off?"

"Right."

"But you didn't hear it?"

"No, I didn't actually hear it."

"Then how do you know it went off?"

"I told you. I had a dream someone stole my car."

Creely shook his head. "Great. Wonderful. You had a dream. What a wonderful defense. 'Gee, officer, I dreamed it.' "

"I had the dream. It must have been because the siren went off and I heard it in my sleep. But it only lasts a minute. So by the time I woke up it had shut off. So I had no recollection of having heard a siren. I just thought someone had stolen my car."

"And what time was this?"

"I don't know."

"Why not?"

"I don't have a watch."

"What the hell kind of a private detective are you, you don't have a watch?"

I didn't want to answer that question. It was embarrassing. But then, that was only one of a number of embarrassing questions I didn't want to answer. And damned if Chief Creely didn't keep shooting them at me.

Creely and I were having a little chat. It was only natural, I suppose. Sincc Chuck had left to take the gun to the police lab, and Davis and the other officer hadn't got back from the morgue with Monica Dorlander and Marvin Nickleson yet, we were the only ones in the station. So

Creely and I were just hanging out, shooting the shit, and killing time.

Waiting for my lawyer.

I'd called Richard right after the gun in the glove compartment bit. I hated to do it, but I figured that little touch had bumped the case up into his league. Not that I was worried about bothering him—I knew he'd actually be thrilled. But Richard is Richard. Involving him in a murder case is kind of like unleashing a pit bull—on the one hand you know it's going to protect you, but on the other hand, are you up to dealing with the resultant chaos?

In this case I had no choice. I was at the stage where it was either call Richard or some local lawyer, and if I did the latter, Richard never would have forgiven me. So I made the call.

I also made Richard's day. When he answered the phone, I could tell he was still in his blue funk, but when he heard why I was calling he perked right up. He told me to sit tight and he'd be right there.

He also told me to keep my mouth shut and not say a word. I had chosen to disregard that advice, for two reasons. For one thing, I figured if I clammed up and refused to answer questions, Creely would chain me to the pipe again. Frankly, I'd had enough of that storeroom. As far as I was concerned, sitting in a chair chatting with Creely sure beat sitting on the floor with my arm in the air.

For another thing—and this was something I couldn't tell Richard on the phone with Creely standing right there at my elbow—despite everything, despite the murder weapon having been found in my glove compartment and all that, Creely still hadn't read me my rights.

Which meant that nothing I told him could be used against me in a court of law. And seeing as how a court of law was where we were apt to be heading, I figured as long as Creely was giving me the opportunity, I might as well get everything in.

And that we did. We went over the code alarm thing again and again. And Marvin Nickleson and Monica Dorlander. And Monica Dorlander's (or Julie Steinmetz's or Judy Felson's or whomever's) evening caller, the man I knew only as Check-hat. Mr. Speedy Gonzales. The in-again-out-again man with no name. Here again the questions proved embarrassing, and Chief Creely's sarcasm withering. But we went over it all.

All except POP. I was holding out about POP. I figured if the cops hadn't tipped to him yet, and it appeared that they hadn't, I ought to have an ace in the hole. If POP was indeed an ace. Though with my luck he was more apt to be a two or a three. But aside from POP, we did the whole schmear.

We were still into it when Davis got back with Monica Dorlander. The real Monica Dorlander, that is, not the phony dead one.

"Well?" Chief Creely demanded.

Monica Dorlander looked a little green around the gills. Apparently she'd never seen a murder victim before.

"Well," she said. "It's just as I told the officer. I've seen her before. She lives in my building. I just don't know her name."

"You got the picture?" Davis asked.

"What?" Creely said.

"Marvin Nickleson had never seen the dead woman before, but he said she looked like the woman in the picture."

Creely jerked his thumb at Monica Dorlander. "What about her?"

"Sir?"

"Had Marvin Nickleson ever seen *her* before?"

"He said no."

"Is that right, ma'am? You ever seen him before?"

"No, I haven't."

Creely grunted. "Here. Take a look at this."

He passed over the picture.

She took a look. Her lip quivered. She looked as if she were going to be sick. "Yes," she said. "That's her."

"How about it, Davis?" Creely said. "Is it her?"

Davis looked at the picture. He nodded. "Yeah. It's her, all right."

All right. Confirmations all around. The woman I was following was dead. I was sorry to hear it, but glad to have it confirmed. The way the case had been breaking, I wouldn't have been that surprised if the dead woman had turned out to be someone I'd never seen or heard of.

At that point, the other officer and Marvin Nickleson arrived, and the whole merry-go-round began again. Monica Dorlander and Marvin Nickleson were given every opportunity in the world to admit that they knew each other. When they failed to take advantage of it, Marvin Nickleson was given every opportunity to admit that he knew the dead woman. He denied that until it became boring, and then he started getting cranky, and demanding to know when he could go home. Which cued Monica Dorlander to start getting cranky and demand to know when *she* could go home. I could tell Chief Creely was getting sick of them, and probably would have sent them both home if he could have only got a word in edgewise.

No one was paying the least attention to me, and I wasn't handcuffed or anything, so if I'd had the guts to do it, I probably could have just walked out the door. I thought better of it, however. For one thing, flight is an indication of guilt. For another thing, if Richard drove up all that distance to get me out of jail, and then found out I'd stood him up, I'd be in a lot more trouble than just facing a murder rap.

It was right about then that Richard arrived. He banged open the front door and came striding into a scene of chaos that must have looked like something out of a "Barney Miller" rerun—two character types bitching and moaning and carrying on, and the cops standing around watching them and scratching their heads.

Richard has tremendous stage presence and an amazing ability to take charge. He did so now. He strode into the center of the confusion, struck a theatrical pose and said, "That will do."

It did. Amazingly, everyone shut up.

"Thank you," Richard said. He snapped his fingers. "First of all, my client's rights are being violated here. One, he's being interrogated outside my presence. Two, he's being interrogated in the presence of other witnesses. Not only does this violate his rights, but it also renders any identification inadmissable in the event the witnesses should subsequently pick him out of a lineup.

"Second of all, what we have here is a case of harassment and false arrest. I hereby serve notice that when I file charges in that case, the manner in which my client and I are treated from this point on shall be relevant to the charge, and shall have an impact on the amount of damages we intend to seek.

"Now. I need to confer with my client alone and at once. Any attempt to prevent me from doing so shall be considered a further violation of his rights, and will substantially increase damages in the civil suit on the one hand, and render him blameless from any criminal charge on the other.

"Is that clear?"

I doubt it, but who would disagree with him? My god, what a performance. He stood there, eyes flashing, challenging the room.

We stood there, gawking at him.

Chief Creely blinked twice. His face wrinkled up, as if he'd just smelled something distasteful.

He cocked his head, squinted sideways at me, jerked his thumb in Richard's direction, and demanded, "Who's *this* cocksucker?"

19

Eventually it all got straightened out, but not before Richard had delivered an impromptu lecture on the laws of libel, by the end of which Chief Creely looked as if he were about to swallow his gum. Richard could get going on any subject if provoked, and before he was done we had all learned more about libel, slander, and defamation of character than any human being could ever wish to know. I must say, distracted as I was, most of it went over my head. I did learn, however, that irresponsible statements are far more damaging when made in the presence of witnesses, and more damaging still if those witnesses happen to be unbiased private citizens rather than public officials. To this end, Richard duly obtained and copied down the names and addresses of Marvin Nickleson and Monica Dorlander.

That's not to say Richard had it all his way. Chief Creely did not take kindly to being used as a punching bag, and managed to get his two cents in. It was a tribute to Richard's powers of intimidation that even in the heat of the argument Chief Creely refrained from using any phrases that could be considered actionable.

When the smoke finally cleared away, Richard got what he wanted—a private conference with his client. The private conference room was—you guessed it—the storage closet. Not my favorite place in the world, but at least this time I wasn't chained to the wall.

I told Richard everything. From Marvin Nickleson to Monica Dorlander, to Monica Dorlander's midnight caller, to my interpretation of dreams, to the subsequent discovery of the murder weapon in my car, to the arrival of the real Monica Dorlander and Marvin Nickleson, to the tentative identification of the body as Julie Steinmetz.

"What a crock of shit," Richard said.

"It happens to be true."

"So what? I'm not interested in true. I'm interested in what I can sell to a jury."

I felt a chill. "You think this will go to trial?"

Richard shrugged. "How the hell should I know. But I'm a lawyer. I have to say, what would happen *if* this goes to trial."

"All right. What would happen?"

"You'd be convicted."

"What?!"

"Don't get upset. I wouldn't let that happen."

"Well, that's a relief."

"I'm just telling you where your story stands."

"It's not a story."

"That's not the point. I'm saying to myself, if this came to trial, what would I have to do to get this guy off?"

"And?"

"A lot depends on the makeup of the jury. Larry Davis got acquitted by ten blacks and two Hispanics."

"So?"

"With your story, I'd have to pack the jury with ten

Martians and two Hollywood producers strung out on coke."

"That's not funny."

"No, it isn't. We have a serious credibility problem here. You shadow the woman for days. You register at a motel under an assumed name. The murder weapon's found in your car. Then you claim the woman you were following wasn't the woman you thought you were following. But you happen to have a picture of her in your wallet, and it happens that the dead woman *is* the woman you were following."

"I was set up."

"Right. You know it and I know it. The problem is to find twelve upright citizens who will buy it. You want to know what the odds are?"

"Damn it, Richard. I know I'm in a mess. The point is, what are we going to do about it?"

"Well, the first thing is to get you out of here. Which may not be easy."

My heart sank. "Oh?"

"Well, they'll probably arraign you for murder. If they do, you'll have to stay in jail until I can go before the judge and make a case for bail."

My eyes widened. "They're going to put me in jail?"

"What did you think they were going to do, name you Man of the Year? They got you dead to rights on a murder rap."

"Richard . . ."

"What?"

"I mean, Jesus Christ, I thought you could do something about this."

"Don't worry. If they make a case, I can fight it. But if they wanna arraign you, they're gonna arraign you.

There's nothing I can do about that. It won't be long. I'll bail you right out."

"I see. So what do we do now?"

"I'll make the pitch for you walking. They won't buy it. I'll say charge him or release him. They'll charge you and whisk you before a judge for prearraignment. I'll make a pitch for bail. The judge won't buy it, because it's murder. So he'll schedule an arraignment hearing."

My world was crumbling. "Schedule?"

"It'll be a day, two at the most."

"Jesus Christ."

Richard jerked his thumb. "Now the two witnesses out there—did they identify you?"

"Well . . ."

"Well what?"

"The woman saw me staking out her office building and her apartment house."

"And she's the real Monica Dorlander, and the guy's the real Marvin Nickleson?"

"Right."

"How'd the cops get a line on them?"

"Well . . ."

Richard's eyes narrowed. "I told you not to talk. What did you tell them?"

"I told them everything."

Richard exploded. "God damn it, I told you not to talk."

"I know, but—"

"Jesus Christ," Richard said. "I listen to your story, and it's such a bunch of bullshit I can't believe it. And the only thing I got going for me, the only thing that gives me any hope at all, is I know no one else on god's green earth is ever going to hear it. Not if I can help it. And then I find out my client went and spilled the whole thing."

Which was neither fair nor accurate. Richard had to know I talked to the cops as soon as I told him about the real Monica Dorlander and Marvin Nickleson. But he hadn't brought it up then. He'd saved his explosion for the right dramatic moment. It was probably just his courtroom training, but it pissed me off to have him try it on me.

Particularly when I was in the right.

I held up my hand. "It's all right, Richard."

"All right? How can it be all right?"

"It's better than all right. It's perfect."

"What the hell are you talking about?"

I played my ace. "No one ever read me my rights. No one told me I had the right to remain silent. No one told me I had the right to an attorney. Even when they found the gun in the glove compartment. Even when I called you. Not a one of them ever mentioned it. So everything I told 'em, the whole story, is inadmissable. They can't use it against me. They can't even bring it up. It's beautiful."

Richard just stared at me. He blinked his eyes twice, slowly. "What are you, a child?" he said, evenly. "What are you, a moron?"

"Richard—"

"Jesus Christ! Why is it, every client in the world thinks they're so fucking smart? I don't believe you. You're smarter than your lawyer, right? What the hell you think I went to law school for? But you don't think about that, do you? No. Why should you? You're smarter than I am, aren't you? I guess you go to the dentist and tell him where to drill the tooth, right? I tell you to shut up, but, oh no, you're smarter than I am. You spill your guts."

"Yeah, but what can it hurt? They didn't read me my rights."

"Imbecile," Richard said. "Come on."

Richard jerked the door open and strode out. I followed.

Monica Dorlander and Marvin Nickleson had evidently gotten their wish, because they, Davis and the other officer had departed, leaving Chief Creely alone at his desk.

Richard strode up to him. "Chief?"

Chief Creely looked as if he'd been stung by a bee. He looked up at Richard with ill-concealed distaste. "Yes?"

"Having conferred with my client, I have come to the conclusion that you may have reason to suspect him of a crime. Therefore, I want him read his rights."

Creely frowned at him. "What?"

"You heard me. I have reason to believe that you suspect my client of a crime. I demand that you read him his rights."

Creely chuckled. He narrowed his eyes. "Are you kidding me?" he said. He pointed. "I read him his rights the minute he walked through that door."

Dorked again.

I was caught completely flat-footed. And who wouldn't be? I mean, after hearing "you have the right to remain silent" on cop show after cop show, after TV show after TV show about bad busts, cops hamstrung by the system and cases thrown out of court on technicalities, it was a huge shock to learn the mighty *Miranda/Escobedo* decision wasn't worth a hill of beans when confronted with a police officer genially willing to lie.

I stared at Creely. "No such thing."

"Stanley," Richard said.

"Richard, he's—"

"Stanley!" Richard interposed himself between me and Creely. "Shut up. As your attorney, I advise you to shut up. If you choose to disregard that advice, you are free to hire another attorney. Make up your mind."

I shut up.

"Fine," Richard said. He turned back to Creely. "Now, if I could park my client in the corner for a minute, perhaps you and I could have a little talk."

"I would feel far more receptive to that," Creely said, "if you weren't threatening me with a libel suit."

Richard shrugged. "Ah, well, what's a little libel suit among friends?"

"That's what I thought," Creely said. "All right, if you can keep this joker here quiet long enough, I'm willing to listen to what you got to say."

"Fine," Richard said. "Stanley? Do me a favor. Park yourself in that chair over there and try to stay out of trouble, will you?" He took me by the shoulders and pointed me to the chair. "There's a good boy."

I walked over and sat down.

They both watched me do it. Their looks were almost paternal, as if they were the grownups and I was the naughty child.

It was a little much. I mean, just a while ago these two had been at each other's throats. Now there they were, all buddy-buddy, as if this were their party and I were a fifth wheel.

In a way I understood. Richard took Creely's lying about reading me my rights as a matter of course. And Creely took Richard's threatening him with a lawsuit as a matter of course. Despite the adversary position, they were two warhorses who understood the system. And I was just a poor schmuck who didn't understand the system. And all they wanted to do was dispense with me and get down to business.

Which they did.

"All right," Creely said. "What can I do for you?"

Richard drew up a chair. "Well, now. We have a situation here."

"That we do."

"Perhaps we could define it somewhat, and then attempt to resolve it."

"Admirable idea."

"All right. Here's the situation. My client's had a rough day and he'd like to go home."

"I'm afraid that's out of the question."

"Suppose I were to say charge him or release him?"

"Then I'll charge him."

"With what?"

"Murder sounds good to me. How does that sound to you?"

"A little harsh."

"Perhaps. But it's the charge that comes to mind."

"It's a charge that won't stick."

Creely shrugged. "Now there, you see, we have a difference of opinion."

"I understand that," Richard said. "I'm wondering if we could resolve it."

"In what way?"

"Well now," Richard said. "You're telling me if I say charge him or release him, you're going to charge him with murder, drag him before a judge and have him arraigned."

"That's right."

"So I'm not saying charge him or release him. We're still talking here."

"*You're* still talking. I'm listening. I haven't heard anything yet."

"All right then. Consider this: if you charge him you're gonna get press. Now admittedly, this is a small town. The local press is probably not too hot. But this is a murder case. The victim is from New York City. My client is from New York City. Which means we're not just talking local press, you're going to have coverage here. And not just the papers. The TV stations too. You're going to have camera crews in this place."

"I know that," Creely said. The prospect obviously did not displease him.

"Right," Richard said. "And right now you're thinking what a swell story it will be—small town boy makes good. But consider this: if you charge him with murder it's gonna be big news. You're gonna have reporters asking you questions, you're gonna be on TV telling 'em how you cracked the case. That's gonna make you a hot shit for a while. Then in a couple of days when this case cracks open and you have to turn him loose, it's gonna get twice as much airplay. You know why? Because the reporters will have found a handle for the story. You know what it is? Big-mouth hick from the sticks jumps the gun and arrests the wrong man."

Creely frowned.

"Oh course, that's not fair," Richard said. "New York City cops do it all the time—arrest the wrong man—and no one thinks a thing of it. Cause they got hundreds of murder investigations going on, and it just gets lost in the shuffle.

"The problem is, you only got one. One murder. One case. You blow it, you're history."

Richard shrugged. "You know that. You got the state cops yapping at your heels right now just waiting for an excuse to move in. You let 'em move in now you got nothin'. You try to handle it yourself and you fuck up, you got worse than nothin'. Cause then you take so much pressure you gotta let the state boys move in anyway, and then to everyone you're just a dumb local yokel who couldn't do the job."

I was watching Creely's face. He didn't like that on the one hand, but he wasn't buying it on the other.

"Says you."

"What?" Richard said.

"Little flaw in your logic. I happen to have your client dead to rights."

"How so?"

"Come on. He bird-dogged the victim for two days, followed her up here, registered under an assumed name, and had the murder weapon in his car. You make it sound like I'm arresting him on a whim."

Richard smiled. "Come on, Chief. If I understand your theory of the case, the guy drove up here, registered at the motel, got up in the middle of the night and killed the woman. Then he put the gun in the glove compartment of his car, went back to his unit and went to sleep, and waited for the cops to come wake him up." Richard jerked his thumb in my direction. "Now, I admit my client's not very bright. But even so, that strikes me as being somewhat short of the perfect crime."

Creely frowned. "Well," he said. "Murderers are often dumb. That's why so many of them get caught."

"I'm not trying to con you, Chief. I'm just giving you a tip. The guy didn't do it."

"You're his lawyer. Of course you'd say that."

"All right. Whose word *would* you buy?"

"What do you mean?"

"My client's a private investigator in my employ, which is why I can vouch for him. But he's also had dealings with the City of New York. Would the word of a New York City cop cut any ice with you?"

"What kind of cop?"

"A homicide cop."

"It might if I knew him."

Richard turned to me. "Who's that homicide cop you're palsy with?"

"Sergeant MacAullif," I said.

I hoped to hell Creely'd heard of MacAullif. I'd done MacAullif a favor once, and though he'd long since repaid it, the precedent had been established, and I would feel no compunction about asking a favor of him. And just vouching for me on the phone wouldn't be that big a favor. Unless, of course, I happened to get convicted of murder. In which case, MacAullif would have really stuck his neck out.

Creely shook his head. "Don't know him."

Shit.

"Anyone else?" Richard said.

I frowned. I had one other name, but I didn't really want to give it. But I realized I had no choice. "Well," I said. "I also know a Sergeant Clark."

Creely pursed his lips. He nodded.

"That cocksucker I know."

My one experience with Sergeant Clark had not been pleasant. I hadn't thought much of the man. I'd even told him so. He'd never expressed his feelings for me, not in so many words, but there was no way they could have been good. Sergeant Clark was a cold, methodical, humorless man, a cop who did everything by the book. I wasn't sure what the book would tell him in this case, but I had a feeling that saying, "Good boy, Stanley," patting me on the head and letting me go probably wasn't it. So I can't say I was bursting with confidence as I watched Creely place the call.

It took five minutes for Creely to get him on the phone. When he did he introduced himself and started to give Clark a rundown of the situation. Of course, I could only hear one side of the conversation. I had to imagine the rest. The old fill-in-the-blanks game. After Creely mentioned the name Stanley Hastings there was a considerable pause, during which Creely frowned and glanced in my direction. My imagination was doing cartwheels over that one.

The first part of the conversation was largely all Creely's. He went ahead and laid out the situation: the murder, the evidence, the two Marvin Nicklesons and Monica Dorlanders, and the whole bit. He didn't slant it any. He just gave the facts. The tone of voice in which he related my version of the story could only be construed as expressing extreme skepticism. But for the most part, I had to admit he was fair.

When Creely was finished, it was Sergeant Clark's turn. That left a big blank for me to fill in. Cause for the next five minutes, Creely did nothing but listen and contribute an occasional "uh-huh," or "yeah." In that time he also frowned, pursed his lips, chewed his gum, played with his glasses, grimaced, doodled on a piece of paper, and by and large looked somewhat less than pleased.

At the end of it all he said simply, "Thank you, Sergeant," and hung up the phone.

I couldn't wait to hear, though I didn't really want to. It was likely the majority of Sergeant Clark's monologue had been a lecture on the preponderance of evidence, and the duty of a police officer to act upon it, regardless of personal welfare.

Creely frowned. Rubbed his head. Took a breath and blew it out again. Took off his glasses, stared at them, put them back on again. Frowned again, and then looked over at me.

"Clark says you didn't do it."

"What?" I blurted.

Creely shrugged. "Clark says you're a major pain in the ass. Not in those words, of course. Very genteel, Clark is. Never heard the cocksucker swear. But that's the general idea. Says you're a goof-off and a fuckup and a bungling amateur. Not at all surprised by any of this. Says it's par for the course for you. Says you're a credulous bastard who could have easily swallowed the improbable story you tell. Not many people who would, but Clark says you qualify.

"That's on the one hand. On the other hand, he says you think you're smart. Smarter than the cops, that is. Says you fancy yourself some fictional hero, outwitting the poor bumbling police. Wouldn't put it past you to withhold evidence and try to solve the thing on your own. Says if I give you the least chance you'll meddle in the case and mess things up. And probably already have."

Creely paused and shook his head. "But as far as the killing goes, Clark says you didn't do it. His most persuasive argument is you wouldn't have the guts. You couldn't stomach it. Says you're a chickenshit who wouldn't know one end of a gun from the other. Again, not in those words."

Creely jerked his thumb at Richard. "He also agrees with your attorney here that it's too stupid, even for you. Here, he says, it's a close call. He wouldn't put it past you to do something incredibly stupid, just not something so *obviously* stupid." Creely shrugged. "It's a fine line, and I'm not so sure, but that's the way Clark seems to think.

"Anyway, he says to charge you with murder would probably be sticking my neck out. Cause I'd probably have to retract. Something, of course, I would not want to do."

"You'll charge him or you'll release him," Richard said.

"Right," Creely said, turning to Richard. "And then there's you. Clark gave me his opinion about you too."

Richard's eyes narrowed. "Is that right?"

"Yeah," Clark said. "He said you're too competent by half. He says if you make threats, you'll carry them out. He seems to feel you're not too bound by moral restraint." Creely held up his hand. "Now don't take offense. I'm not quoting word for word. I'm just giving you the general impression. None of this is actionable. Against me or

Clark, if that's what you're thinking. The word shyster was never mentioned. All Clark told me basically was to watch my step."

Creely took his gum out of his mouth, wrapped it in a small piece of paper, and tossed it in the wastebasket. "So," he said, "we have a situation here. According to Sergeant Clark, if I charge this guy with murder, I'm in deep shit. On the other hand, if I let him go with so much evidence against him, I'm in deep shit. So it seems to me, there's only one way to go."

"What's that?" Richard said.

"Charge him with something else."

"Such as?" Richard said, and just like that they were off into plea bargaining, happy as pigs in shit, and sounding just like schoolboys trading two Yogi Berras for a Mickey Mantle as they bargained for my future. Creely opened the bidding with illegal possession of a firearm, Richard countered with a misdemeanor charge of disturbing the peace, and they battled it back and forth for a while and finally settled on obstruction of justice. When they finally did, I got the impression everything else had been for show, and that was what they were shooting for all along. I wasn't that clear on what obstruction of justice was, but Richard seemed happy enough with it, so I figured that was good enough for me.

Once they'd gotten the charge squared away, Creely put in a call to the local liquor store, the proprietor of which turned out to also be a judge, and we all moseyed over there to get me prearraigned.

We moseyed in two cars, Richard in the back of his rented limo, and me in the back of Chief Creely's cruiser, which was nothing more than a beat-up old Chevy, with grillwork between the front and back seats, a police radio, and a light to slap on top.

The judge turned out to be a dapper old coot with no

hair but a lot of adam's apple, and an eye on the main chance. Not only did he not close up shop while I was prearraigned, he actually waited on customers during the course of the proceedings.

Which seemed to puzzle him. The proceedings, I mean. Selling liquor he had no problem with. He didn't really have any problems with procedure either—I wouldn't want you to get the impression that just because he lived upstate and ran a liquor store, he didn't know his law. No, what confused him was why in the face of so much evidence I was being charged with obstruction of justice rather than murder. He was so skeptical in fact, that at first I was afraid he wasn't going to ride along, and it occurred to me Richard might have to bribe him by buying a case of cognac. But after Creely made it clear that obstruction of justice was really all he wanted, the judge was perfectly willing to oblige. In no time at all he'd scheduled an arraignment hearing for a week from the following Thursday, released me on my own recognizance, and sold two bottles of burgundy and a pint of gin.

And that was that. Five minutes later Richard and I were in the spacious back seat of his stretch-limo, tooling over to the motel to pick up my car, as if the whole thing had never happened.

Alice wasn't on the computer when I got home.

She was on the phone.

Talking about the computer.

That's the thing about these computer junkies. They have a whole network set up. A computer freak society. And they hold monthly meetings and exchange information. And in between they call each other up and talk animatedly and endlessly, employing digital linguistics only they can understand.

Which drives me nuts. I mean, Alice was big on the phone *before* we got the computer, what with her network of mother junkies calling up to discuss their respective offspring. But lately, the problem had escalated out of all proportion.

When I get home, I'd like to say hello to my wife. Even if I have no specific news to impart, it's still nice to make contact. But I never can. Cause she's always on the computer or the phone. When I have nothing pressing to discuss, this is mildly annoying. When I have something important, it's excruciating.

I used to stand in the kitchen and wait for her to get off the phone. Alice broke me of the habit. "Don't stand there staring at me," she'd say. "I'll get off the phone when I'm off the phone. If it's important and you need something, just say, 'Excuse me.' "

It was important and I needed something, so I walked up to Alice and said, "Excuse me."

Alice said, "I'll be off in a minute," and went on talking.

I waited a minute and said, "Excuse me," again.

She waved her hand at me impatiently and went on talking.

I tried one more, "Excuse me," which drew an exasperated grunt and an, "I'm sorry, my husband's bothering me, go on."

I went into our office, hunted up a piece of paper, wrote SHE'S DEAD on it in block capitals, went back in the kitchen and held it under Alice's nose.

That produced the desired effect. Alice said, "I'll call you back," and hung up the phone.

I told Alice the whole thing. She took it well. Or as well as any wife could be expected to under the circumstances. On the whole she was a brick. She didn't blame me for anything. She didn't point out that I was stupid. And she told me not to worry. From which I gathered that she was fully prepared to do the worrying for both of us.

About then Tommie got home from a playdate at a friend's house, and then we were into what I call the crazy hours, the period from five to nine during which we have to have dinner and get Tommie into bed. It always seems long. Today it seemed interminable.

As if he read my mood—I don't know how kids sense these things but they do—Tommie chose tonight to stall. By the time I finally got him to brush his teeth and wash his hands and face and put on his pajamas, it was after nine-thirty. Then I had to read him a bedtime story. I don't know about other fathers, but after years of reading bedtime stories I find I can put my mind on automatic pilot and read perfectly well and with expression while thinking of something else. I read Tommie *Yuck* by James Stevenson, complete with cackling witches and a bear that goes oo-bop-a-dop, and all the while thought about Marvin Nickleson.

What I thought about was not the whole mess I was in, but just how much it had cost me. Discounting the obstruction of justice charge—Richard, for all his stinginess, has never once billed me for professional services for coming to my aid, and I didn't expect him to now—I had still not acquitted myself with valor. The bogus Marvin Nickleson had advanced me two hundred dollars. What with garages, taxis, tolls, gas, motel reservations, etc., that was long gone and I was into my own pocket. Which left me having worked four days for free. With more on the horizon, if I ever expected to get out of this mess. I don't know how other private detectives conduct business, but I had a feeling this wasn't it.

I finished *Yuck,* kissed Tommie goodnight, and went in the bedroom to find Alice. She wasn't there, but by then it was ten o'clock, so I turned on Channel 5 to see if the murder of Julie Steinmetz had made the news.

I shouldn't have wondered. It was one of the lead stories. Julie Steinmetz was an attractive young woman, and turned out to have been both a high fashion model and an executive for a prominent Manhattan agency. As Richard predicted, Channel 5 had dispatched camera crews to Poughkeepsie, and I was treated to the smiling face of Chief Creely, chewing his gum a mile a minute and confidently asserting that he was pursuing a number of leads, and expected to have the murderer in custody before long. That might have cheered me some if I hadn't known damn well the son of a bitch was talking about me.

I went back to the office to tell Alice, and she was on the computer again.

She heard me come in and turned around. "I'm sorry," she said defensively. "You wanna talk, we'll talk. I don't mean to be insensitive. I'm upset by what you told me. This is like therapy, to get my mind off it. You know?"

I did know. I go to the movies to get my mind off things. I didn't feel like going to the movies now. And I didn't feel like raining on her parade either.

"So what are you doing?" I asked. I figured it couldn't hurt to show some interest, although I didn't really care.

"You wouldn't be interested."

"No, you're right. Take my mind off things."

"You sure?"

"Sure."

"O.K. Look at this."

Alice punched some buttons. A straight line appeared on the screen. She punched a button—it got longer. Another—it got shorter. Another—it tilted on its side. Another—it rotated 360 degrees. Another and the pattern it had traced doing all that appeared on the screen.

"What is it?" I asked.

"Line-sketch."

I frowned. "You bought another program?"

"No. I designed it."

"What?"

"I programmed it myself. It's my own program."

"You did that?"

"Yeah. Look what else it can do."

Alice pushed more buttons. Various geometric shapes appeared, turned, rotated.

"Neat," I said.

"It's not done," Alice said. "When I get finished, I gotta make copies and then print out the documentation."

"Documentation?"

"Yeah. Like an instruction manual. I'll type it up in WordPerfect and print it out. I'm trying to get it ready for next month's meeting."

"What for?"

"To exchange with people for other programs."

"Oh."

"I'll show it off and talk it up, and they'll advertise it in the newsletter."

"Newsletter?"

"Yeah. The group's getting a mailing list and putting out a newsletter. I can advertise my program in it and sell it to people on the mailing list."

I was rapidly losing interest. Another harebrained scheme, just like the résumés and letterheads. And that only wasted paper. For this, Alice would be using up floppy disks at two or three bucks a pop.

"I see," I said. I tried to underplay my lack of enthusiasm. I'd had it with computers and computer programs. It was time to tell Alice nice job, kiss her on the cheek, and go back in the bedroom and give some thought to my own problems.

"That's real nice," I said. "Tell me something. How much would someone pay for a program like this?"

Alice shrugged. "I don't know. The more complex programs go for anywhere from fifty to seventy-five bucks."

I pulled up a chair and sat down. "Tell me more."

23

Sergeant MacAullif unwrapped a cigar and surveyed it gloomily. His doctor had ordered him to give up cigars. He hadn't. He'd just given up matches. He smelled the cigar, put it in his mouth and chewed on the end.

"What a crock of shit."

"That's what Richard said."

"Richard?"

"Rosenberg. My boss."

"Oh. Him." MacAullif snorted. "He says a lot, don't he? Well in this instance, he happens to be right."

"No argument there. It's a crock of shit. It's a holy mess."

"And you seem to have acquitted yourself with something short of valor. Well, I guess you just chalk it up to experience."

"I can't chalk it up to experience. I'm on the hook for obstructing justice. That charge could be changed to murder."

MacAullif waved it away. "I wouldn't think so. They got you dead to rights on means and opportunity. But they'll have a little problem with motive. Why would you wanna kill her? That's gotta be a little difficult to buy."

"Even so, I got a local cop in charge of the investigation. It's probably his first murder case, and he doesn't seem particularly swift."

"Now, let's not sell a fellow officer short," MacAullif said. "Standing up to the state boys took guts. Besides, if you don't like him, it's practically an endorsement. I mean, your judgment of character's so bad. I remember what you thought of Sergeant Clark."

"That was different."

"How so?"

"Never mind. The point is, if this guy can't find anyone else, I wouldn't put it past him to charge me with murder."

"He hasn't charged you yet."

"He would have, if Richard hadn't threatened him with adverse publicity."

"From what I remember of Rosenberg, the guy has my profoundest sympathies. But the hell with that. What are you here for?"

"What?"

"You didn't come down here just to tell me your troubles. Whaddya want?"

"Well. So far I've just given you the facts. We haven't talked about what it all means."

MacAullif's eyes widened in mock surprise. "You're going to let me in on your theories of the case? What a treat." He dropped his cigar and snatched up a pencil. "Perhaps I should take notes."

"Shit."

"Wait a minute," MacAullif said, pretending to write. "Shit. Is that one 't' or two?"

"Maybe I should skip the summary and just tell you what I want."

"See, I knew you wanted something," MacAullif said. "Well, if you think you're gonna get it without telling me why, you must be dreaming. I happen to have an ax murder on my hands, and I'm not in a particularly good mood."

"An ax murder. Do you know who did it?

"Yeah. The guy with the ax. No, I don't know who did it, and I have to find out before he does it again. The only thing that gives me any satisfaction at all is, as far as I know, you're not involved."

"I swear to god."

"Good. Now lay this on me, cause I gotta get back to work."

"Fine. Now to begin with, I was set up as a patsy."

"This is your expert analysis? Let me help you out here, cause I'm pressed for time. This guy who posed as Marvin what's-his-face wanted a fall guy for murder. So he got himself a private detective hungry enough to want the money and credulous enough to buy the story. He fed you a bullshit spiel, ran you around town a couple of days to get you used to the idea, and then at the first opportunity pulled the job. The idea was to leave you with the murder weapon and an impossible story. By rights, the perfect frame.

"Which tells us a lot. To begin with, this guy must have had a reason for killing the woman that on the one hand isn't obvious, but on the other could be uncovered with a little effort. Why? Because he bothered to frame you. It's a kind of clumsy, half-assed frame. But in a way, that's the beauty of it. Everything you know just tends to confuse the situation. The more you explain, the more ludicrous it gets. The cops may not be able to nail you for this murder, but chasing you mixes things up. That's what the murderer wanted. To ball up the investigation and keep the police from going off on the right track."

"Which is?"

"How the hell should I know? We're talking theory here. Where was I? O.K., we know for certain that messing up the investigation is important to the murderer, because in order to do it he took a big risk. He saw you in person. Face to face. You can identify him. Now you can say even if you did it would be your word against his, but that's not good enough. Once you find him, find out who he really is, he'll be sunk. Cause he must have some connection with the dead woman, and once you know who he is it wouldn't be that hard to figure it out. So he must be counting on never seeing you again."

"All that's obvious," I said.

"Yeah, but with your track record for seeing the obvious, I like to state it just the same. All right. That's the situation as I see it. Whaddya want?"

"All right. Here's the thing. The dead woman. Julie Steinmetz. I was told she lived on 83rd Street and she did. But I was also told she worked at Artiflex Cosmetics on Third Avenue. I was told that because that's where the real Monica Dorlander works."

"So?"

"But she didn't work there. She worked at another place a few blocks up the street. But I was told to stake out that building and pick her up leaving work. Well, she wasn't there often, and now I know why. But she was there once. Tuesday, my first day on the job. She showed up around three-thirty, went in, and was out about ten minutes later."

"She had business in the building."

"Right. But how did this guy know that? The way I see it, that's the weak link. Either the woman had a real appointment and he knew it, which is too farfetched and I can't buy it, or he *set up* an appointment for her to get her into the building, just so I'd see her and pick her up. If so, he must have a confederate in the building. Maybe an unwitting one, but still a confederate. And that's the link."

MacAullif frowned. "Sounds farfetched to me."

"Yes, I know. But there's one other thing. The guy really wanted me to start work on Monday. Only when I absolutely refused did he agree to let me start Tuesday. The way I see it now, the reason he was so hot for Monday was he had *already* set up this bogus appointment, and when I wouldn't come around, he had to somehow get it switched to Tuesday."

MacAullif frowned again. "I see the point. I don't buy it, but I see it. So whaddya want?"

"I want to know where she went. I wanna know if she had an appointment in that building on Tuesday. More particularly, if she had an appointment for Monday that was changed to Tuesday."

"So?" MacAullif said, suspiciously.

"So, she was a businesswoman. She must have had an appointment book and—"

"Forget it," MacAullif said. "I thought I saw where this was going, and the answer is, forget it. This is a murder investigation. It's outside my jurisdiction. You may think that upstate cop's a doofus, but he happens to be in charge. I can't go poking my nose into this woman's business, asking to see her appointment book.

"And neither can you. You've already been charged with obstructing justice. You try to get your hands on that book, not only is that charge gonna stick, but the counts of it are gonna mount up."

"I gotta know where she went."

"I doubt if it's gonna do you any good. Most likely this was all arranged by phone. Whoever arranged it was a dupe and won't know beans.

"But if you really wanna do it, why don't you start from the other end?"

"Whaddya mean?"

"You got a picture of the dead woman, right?"

"Yeah."

"So go in the building and ask people where she went."

I thought that over. It wasn't my idea of a good time, but it was something I could do.

"I guess so," I said.

"Fine. So go do it. Get out of here. I got work to do."

"There's one more thing," I said.

"Shit. There's always one more thing. What is it?"

I told him about the license plate named POP.

MacAullif wasn't pleased. "You held this out on the cops?"

"Well, I wasn't sure it meant anything, and—"

"Save it for the judge. Jesus Christ. Yet another obstruction of justice."

"All right. I'm a bad boy. The point is, can you trace it?"

"Trace what? You got three letters there. You got any numbers?"

"No."

MacAullif stared at me. "You want me to trace *every* license plate number starting with POP?"

"How many of them can there be?"

"A thousand, you moron. Three digits is nine hundred and ninety-nine, triple zero makes a thousand."

"They don't issue 'em all, do they?"

"They issue enough. Say it's only five hundred—what the hell good's it gonna do you? You'll have names and addresses of people spread out all over the state, and what's the point? How are you gonna pin 'em down?"

"I don't know."

"Well, let me help you. What make of car was it?"

"I don't know."

"You don't *know*?"

"I was being arrested. I was a little distracted at the time."

"You saw the car. You saw the plate."

"Yeah."

"So what kind of car was it? Big? Small? A foreign job?"

"I'm not sure. Medium size. I think it was American."

"That's a big help. What color?"

"A light color. Gray or tan."

"Gray *or* tan?"

"Or light blue or green."

"Shit."

"Sorry."

"It ever occur to you you're in the wrong line of work?"

"Constantly."

MacAullif rubbed his head. "Great. You got no way to pin it down. So what's the point?"

"I don't know the point. I'm desperate. It's my only lead. If you don't wanna do it, you don't have to do it."

I got up to go.

"Wait a minute," MacAullif said. "Don't get so huffy. Did I say I wouldn't do it? I just asked you what's the point."

"I tell you, I don't know."

"Fine. That's good enough for me. Call back this afternoon. I'll get you your damn numbers. Now, was there anything else?"

"No, that will do."

"Jesus Christ, I should hope so. Now get the hell out of here, will you? I wasted enough damn time already. Now I gotta run a thousand license plates."

MacAullif picked up the cigar again and leveled it at me as if it were a gun. "Let me tell you something. If there's another ax murder, it'll be your damn fault."

24

It wasn't that bad. Actually, it was kind of fun. Going into the office building and asking people if they'd seen the woman in the picture. It was almost like *real* detective work somehow. After my usual initial nervousness, I kind of got into it. By the fourth or fifth office I was even asking the receptionist relevant questions, like, "Were you working here last Tuesday?" No one was remembering the woman in the picture, but no one was throwing me out on my ear either. So it was almost fun.

I had a feeling most of the receptionists thought I was a cop. Of course, I was doing my best to promote that image. I wasn't saying I was a cop, but I wasn't saying I wasn't, either. In a crunch, no one could accuse me of impersonating a cop. In point of fact, the only misleading word I was using at all was the pronoun 'we.' As in, "Excuse me, but we're trying to trace the movements of this woman. Have you seen her?" Somehow that one small word made me sound like the whole damn police force. But I could justify it—I knew a private detective in Atlantic City who used the word 'our' to refer to his one-man operation, so I guess I could use the word 'we' to refer to mine. At any rate, it sure worked. No one asked to see my I.D., and receptionist after receptionist was damn cordial.

Of course, some of them recognized the picture as that of the woman they'd seen on the news or in the morning paper, but that didn't hurt me any. If anything, it helped. But not many made the connection. I guess a lot of people just don't equate what they see in the media with real life.

I struck pay dirt on the sixteenth floor. I'd started at the bottom and worked my way up, and by that time the thrill had worn off and I was damn glad to get a nibble.

It was an ad agency, and if I were smart, that was where I would have started, looking for a place a high-priced fashion model might be expected to go, rather than checking all the offices in turn. But then again, if I were smart, I wouldn't be in this mess to begin with.

The receptionist was a genial young woman who probably could have been a fashion model herself if she'd lost a hundred pounds, bought a new wardrobe, and cut her hair. She took one look at the picture and said, "Yeah. I know her. She was in here last week."

"Tuesday?"

"Could have been Tuesday. I don't recall."

"Can you recall where she went?"

"She had an appointment with someone. Either Mr. Metzer or Mr. Saltzman."

"Are they in today?"

"Yes they are."

"Then I'll need to see them."

She frowned. "What's this all about?"

I gave her what I hoped was an enigmatic smile. "I'm sorry, but I need to be the one to tell them. Could you ring them one at a time and send me in please?"

She gave me a look, but picked up the phone.

Mr. Metzer turned out to be an overweight middle-aged

man with horn-rimmed glasses and a paranoid fear that I was a private detective employed by his wife. He barely glanced at the picture before denying he knew the woman in question. In fact, he began his stream of denials before I even handed him the picture. It was only after I got him to take a good look at it and he suddenly came to the happy realization that he really *didn't* know the woman, that I was able to calm him down.

Of course, that's just my analysis of the situation, and I'm not that good a judge of character, so I couldn't really be sure if that were true or if he actually did know her and everything else was just an act.

Until I met Saltzman.

Mr. Saltzman was a tall, thin young man, with the calm assurance of someone with executive ability. He took one look at the picture and said, "Yes. I know her. She was in last week."

"Oh?"

"Yes. Tuesday, I believe. Tuesday afternoon."

"She had an appointment with you?"

He smiled. "Well, now, that's the thing. She *thought* she did."

"Oh?"

"But she didn't. I'd never heard of her, and I'd never made any appointment."

"But she claimed you had?"

"Exactly. She said I'd called her and made the appointment."

"You or your secretary?"

"Me. She said she'd talked to me personally."

"And you hadn't?"

"No, of course not. Well, I shouldn't say of course not. She's a model, and we employ models. In fact, we may have even used her agency."

"But not this time?"

"No. It hadn't happened. It was a mistake."

"How'd she take it when you said you hadn't called her?"

"Not well. She was put out. She tried to argue with me. I understood her feelings, but she should have understood mine. Someone played a joke on her, a nasty kind of joke, but it wasn't my fault."

"I understand. Did she say anything else?"

He frowned. "Why is it important?"

So far he had all the right answers. I decided to give him a jolt. "Because she wound up dead."

His eyes widened. "What?"

I nodded. "That's right."

"Dead? That woman? Dead?"

"That's right," I said. I added, "Murdered."

"Murdered!" He frowned thoughtfully. "I see."

"So you see why it's important. We need to know the events leading up to her death. Particularly anything out of the ordinary. If she thought she had an appointment that she actually didn't have, that's interesting. It means someone tricked her. And someone also murdered her. It doesn't mean they're necessarily one and the same person, but you can see why it would be important."

Saltzman frowned and shook his head. "Yes. I see."

"So if you can recall anything about the incident. Anything that she said."

He thought a moment. "Well, one thing. When she was arguing with me—when she was still insisting that I had made the appointment, that I'd called her myself—she said I'd actually called her twice. She said I'd called her first Monday morning to make the appointment for Monday afternoon. Then I'd called her back later in the day, told her I had a conflict, and changed it to Tuesday."

"I see," I said.

And I did. That fit in with everything as I knew it. The

bogus Marvin Nickleson would have called her Monday morning to make the Monday afternoon appointment. When I refused to work on Monday, he'd have had to call her back and change it to Tuesday.

Which was too bad. Because if that were true, it meant the bogus Marvin Nickleson had arranged the whole thing, and Saltzman wasn't an accomplice after all, just another dead end.

I asked a few more questions which accomplished nothing, and got the hell out of there.

By then it was afternoon, so I headed downtown to check in on MacAullif.

MacAullif had been busy. He hadn't solved his ax murder, but he had managed to trace my license plates for me.

"You traced them all?" I said.

MacAullif snorted. "Yeah, well I caught a break. There weren't a thousand, just five hundred and seventy-six."

"What?"

"Yeah. Some days you get lucky."

"You traced five hundred and seventy-six license plates."

"Uh-huh. Don't say I never did you any favors. I got you names, addresses, the whole schmear."

"How the hell'd you do that?"

MacAullif shrugged. "Piece of cake, really. It's all computerized. The guy typed in "P-O-P asterisk, asterisk, asterisk," and asked the machine to do a search and printout." MacAullif jerked open a desk drawer. "Here you go."

MacAullif pulled out a sheaf of papers. I recognized it instantly, being in a computer family now. The pages were joined together and had perforated strips with holes in them on the sides.

I picked it up. "Thanks a lot."

"Yeah," MacAullif said. "I don't know what you're going to do with it, but for what it's worth, it's yours. O.K., you've worn out your welcome today. I traced five hundred and seventy-six cars for you. Now let me get back to work."

I thanked MacAullif again, took the computer printout and went home.

Where Alice pounced on it the minute I got in the door. Perforated paper is like catnip to a computer junkie. Before I even had my coat off Alice had it out of my hands and was demanding to know what it was. When I told her, she was quick to offer an expert opinion.

"Ha," she snorted. "Cheap dot-matrix printer. Terrible font."

"It's not supposed to be artistic. Just functional."

"It's not even that. It's just a list of the plates in numerical order."

"Sure," I said, parroting back what MacAullif had told me. "The machine searched for P-O-P blank, blank, blank, and it printed out the numbers in order. That's the beauty of doing a search, right?"

Alice shook her head. "That's the first step. You can do so much more than that. What do you want the numbers in order for? That doesn't help you at all. Wouldn't you rather have them grouped by geographical location?"

"Sure, but they can't do that."

Alice gave me one of her withering looks. "Of course they can. It's easy."

"How?"

"Any way you want. Just tell the computer to do it."

Another thing about computer junkies is they always talk as if everyone knows what they're talking about, and tend to get angry when it turns out they don't.

I didn't want Alice to get angry. "O.K.," I said. "What could I tell the computer to do?"

Alice got angry. "Oh, come on. For an intelligent man, sometimes you're a moron. Think."

"I don't know anything about computers."

"You don't *have* to know anything about computers. You just have to know what you want. What do you want?"

I wanted Alice to leave me alone and let me look at my list, but I didn't think that was the answer she was looking for. "What you said. To group them geographically."

"Fine. So that's what you tell the computer to do."

"How? What do I do, type in 'group them geographically?' "

"No, of course not. You have to give the computer a command that it can understand."

"Such as?"

"Well, it can alphabetize. You could order it to list them alphabetically by town. What about that?"

"Yeah. That would do it."

"Or numerically by zip code."

"Yeah. That would do it too. So, can you do it?"

"What?"

"Can you do that for me? On the machine?"

"Of course not."

"Why not?"

"Because the data isn't in the computer."

"You mean you'd have to type it in?"

Alice nodded. "Unless we had a floppy disk with the data on it."

"Which we don't."

"Right. Or unless we had a scanner."

"A what?"

"A scanner. You run it over the printed page and it reads the information into the computer."

A warning light had gone on. I could see Alice leading up to making a pitch for the purchase of an expensive piece of sophisticated machinery.

"Too bad," I said. I picked up a pen from the desk. "I'll just have to make do with this." I smiled at Alice and fled for the living room to tally up the names on my list.

Some fun. To the best that I could determine, in the New York City area there were two hundred and twenty-seven POPs. That was including all five buroughs, Long Island, and Westchester County. Of course, there was no reason to assume POP came from the New York City area just because Julie Steinmetz did. After all, she'd been killed in Poughkeepsie.

There were three POPs in Poughkeepsie, and several more in the immediate vicinity. It was hard pinpointing those, cause I wasn't familiar with the towns, and I had to keep looking at the map.

Going over the list was beginning to give me a headache. And I rarely get headaches. So this alone was enough to point up the tedium and futility of the task.

I was getting nowhere, so it was actually a relief when Tommie got home and wanted to play with me.

I heard the door open and close when he came in, and then I heard Alice intercepting him in the foyer and trying to protect me, saying, "Don't disturb Daddy, he's very busy now." I sprang up, opened the living room door and magnanimously offered to take time off from my work to play with him.

Tommie wanted to play "Zelda," one of the adventure games in his Nintendo Entertainment System. I'd figured he would. We'd been playing it off and on all weekend. And it's a very addictive game. That's because you don't start over at the beginning each time, as you do with most video games. Everything you've earned, hours and hours of playing time, is stored in the memory of the gamepack. So you can pick up where you left off. And it's not just fighting—it's finding things and figuring things out. It's really challenging, and when you get stuck and can't do it, it drives you crazy.

At the moment, Tommie and I were going crazy. We

were in the fourth level of the second quest, and we couldn't find the raft. We'd already been through the whole labyrinth, and we'd killed Digdogger and gotten our extra heart container and our piece of the Triforce, which raised our energy level and transported us outside the labyrinth again, since once you've gotten the Triforce you've supposedly completed the level.

Only we hadn't gotten the raft. And without the raft, you can't get to level five, because level five is on an island.

So we were going nuts. The treasures in the labyrinths are always in underground chambers that you reach by killing all the enemies in the room above, and then moving a stone to open a secret passage in the floor. Well, we'd been in every room in the labyrinth, and killed everybody in every room with a stone in it, and tried to move every one of those stones, and still nothing. Zip. Zero. So now we were running around killing everybody in the rooms that didn't have stones, even though that had to be a futile exercise, since without a stone to move, there could be no secret passage. But we were desperate, and we were trying everything.

In one room, in a far-off corner of the labyrinth, were six blue Darknuts, which look like little cats with shields. We'd never killed them before, first of all because there was no stone in the room, and second of all, because they're so damn hard to kill. You can't hit 'em from the front because of their shields, and the moment you make a move on them, they turn toward you. And the blue ones are twice as tough as the red ones, and take twice as many hits to kill. So out of the kindness of our hearts, we had previously left them alone.

Now it was death to the Darknuts. Armed with the white sword, twelve bombs, and the water of life, the red potion that costs sixty-eight rubies and allows you to fill up your life-hearts twice during the course of a battle, we waded in and took them on.

It was close. We'd used up all our bombs, both bottles of potion, and were down to two and a half life-hearts when the final Darknut breathed his last. As expected, no secret passage opened in the floor.

But the map appeared. The map of the labyrinth. It was lying there on the floor.

We pushed the buttons and made Link, our young protagonist, walk over and pick it up.

Immediately, a diagram of the layout of the labyrinth appeared in the upper left-hand corner of the screen. It always does when you get the map.

Tommie and I looked at it and said, "Wow!"

There were three rooms we'd never been in. They were beyond the Triforce room, where we'd never thought to look. And why should we? After all, we'd been through nine labyrinths in the first quest, and three labyrinths in the second quest, and there was never anything beyond the Triforce room. You got the Triforce and that was it. But there they were.

Tommie and I were hot to check 'em out. But first we had to get out of the labyrinth and go to the fairy pond and fill up our life-hearts, and get twelve more bombs, and buy more water of life. That accomplished, we returned to the labyrinth, fought our way to the Triforce room, walked behind the altar, pushed the up button on the controller, and disappeared through the wall.

Into the promised land.

We fought our way through a room of red Darknuts, knocked off three Dodongos, and, with our last life-heart ebbing away, polished off an assortment of enemies in the third room. We pushed all the stones in the room until one moved. A passage opened and we went down and grabbed the elusive raft.

I can't tell you what a feeling of accomplishment that gave us. Tommie and I were both jumping up and down and yelling and giving each other high-fives. And Alice heard the commotion and came popping in from the kitchen, saying, "You got the raft?" cause we'd been talking about it all weekend and what else could it be? And she stayed and watched while we took the raft to level five, and a grand old time was had by all.

But eventually, all good things must end. Tommie had to stop and do his homework.

I had to stop and do mine.

But with a fresh new outlook.

Now, I wouldn't want you to think that finding the map in "Zelda" told me I had to look at my map. After all, I had the map out already, checking the towns around Poughkeepsie. And it wasn't even as if finding the three rooms beyond the Triforce room told me I hadn't gone far enough and wasn't looking in the right place. Though all that did occur to me later.

No, I think it was just the whole "Zelda" experience was so exhilarating it raised my expectations. It made me feel a seemingly insoluble problem *could* be solved, if you just approached it in the right way. So I was full of confidence when I pulled out the map.

My confidence quickly ebbed. The map looked just as it had before. There was Poughkeepsie. There were the outlying towns with their potential POPs.

So what?

In "Zelda," aside from getting the map, you can also get a compass. When you pick up the compass a light goes on on the map, telling you where the Triforce room is.

That was the problem. I had no compass. No light went on on my map.

As I stared at the map my eyes began to glaze over, my

feeling of exhilaration was gone, and I was right back where I started again.

I set the map aside, leaned back and rubbed my head. All right, the hell with the map. Let's just try to figure this out.

I thought about it, and I decided what the "Zelda" experience really taught me was, I'm not as smart as I think I am. And whatever the hell it is I'm thinking is probably wrong, so I ought to take a good hard look at it and try thinking something else.

So that's what I did.

Julie Steinmetz had driven up to Poughkeepsie and registered at a motel. Not to mention the murderer, she'd had at least two callers, Check-hat and POP. I didn't know why she'd gone there, or why they'd come to see her, or what it was all about. But it had happened in Poughkeepsie. Why? I mean, what the hell's in Poughkeepsie anyway?

I didn't know.

But I did know this. Julie Steinmetz had gotten involved in something important enough to have gotten her killed. Now what the hell could that have been?

Well, organized crime would fit the bill. But I couldn't see an attractive young fashion model getting involved in organized crime somehow. Or maybe I just didn't *want* to think that. Because if that was true, then I was in way over my head, and the situation was so bad there was nothing I could do about it. The saving grace was, if she was somehow involved with the mob, surely the police would uncover the connection. Though, on reflection, with Chief Creely in charge of the investigation, they probably wouldn't.

Organized crime was a thought, but for practical purposes I could pretty well wash it out.

What did that leave? What other motivations for murder were there?

Sex? Always a biggie, but not likely here. Not with Check-hat in and out in five minutes flat.

Drugs? Slightly more likely, but even so. I mean come on, Julie Steinmetz, high-class fashion model, leading a double life as the Poughkeepsie Connection? Well, if that were true, wouldn't the cops have found some evidence of it? No. Any drugs involved, the killer would have taken away. But even so, could there really be two big time drug dealers in Poughkeepsie, POP and Check-hat, and yet another who had seen fit to kill her and rip her off? Somehow I didn't think so.

Blackmail?

Hmmmm. Blackmail.

A blackmailer's a good target for murder. And a person paying blackmail doesn't need more than five minutes to pop in and out again. And an attractive young woman just might be in a position to put the squeeze on some people. Yeah, blackmail seemed a lot more likely.

But why would the people she was blackmailing happen to live in Poughkeepsie? I mean, a blackmail victim's gotta be someone important, most likely a wealthy businessman or a politician. From what I'd seen driving through Poughkeepsie, it had no large industry to speak of. And the local government couldn't be that important, could it? I mean maybe Poughkeepsie was the county seat or something, not that that would mean much.

So what the hell was so important about Poughkeepsie?

I had no idea. But it occurred to me I could find out.

I went in the office and dug out Tommie's class list, which had the addresses and phone numbers of all the parents. Frank Wilkes, the father of one of Tommie's classmates was a sociology professor at NYU. I got the number and gave him a call.

He was home, but just going out the door. I told him it was important, I needed information about Poughkeepsie. He grumbled a bit, but put down the phone and was back a minute later saying he had two reference books that might help.

"Great," I said. "I'll run over and pick 'em up."

"I can't wait."

"So leave 'em with your doorman."

"There's no doorman. It's a brownstone."

"Look, I'll run right ovcr."

"You don't understand," he said impatiently. "I've got a class. I can't be late."

He had a class, but I had a murder. "Please. I'll leave right now."

He exhaled. "Where are you?"

"At 104th."

"All right. Meet you halfway. Broadway and 96th. Southwest corner."

"Great."

I slammed down the phone, grabbed my jacket and dashed out the door.

I'd already rung for the elevator when it hit me. *Meet you halfway.*

Shit!

The compass!

I jerked the door open, dashed back inside. As I did, I heard the clang of the elevator man opening the door to discover no one. "Just a minute!" I yelled. I'd have to meet Frank all right, so I wouldn't hang him up, but I didn't need his books anymore. Cause I'd been right all along. There was nothing in Poughkeepsie. *Meet you halfway.*

I snatched up the map just to verify it, though I didn't

really need to. Somehow it just had to be.

Sure enough, Poughkeepsie was almost exactly halfway between New York City and Albany.

The state capital.

25

I'd never been to Albany before. But apparently other people had, because the Thruway went right there. I came over a rise in the road and there it was in front of me. A cluster of official-looking buildings, and a huge stone egg, which I later learned was the Arts Center, and was actually called The Egg.

You couldn't miss the government center because there were huge signs proclaiming EMPIRE STATE PLAZA, STATE CAPITOL, GOVERNMENT CENTER, and what have you. While I was reading the signs I missed the exit and wound up in Menands. When I did, I found I couldn't get back on 787 going south because I couldn't make a U-turn. But the road I was on ran parallel to it, so I figured I could just follow it back to the center of town. I followed it back until I'd gotten myself pretty thoroughly confused, and finally spotted a sign for 787. I figured I must have worked my way past the government center by now, so I got on 787 going north.

Wrong again. As soon as I got on the elevated road, the stone egg winked at me like a giant eye, behind me and to the left, and I wound up in Menands again.

This time I didn't give a damn. I drove down the parallel road, turned off on another road, hung a U-turn on that road, hung a left on the parallel road, came back to the turnoff, and got on 787 heading south. I kept an eagle eye open, and managed to make the turn into the government center this time, on only my fourth pass.

I followed the signs and suddenly I was underground. In an immense parking lot. There were signs saying VISITORS PARKING so I followed them and eventually came to an automatic gate where the machine failed to dispense a parking ticket. I sat there with my window open looking futilely at the machine for some button I might be supposed to push, until an attendant finally came over and glared at me as if the whole thing were my fault. He stuck a key in the machine, did something, and the ticket came out and the gate went up.

It took me ten minutes to find a place to park. I was in section C 7 BLUE. I was afraid I'd forget it, and I went to write it down and discovered I'd forgotten my pen and notebook. All right, let's remember it. 7—lucky 7, roll of the dice. C—Gentleman's C in college. Blue—I'm Mr. Blue, wa wa oooo, when you say you love me. Got it. O.K. Now to get out of here.

But how? There were a lot of signs saying EXIT, but they were for cars. Where the hell did *people* go? Well, they went somewhere, because they weren't here. I looked around the vast garage, and while it was packed with cars, aside from myself, there wasn't a person in the place. What was this, an episode of "The Twilight Zone"? I stood there looking around like an idiot, and then I spotted it. In the far corner, movement. A car circling, and, yes, finding a parking space. I headed for it.

I'd managed to go enough rows so that I wasn't sure any

more where C 7 Blue was, when the man himself appeared, walking between two cars. I tailed him across the lot until he walked around what looked like a pillar, and turned out to be the back of an elevator. He got in and so did I. There was only one level above ours and he pushed it, so I didn't have to do anything. The elevator went up, the doors opened and I got out.

And discovered I was still underground. In a huge corridor that signs proclaimed to be NORTH CONCOURSE. It was weird. It was like a New York City street fair. The center of the corridor was lined with tables of merchants hawking their wares. Jewelry, clothes, knickknacks, what have you. I walked along it, wondering what any of it had to do with government, and what one had to do in this city to get out from underground.

At the far end of the corridor was a booth that said INFORMATION. That was for me. I walked up to it and found it was manned by an attractive young woman in a guide's uniform.

"May I help you?" she said.

I had a wild impulse to say, "Yes, could you tell me where I can find a man with a check hat and another man named POP who may have killed a woman?" I stifled it and merely asked her where the capitol was. I'm sure it was a good choice, because she seemed well versed on that subject—the capitol, I mean. She reached into a cubbyhole and pulled out what proved to be a black and white sketch map of the government complex.

"You're here," she said, making an *X* on the drawing. "The capitol building is here." She pointed down the corridor. "Go through those doors, keep going straight, go up the escalator, and you'll be there."

I followed her directions and found myself in a building of no distinction whatsoever. I walked down the hall and came to a dead end in a tiny lobby with a hole in the wall newsstand and not much else. Damn. Could this really be the capitol?

I went back the way I came and found a corridor leading off to the right. I took it and soon came to an immense staircase. Immense was the right word, but I'm afraid does not really do it justice. I mean I'm talking big here. This was one big mother staircase. It went up the center of the room to a landing, then branched upwards at right angles in both directions, and down again in the direction it had been going. The up branches led to the second floor, where the whole pattern repeated again. The staircase was like some huge stone plant growing up in the middle of the building.

A sign on it said, THIS IS AN HISTORIC STAIRCASE. PLEASE USE CAUTION. That puzzled me somewhat. Caution? Caution not to harm it? Caution not to fall? Caution because some historic figure might leap out at you on some landing?

I climbed the stairs with caution. I explored the corridors on the higher floors. On the second floor, I found the Department of Criminal Justice. That started several associations in my mind, but in terms of what I wanted, didn't seem promising.

I struck paydirt on the fourth floor. At the end of a corridor was a door. It was open, and when I walked through it, I stepped out onto a small balcony overlooking a huge assembly room. Countless small desk units arranged in a semicircle facing a large main desk, which was right below me. I had to lean out over the balcony to see it. It was a long, sprawling affair, the type I would have expected to find in a legislative chamber. But what surprised me was that built into the middle of it were a whole bunch of electronic controls and a TV monitor. I don't know why that surprised me so much. I guess I'm just so apolitical that my views of government come from watching Jimmy Stewart in *Mr. Smith Goes to Washington,* making TV seem an anachronism.

At any rate, I figured I'd found what I was looking for.

As I was standing there looking around, a man came out of an office down the corridor. I figured he was as good a person to ask as anyone, so I hurried after him and stopped him.

"Excuse me, sir," I said, pointing. "Is that the Senate?"

He shook his head. "No. That's the Assembly."

"Oh," I said. "And who meets there?"

He looked at me a moment before answering. "The Assembly."

I blinked. I realized the man realized he was dealing with an idiot. "I'm sorry," I said. "I really don't know anything about the government. What is the Assembly?"

The man was younger than I, but twice as wise. He adopted a fatherly, educational tone. "It's a legislative body."

"State legislature?"

"Of course."

"They pass laws?"

"That's right."

"Just like the Senate?"

"Exactly."

"State laws?"

"Right."

"Well, what's the difference, then? Between the Assembly and the Senate, I mean? Are there different areas of jurisdiction? Different types of laws involved?"

He chuckled and shook his head. "No, no, no. You don't understand at all."

"I'm afraid I don't."

"The Assembly votes on legislation. If it passes the Assembly, it goes to the Senate and they vote on it. If it passes the Senate, it goes to the governor."

"Oh," I said. "Kind of like the Congress and the Senate of the United States."

"In a way."

"I was thinking maybe one was City and one was State."

"Not at all."

"I see. Tell me. How many assemblymen are there?"

"One hundred and fifty."

"And how many senators?"

"Sixty."

I smiled and nodded, but I was dying inside. Jesus Christ. Why couldn't it have been something simple? Two hundred and ten candidates to choose from. With just a check hat to go on.

"When's the Assembly meet?" I asked him.

"Two o'clock this afternoon."

By reflex action, I looked at my watch, which of course wasn't there. However he looked at his and I saw it was nearly twelve.

"What about the Senate?"

"Same thing."

"Where does that meet?"

He pointed. "Go down the corridor, turn left, walk across the building. You'll be able to look down through the windows."

I thanked him and followed his directions to the other side of the building. Sure enough, there were windows looking down into another large assembly room. It was sort of like the other room, only more plush. The furniture was older and more established, and more of what I thought a legislative body should be. The desks were of aged wood. Large, more spread out. And fewer, of course. It had a sort of British clubroom atmosphere. I don't know why that image came to me, never having been in a British clubroom, but that was the impression I got.

I followed the windows around looking for the door. When I found it, I realized why the man had told me to look in the windows. Unlike the Assembly room door, this door was locked. Not only that, it had a metal detection device in front of it, one of those door frames you step through, like they have in airports. Apparently the senators were slightly more selective about who watched them legislate then the assemblymen.

All right. Two hours to kill. Where the hell were these guys when they weren't passing laws? Shit. I should have asked my buddy. Did they have offices in the building or what?

I went down to the third floor and looked around. I found a hallway where the doors started saying Assembly, then one grand looking doorway marked ASSEMBLY, which was closed. Of course. I'd seen the room from the balcony level. This would be the main room down below.

But where the hell were the offices? There was a desk outside, but there was nobody at it to ask. But there were notices tacked to the wall behind it. I stepped behind and read them. One was a list of the various branches the assembly had jurisdiction over. Another was a list of all the assemblymen with the room numbers of their offices. At the bottom of the list it said, "All room numbers, except those marked (C) (for capitol), are in the Legislative Office Building."

I whipped out my map. I was in the State Capitol, building number one. The State Legislative Building, building number four, was a long black rectangle directly across the street from it. Great. If I could ever *find* the street.

I went back down to the first floor and there over a doorway, as if it had been put there just for me, was a sign reading, TO LEGISLATIVE OFFICE BUILDING. I went through the door, down a hallway, down some stairs, and found myself in a long, mineshaft-like tunnel that seemed as if it might go on forever. It didn't, it finally surfaced inside another building.

It was too much for me. I mean, I'd been in town for a couple of hours, and aside from some black squares and rectangles on a sketch map, I hadn't the faintest idea where I was.

I was on ground level and there was a door. I pushed it open and walked outside.

Wow. Fresh air. Sunlight. What a bizarre concept.

Before me was a spacious lawn. Around it were buildings reflecting a clash of the old and the new. I admit I know nothing about architecture, but one was a modern office building, and one was a massive stone affair with peaked towers on its center and sides.

It was quite a sight. I wondered if the politicians had ever seen it. Or if they just drove into the garage in the morning, went about their business, and drove out again. By now I'd begun to think of New York State politicians as mole-men, strange furtive creatures who never saw the light of day.

I looked back at the building I'd just come out of. A sign over the door said, ALFRED E. SMITH BUILDING. Damn. I'd taken a wrong turn somewhere in the underground. I looked at my map. Let's see, Alfred E. Smith was building number three. The building over there said, STATE EDUCATION BUILDING. That gave me the orientation. So the modern building was building number four, the State Legislative Building. Which made the old building with the pointy towers building number one. The State Capitol.

While I was standing there, a woman parked her car, got out, looked around and came up to me.

"Excuse me," she said. "Do you know where the State Capitol is?"

I smiled. Incredible. What with me being a stranger in these parts, and knowing so little about government, and having no idea what was really going on, it was funny someone should happen to ask me the one question to which I knew the answer.

"Yeah," I said, pointing, "It's the building right there."

She looked, said, "Oh?"

"Yeah, me too," I said. "I guess I was expecting a dome."

She smiled, thanked me and walked off.

I checked the map again, crossed the street, and went into the Legislative Office Building.

It was a huge long building. With a huge long lobby. With elevator banks at either end. I was on the street level, but there was of course a lower level, the underground level for the mole-men. The middle of the lobby was open, so I could look down on the lower level, where there were other banks of elevators and corridors leading off in various directions.

So what the hell did I do? Take the elevator up and go through the offices one by one—"Excuse me, sir, do you happen to own a check hat?" Or did I pick an entrance, any entrance, and wait to see who went in and out? I mean, a check hat was a long shot to begin with, but to pick one out of possibly ten entrances, made the odds somewhat like those of winning the lottery.

I was beginning to feel rather stupid. I was also beginning to feel hungry. I went down to the lower level and sure enough found a tunnel marked TO NORTH CORRIDOR. I made my way along it and back to a cafeteria I'd spotted on the way in. I went in and had lunch, and discovered to my satisfaction that politicians don't eat any better than anybody else.

By the time I finished it was nearly two, so I caught my bearings again, and mole-manned my way back to the capitol.

Where I had another choice. Assemblyman or senator? Two separate entrances on two sides of the building, can't watch both.

I picked the Assembly. I figured there were one hundred and fifty assemblymen and only sixty senators, so that made the odds five to two.

I took up my position right outside the main entrance to watch the assemblymen file in. Apparently these sessions didn't start on the dot, because nobody was there at two o'clock. The first assemblymen arrived around two-ten.

And reminded me once again I'm a total schmuck.

They were wearing suits and ties. But not coats and hats. They didn't wear their coats and hats into the assembly room, take 'em off and hang 'em over the backs of the chairs. They hung 'em somewhere else. And if they did, it was a sure thing the senators did too.

I thought about asking. "Excuse me, where do the assemblymen hang their coats?" And then finding it somehow. And getting in and searching through it for a check hat. Going to jail for obstruction of justice almost seemed preferable.

I decided to wash it out. Come back at the end of the session, try to spot them leaving. I mean if I just knew where the coatroom was I could stake it out, and—

Then it hit me. Schmuck. You're in the city of the molemen. No one needs coats. They leave their coats in their offices and walk around underground all day.

That decided it. All right, the hell with Check-hat. It was time for Futile-Plan-B. Buy a map somewhere and check out the addresses of the local POPs.

I went down to the first floor and found the tunnel back to the North Concourse. I was getting pretty good at it by now. I even found what I thought was the right elevator door, if I remembered the vendor opposite it correctly.

Let's see, I went one stop, so I was on the top level. That's level 3C. C, that's right. Part of my formula. Lucky 7, Blue wa wa ooooo.

I found my car. I found the parking ticket that the machine had been so reluctant to give me. I paid my parking toll, and followed the arrows around and into the light of day.

All right. Now to find a store and buy a street map.

I pulled up to a light and stopped. I looked around. I discovered I was in the same place where I'd come up for air before. There's the capitol, there's the State Education Building, there's Alfred E. Smith. That's Washington Street, which will be on my map, and—

I gawked.

I blinked.

You could have knocked me down with a feather.

The license plate on the car in front of me was POP-422.

26

I'm not big on coincidence. And I'm usually not long on luck. But this had to be one or the other, if not both.

I grabbed for the computer printout. I'd circled the Albany POPs. That sounds like a symphony orchestra, doesn't it? Yes, P-O-P-422. Keven Drexel. Hello, POP.

Keven Drexel, if it was indeed he, was alone. All I could tell from looking at his back was that he had short dark hair and was wearing a coat. He wore no hat. Unless it was beside him on the seat.

That thought set up a chain reaction in my head. Holy shit. Suppose it were beside him on the seat? And suppose it were check?

In the whole time I'd been thinking about POP and Check-hat, it had never occurred to me that they might be one. But I hadn't seen Check-hat's car at all. And I hadn't seen the driver of POP's car at all. But what would be more natural if Check-hat had called on her once, than that he might come back and call on her again? I'd never even thought of that.

Until now.

The light changed, and POP turned right and drove down Washington Street alongside the capitol. I followed. We were going to have to turn again, because at the next corner Washington Avenue ended. There was a small rotary with a monument in it, and a large brown and white marble building with a tall clock tower. So POP was going to have to turn left or right.

He didn't. He pulled up around the rotary and parked by the monument. There were signs all around saying NO PARKING-TOW ZONE, but that didn't seem to bother POP. He got out and walked toward the large marble building. Well, if he can, I can. I pulled up next to him, parked my car and got out.

I followed him into the building. The sign over the door said, CITY HALL. Inside was a big lobby with an elevator to the right and the left. POP walked over and pushed a button on the one on the left.

As far as I knew, he didn't know me. Unless he'd caught a glimpse of me standing with the cops when he'd pulled into the motel. But he'd have had to be awful observant to have done that, what with spotting the cops and being in such a hurry to back out and get turned around again. Assuming, of course, that he was the right POP.

At any rate, I wasn't going to take the chance of letting him get away. I walked over and got in the elevator with him.

He went up to the second floor. He walked down the hall and went into a door marked 202.

I gave him a little head start, then walked up and looked at the door. On it read, CITY CLERK, and DEPARTMENT OF LEGISLATURE.

I went inside. It was a room with a long counter. Behind it, three women clerks worked at desks. One was a black woman with a broad, open, friendly-looking face, one was an older woman with glasses and a gray hairdo that looked as if it had been glued into place, and one was a younger woman in a nicely-filled-out sweater.

POP was at the far end of the counter talking to the younger woman. He was a young pretty boy type, and he seemed to be handing her a line, or at least telling her a dirty joke, because I heard her giggle and say, "Really, Mr. Drexel," before he grinned at her and ducked through a door into a room at the far end of the counter.

I walked up to the counter. The gray-haired woman got up from her desk. She frowned at me and said, "May I help you?"

"Well, yes," I said. "I was hoping you could. I'd like to get some information."

"About what?"

"About the city government."

"What about it?"

"Well, for instance," I said, pointing in the direction POP had gone, "what's that room there?"

"That's the City Council."

"City Council. I see. And what do they do?"

She frowned. "Could you give me an idea of what you want to know?"

"I'm trying to get some insight into the workings of city government."

"Why?"

Time to improvise. I'm not that fast on my feet, so I always figure the closest to the truth the better.

"Well, you see," I said. "I'm a writer. I'm doing an article on the government."

Her eyes narrowed. "The city government?"

"Yes."

"The Albany city government?"

"Yes."

"And the City Council in particular?"

"I would like to know about the City Council, yes."

She was looking at me very suspiciously. I'm paranoid as hell, so when I start feeding someone a bullshit spiel such as that, I kind of expect them to be suspicious. But in this case I couldn't figure out what I was doing wrong.

"Are you from Albany?" she asked.

"No. I'm not."

"Where are you from?"

"New York City."

Her lips clamped in a firm line. "I knew it," she snapped. "You're a reporter, aren't you?"

"No, I'm not."

"Oh yes, you are. You think I don't know that? And you probably think you're the first one, too. Well, let me tell you, there've been others before you, and they didn't get a damn thing."

"What are you talking about?"

She smiled and shook her head. "Don't play dumb with me. You New York City reporters, you're all alike. You think cause New York City's got a parking violations scandal, Albany's gotta have one too. Well, guess what? We don't. We have a clean city government, and I won't have anyone printing anything any different. You want a story, you know what you'll have to print? Lies and innuendo. You won't get one hard fact. The others didn't, believe me."

"That's not what I'm after."

"Of course not. That's what they all say. But just let one spiteful malcontent make the slightest insinuation, you'll change your tune."

Spiteful malcontent? Good lord. I was dealing with a paranoid government clerk who slept with a thesaurus.

"I'm not a reporter. I'm not interested in parking violations. I'm interested in the City Council."

"Why?"

"I told you. I'm doing a story on the functions of local government."

"So you say."

I was getting nowhere. "All right, look," I said. "You tell me there's no corruption in the City Council—"

It was the wrong opening. Her eyes flashed. "I *knew* that was what you were after."

I held up my hands. "No, no, no. Time out. False start. Flag on the play. Let's try again. Your City Council is honest. You haven't a bad word to say about 'em. Believe it or not, neither have I. If you'd let me ask my questions, you'd see that. So why don't you let me ask 'em? If I ask anything you find offensive, you don't have to answer."

Which was the wrong thing to say again. I have a knack for it. She was more suspicious than ever.

"Then you'll print my refusal, won't you? 'Declined to comment.' "

I took a breath. "I'm going to try one anyway. How many members on the City Council?"

She looked at me. "Are you kidding?"

"No. How many?"

"Fifteen."

That was a break. With my luck, it could have been two hundred and forty. But there were only fifteen.

"And what do they do?"

"Do?"

"Yeah. What does the City Council do? You say that's their meeting room. When they have a meeting, what do they do?"

She frowned. "I don't understand."

"I know," I said. "That's because you've mistaken me for a muckraking journalist. If you'd figure me for a second-grader on a class trip, you'd be on the right track."

She softened somewhat. "What do you want to know?"

"The City Council. Do they vote on things? Do they pass laws?"

She blinked. "Yes, they do."

"Such as what?"

She hesitated.

"Aside from traffic violations, which I don't care about," I said quickly. "What else do they do?"

"They pass city ordinances."

"Such as?"

"Well, regarding noise pollution, sanitation, housing, traffic . . ." Her eyes blinked, nearing a dangerous subject. "Zoning ordinances. Stuff like that."

"Does it have anything to do with the State government?"

She looked at me as if I were an idiot. "Absolutely not. It's totally separate."

"I see."

She looked at me. "What else did you want to know?"

I had no idea. It was a dead end as far as I was concerned. And the thing was, it had seemed so promising. I mean, Albany had seemed the right answer. And then finding POP. And finding him connected to the government. True, not the State government, but still the government.

But Jesus Christ.

Julie Steinmetz could have been blackmailing a politician. Or, even if it wasn't blackmail, it was possible she could have gotten involved in something of enough political importance to have gotten her killed. But the way I saw it, in either case that had to mean at least a Senator or Assemblyman. But some dipshit city councilman engaged in passing local ordinances on such weighty matters as noise pollution and zoning, just didn't add up at all. Frustrating as it might be, I was just gonna have to chalk POP up to coincidence and wash the sucker out.

I smiled at the perplexed looking woman, said, "No, I guess that's it," which puzzled her all the more.

I nodded at her again and turned to go.

And in walked a man with a check hat.

27

If my friend, the gray-haired clerk, had been confused before, she must have been utterly baffled now. Because I suddenly remembered I had a zillion other things to ask her. I paused in the doorway just long enough to hear the clerk in the pink sweater address Check-hat as Mr. Fletcher and see him disappear into the City Council room, when I was back at the counter saying, "Excuse me." Which is the sort of thing Peter Falk used to do in the old "Columbo" series, when he had the suspect on the run, telling him, "That's all," starting to go, then turning back in the doorway saying, "One more thing." It was a marvelous technique. It always irritated the hell out of the suspect and caught him off his guard.

It sure did this woman clerk. She must have been patting herself on the back at how well she'd brushed off the nosy reporter, when there I was again with more questions than ever.

And this time I realized what I'd missed the first time around. When she'd said, "Then you'll print my refusal," the woman had actually been voicing her deepest dread.

She didn't want to have anything to do with me, but she was afraid *not* to answer.

So I asked everything. Everything I could think of. About the councilmen. And when they met. And what they did. And was it a matter of public record. And where could I look it up. And the whole shmear.

That's not to say that I got anything. I didn't. I was pretty sure I hadn't learned one damn thing useful. But I'd sure learned everything. This time around I covered the whole ground.

I also tailed Check-hat when he left, which was about a half-hour later. This hadn't been a City Council meeting of any sort. In the half-hour, aside from POP and Check-hat, one other city councilman had come in. I didn't know why any of them were there, unless it was to check their mail, or whatever it was city councilmen do. The gray-haired clerk didn't know either. At least she said she didn't, and I had a feeling if she'd known she would have told me. I really had her going the second time around.

POP left first, but I let him go. After all, I had his name and address. It was Check-hat that I wanted to tag. All I knew was that he was a Mr. Fletcher, and there were probably a few dozen Fletchers in Albany.

I suppose I could have asked the gray-haired clerk for a list of the names and addresses of all the councilmen. But I figured that would have been pushing it. If that's the real reason. If it wasn't just that it had been a particularly boring day, and having a suspect to tail was sort of fun.

Mr. Fletcher had parked next to the monument too. I guess it was the city councilmen's place to park. He hadn't gotten a ticket, but I had. Wouldn't you know it. I tore it off the windshield, stuck it in my pocket, and hopped into my car just as Mr. Fletcher pulled out.

In a perfect world, my car would have started on the

first try. As it was, it coughed twice and died. I avoided flooding the engine, and got lucky on the third attempt. The motor roared to life, and I lurched away from the monument and took off after Fletcher. He had about a block head start. I caught him at a traffic light three blocks later. After that I played it cautious, dropped back a bit, tried to keep from being seen.

I tailed him out of town to a residential section of nice-looking houses and lawns. He pulled into the driveway of one of them, parked his car, and went in.

There was a mailbox at the bottom of the driveway that said, FLETCHER. The street number was on the house, so I had the guy tagged. I also had his license plate.

So what did I do now? Did I go in and talk to him?

There was another car in the driveway and a swing and slide set in the side yard. So presumably Fletcher was a young city councilman with a wife and kids. So asking him what he was doing calling on young fashion models at motels would have to give him a bit of a jolt.

I couldn't see it getting me anywhere, though. The car meant the wife was probably home, and he wouldn't want to say anything in front of her. The best I'd get would be indignant denials. All I'd accomplish would be to fuck up his married life.

On the other hand, I realized, that made the information a hell of a club. If I could get him alone away from home and spring it on him, he might be willing to tell me anything just to keep it from getting back to his wife.

That was a cheery thought, and showed me how much this draggy case had gotten to me. The most productive idea I could come up with was to blackmail some poor city councilman.

Who probably had it coming. I shouldn't forget that. If this was indeed Check-hat, Speedy Gonzales, the in-again out-again man, then he had called on Julie Steinmetz the night she died. Furtively. Clandestinely. Not even driving into the motel lot, but leaving his car parked on the road. So I shouldn't be wasting any false sympathy on him. No, if I wanted to talk to him. I had every right and every motivation.

But did I want to talk to him? That was the thing. Odds are he wouldn't tell me anything useful. He'd just deny everything and clam. And that would tip him off. Put him on his guard. If he were in cahoots with POP somehow, he'd tip him off. I didn't know what these guys were up to, and I didn't know what it was all about, but until I did, I didn't really want to show my hand.

Or did I?

Fuck it. I had to do something. I realized I was just hesitating cause I didn't want to talk to him, cause I figured I'd blow it. But what the hell. How could I blow it any worse than it had already been blown?

One way to find out.

I got out of the car, walked up the front steps and rang the bell. There was a pause, and then the man I had been tailing opened the door.

It was my first good look at him. He was a pleasant-faced man in his mid-thirties, with a kind of a homey quality about him, not farmboy exactly, but a certain open, down-to-earth look that would probably appeal to voters. He'd taken off his jacket and tie and unbuttoned his shirt and had probably been in the process of mixing himself a drink when I rang the bell.

"Yes?" he said.

"Mr. Fletcher?"

"Yes?"

Being a potential member of the press had worked so well with Gray-hair, I decided to stick with it. "Stanley Hastings. I'm with the Albany *Times.* I wondered if you could give me a few minutes."

He frowned, and glanced toward the door to the living room. The TV was on, and over it I could hear the sound of children's voices. In some back bedroom a baby was crying.

He looked back at me. "It's not really a good time. What's this about?"

I decided to shoot from the hip. "Julie Steinmetz."

It shook him. I'm sure of that. He was a politician, so he was probably used to taking potshots in his stride, and he covered it pretty well.

But he covered it.

And that's what I caught.

"I beg your pardon?" he said. "Who did you say?"

"Julie Steinmetz," I repeated. "A fashion model. She was murdered last Thursday night."

His jaw dropped open. "Murdered!"

"Yes."

"That's impossible."

"Why? You don't know her."

He blinked twice. "Yes, but still. You come in here and ask me if I know someone, and then tell me she's been murdered. I mean, it has to be some kind of joke."

I shook my head. "No joke. Julie Steinmetz was murdered. Shot through the heart. In a motel somewhere near Poughkeepsie. The Pine Hills Motel. Ever hear of it?"

He'd recovered his composure. "I never heard of it, and I never heard of her."

"That's funny. Because there's evidence linking her to the City Council."

He stared at me. "What?"

"That's right."

From the living room a woman's voice called, "Steve? Who is it?"

He winced slightly. "Nothing, dear," he called out. He

turned back to me. "I really know nothing about this. You'd better go."

"A couple more questions. You never heard of the Pine Hills Motel?"

"No."

"You've never been there?"

"No."

"Last Thursday night. You didn't go there last Thursday night?"

"Certainly not."

A woman came through the door carrying a baby. She looked hassled, and I didn't blame her. I have one kid and know it's a handful. She had at least three.

"Steve?" she said. "What is it?"

Fletcher looked hassled too. "Nothing, honey. This is a reporter, and he's just leaving."

"A reporter?"

"Mrs. Fletcher?" I said. "I'm sorry to disturb you. I have a kid of my own, I know what it's like. But you could help me out too. I'm covering the story of a woman who was murdered last week."

Her eyes widened. "Murdered?" she said. They all seem to say that.

"Yes."

"But what does that have to do with us?"

"Nothing," Fletcher said.

"Your husband's right," I said. "Probably nothing at all. This is a young woman from New York City. Her name was Julie Steinmetz. She was murdered at the Pine Hills Motel near Poughkeepsie some time last Thursday night."

Mrs. Fletcher looked totally baffled. She turned to her husband. "Steve?"

Fletcher threw up his hands. "Don't ask me, honey. I know nothing about it."

She looked at him a moment, then turned to me. "Then why are you here?"

"It's silly, I know. But there is evidence linking Miss Steinmetz to the Albany City Council."

"What?"

"That's right."

"To my husband?"

"No, ma'am. That's how you can help me. Your husband says he doesn't know the woman. And that he wasn't at the Pine Hills Motel last Thursday night. I'm sure he wasn't, and it would be nice to eliminate him from consideration. So last Thursday night I would assume he was home with you. Could you confirm that fact?"

Fletcher's face reddened. "Now see here," he said. "I will not have you cross-examine my wife."

My eyes widened in mock surprise. I put up my hands. "I'm terribly sorry," I said. "I didn't want you to get that impression. Please try to understand. I have to follow up this lead to the City Council. But I am not a muckraker, I am a responsible journalist. You are a respected politician and a family man. If you weren't involved in this, I don't even want to print your name. That's why I'm asking your wife the question. Because I would like to wipe you off the list.

"But you have to understand, I have a responsibility to follow up the story. And in the event you refuse to let your wife answer the question, then I *have* to print it. Because then it's news. 'Councilman Fletcher declined comment and refused to disclose his whereabouts on the night of the murder.' You see what I mean?"

The power of the press. That line worked as well on Fletcher as it had on the gray-haired clerk. He frowned and bit his lip.

When he did, his wife jumped in. She was a feisty young woman, who had been wanting to answer all along.

"Oh yeah?" she said. "Well, you print that and you're going to have a libel suit on your hands. I don't know what it is you're talking about, but my husband was not involved, and he can prove it."

"He was with you, then?"

"No, he wasn't. Thursday night is his poker night. He played till two in the morning. You see, it's better than if he'd been here with me. He'll have six witnesses to confirm it."

I turned to Fletcher. "You played poker that night?"

Fletcher frowned. "Please. My wife sometimes speaks without thinking—forgive me honey—but let's say 'cards.' I met some friends to play cards." He smiled for the first time since I'd opened the door. "The word 'poker' has certain connotations. I'm a public figure. I would not like to read in print that I had been gambling."

"I assure you that won't happen." I said. "Well, I guess that does it. Councilman. Mrs. Fletcher. Thank you very much, I'm sorry to have taken up your time."

I bowed and smiled myself out the door. I went out and got in the car.

Well, about what I'd expected. No new information. Just a confirmation, if you could call it that, that Councilman Fletcher was Check-hat. Not a dead certainty, but a damn good bet. And despite my assurances that I would let the matter drop, it was another good bet that high on Councilman Fletcher's priorities would have been sneaking calls to his poker buddies to ask them to confirm that last Thursday he'd been there all night and never left the game.

Yeah, that was the picture all right. But what did it get me? Nothing, expect for the fact that in my opinion, his surprise at hearing Julie Steinmetz was dead had been genuine. Which would, of course, clear him of being the murderer. And while I didn't really want a family man with a wife and kids to be guilty of murder, I sure would have liked to have come up with another suspect besides me.

Well, so much for that. Check-hat was pretty much of a washout. But at least I'd tried. Now, while I had the adrenaline flowing, it was time to opt for POP.

I checked the computer printout. Keven Drexel's address was on Clinton Avenue. I'd have to buy a street map somewhere and find out where that was.

Before I did I checked the black and white sketch map of the government center, and I got lucky. Clinton Avenue was on it, just half a dozen blocks from the government center, the one thing in Albany I had any chance to find.

I turned around and headed back the way I came. Before long, I caught sight of The Egg, and took my bearings off of that.

The way I figured it, POP was a good bet. From what little I'd seen of him, he struck me as a young, aggressive, hustler type, the kind of guy who could conceivably be involved with a girl in Julie Steinmetz's league. I figured him to be single and live alone. Of course, as MacAullif tells me, my judgment isn't that hot, so I couldn't really be sure. But I figured him for an apartment rather than a private home.

For once I figured right. The address on Clinton was an apartment house. As I drove up, I tried to spot POP's car to see if he was home. It couldn't have been easier. It was double-parked with the flashers on right outside the door. I pulled in by a fireplug half a block away and waited.

He was out in ten minutes. He hopped in the car, cut the flashers, snapped on his headlights and pulled out. I snapped on my lights and pulled out after him.

It was getting on toward dinnertime, so I figured that was where he was heading. If so, I hoped he wasn't picking up a date. I didn't want to have to strut my stuff in front of her. I wanted to talk to him alone.

I got my wish. POP drove about a mile out of town and pulled into a rather posh-looking restaurant. He parked his car in the lot and went in. I parked in the lot and went in too.

Just inside the door was a hatcheck room. Beyond that, the door to the bar and restaurant.

POP had checked his coat and was already heading for the bar. I checked my coat too. Even if I didn't have dinner, talking to POP was going to cost me a buck.

I walked over to the bar. POP had already given his order, and the bartender had moved off and grabbed a cocktail shaker. There was an empty seat next to POP. I slid into it, turned to him and said, "Councilman Drexel?"

He turned, looked at me. If there was any sign of recognition, I didn't catch it.

My initial impression of POP had been pretty accurate. He was young, say late twenties, with carefully groomed hair and the features of a soap opera star. He also had a sporting, competitive air to him. The type of guy who does well with women and prides himself on it. The type of guy women admire and men want to kick in the butt.

"Yes?" he said.

"Stanley Hastings, Albany *Times.* I wonder if you could give me a few minutes?"

He smiled what I took to be a politician's smile. "I always have time for the press," he said. "What can I do for you?"

"I was wondering if you could give me a statement."

"A statement? About what?"

"Julie Steinmetz."

He winced perceptively. Then he recovered. If that indeed was what he was doing. Because the recovery was so good, frankly I couldn't tell.

He frowned and shook his head. "You reporters," he said. "You're all the same."

"What?"

"Look here, Mr. . . . uh . . ."

"Hastings."

"Mr. Hastings. Look here. I'm a city councilman. I'm also a bachelor. I happen to date a lot of women." He smiled. "Women seem to like me." He gave me a roguish, man of the world look.

I wanted to kick him in the butt. "Yeah? So?"

"So every few weeks some enterprising reporter hunts me up and throws the name of some woman at me. And then it gets in the papers. I can't say I mind that much. It probably helps me with as many voters as it hurts. But that's beside the point. The point is, half of these stories are true, and half of them aren't. And I beg your pardon, but on the whole the press doesn't give a damn which is which."

I felt defensive, which was strange, since I wasn't really a reporter. But I guess I just disliked the man so much, I felt he was attacking my bogus profession. "That's not true," I said.

He held up his hands. "Of course, of course. Far be it from me to malign the press. But you know how it works. A reporter throws a name in my face. If I say I know her, it gets printed. If I say I don't know her, *that* gets printed—'Councilman Drexel denied rumors linking him with Miss So-and-so.' If I say 'No comment,' that gets printed—'Councilman Drexel declined to comment on . . .' So you see, whether I actually knew the woman or not is scarcely the issue."

"That's interesting," I said. "You know, Councilman, I don't think I've ever heard a person evade a question more persistently than you're doing."

He frowned. "Exactly what I was talking about. You prove my point. I tell you my position, you tell me I'm evading. You didn't let me finish. I'll have you know I've consulted an attorney to know what to do in cases like this. Now my attorney tells me whether it's a paternity suit, a breach of promise, or merely a simple question of whether I knew the woman, I'm to decline comment and simply let the press print what they like. Because they will anyway, and that way at least I stay out of any legal difficulties." He smiled a superior, condescending smile.

"That's fine," I said. "Then let me define the situation you're not commenting on. The woman in question is Julie Steinmetz. The allegation is that you called on her at a motel."

He raised his eyebrows. "A motel?"

"That's right."

He chuckled. "Well, that is one area I can comment on. As I said, I'm a bachelor. If I want to see a young woman, I'll bring her to my apartment. I don't have to go to a motel."

"You're denying you called on Julie Steinmetz at a motel?"

He waved his hand. "Not at all. Regarding your questions, I have no comment. I'm merely making a general statement that I would not take *any* woman to a motel. And any person that says that I did would be printing a falsehood."

"I see," I said. "Then the falsehood that I'll be printing will be that you called on Julie Steinmetz at the Pine Hills Motel in the vicinity of Poughkeepsie."

He frowned. "Poughkeepsie?"

"That's right. And the woman you didn't call on was Julie Steinmetz of New York City."

"New York City?"

"That's right."

I must say the guy was good. He managed to put just the right tone of incredulous skepticism in his voice so that, even though I knew better, I couldn't help feeling like a fool.

"You intend to print that I called on a woman from New York City in a motel in Poughkeepsie?" he said.

"Unless you'd care to comment."

"I most certainly don't. I must say even the most sordid gossipmongers, who are happy to believe everything they read in the papers, will find that stretching it a little thin."

"Maybe not," I said. "You see, I have a handle for the story."

"What is that?"

"She was murdered."

He raised his eyebrows. "Murdered?"

I was right. They all did it.

"That's right. Murdered. Which makes it a bit more of a story, don't you think? Now in light of that, would you care to comment?"

He drew himself up. "In light of that, I don't think I should give you the time of day." He shook his head. "I had no idea to what depths you reporters would stoop, but this takes the cake. You find some woman who's been murdered. You come throw her name at me. You don't tell me why. You go through the usual song and dance, and then tell me the woman's been murdered. Now you'll print my refusal to comment and make a big stink out of the whole thing." He shook his head, piously deploring the wickedness of the world in general, and me in particular.

A knockout of a young blonde came up to the bar and put her hand on his shoulder. "Hi, Keven," she said.

He looked at her, smiled, put his arm around her. "Hi, honey."

She looked at me. "Who's this?"

"He's a reporter, and he's leaving."

"Oh," she said. "Another reporter. And what does this one claim?"

"That I took some girl to a motel."

She smiled. "Oh? Did you?"

"No, but I have to decline comment. You know the bit."

"Of course." She turned to me. "But you'll print it anyway, won't you?" she said archly. "Even though it isn't true. Well, Keven happens to be with me now. That's Jean Carr. C-A-R-R. You could print that if you wanted, but you won't. You know why? Because it happens to be true."

"No," I said. "Because it isn't interesting. Julie Steinmetz *is* cause she happened to get murdered."

Her jaw dropped open. "Murdered?"

Chalk up another one. That made it unanimous.

"That's right. At the Pine Hills Motel. The motel he didn't take her to."

She stared at me a moment. Then she smiled. Then giggled. Then looked slyly up at him. "Gee, honey," she said. "You didn't tell me you'd killed anyone."

He smiled back. "Must have slipped my mind." He slid down off his barstool. His face got hard. "Now you see here," he said. "You print any damn thing you want. I can't stop you. But I can sue you for libel, and don't think I won't. But that's neither here nor there. This young lady and I are going to have dinner, and you're not going to spoil it. So, as the saying goes, go peddle your papers." He smiled a superior smirk. "That's what you people do, isn't it?"

He turned and led the young blonde off toward the dining room.

I stood and watched him go.

I can't say I liked him much. For one thing, he was lying—I was almost sure of it. He was a pompous, pretentious, son of a bitch, and he was lying his ass off. In a murder investigation. One in which I was a prime suspect. Which was infuriating.

If that was all of it. If it wasn't also that he was a young, handsome playboy, picking up attractive blondes as if they were a dime a dozen, and then flaunting them in my face, as if realizing I was an old fart of a family man whose days of dating attractive young blondes were far behind him. And even then were few and far between. And approached without finesse, confidence, or savoir faire.

I bought my coat back for a buck, went out to the parking lot, got my car, and headed home.

I can't say I felt great. Every instinct had told me talking to POP and Check-hat would be a waste of time. I'd done it anyway, and it had been a waste of time. I didn't know whether I should feel good about having my judgment vindicated, or stupid for not trusting it to begin with.

There was no reason for me to feel so bad. Keven Drexel must have really gotten to me. Because Albany had been a thin thread to begin with and, I had to admit, it had more or less panned out. I'd found Check-hat. I'd found POP. I was a lot farther along than when I'd started the day.

Yeah. That was the trouble. I was farther along all right. By talking to Check-hat and POP and coming up empty, I had advanced all the way to a dead end. Which left me right back where I started, not knowing what to do next.

Worse, I had advanced to the point where I had to abandon my original theory. About it being blackmail, I mean. Because, like it or not, the City Councilmen just weren't involved in anything important enough to be blackmailed about. So she couldn't be blackmailing them about their jobs. And if she was blackmailing them as individuals, then it was just too much of a coincidence that both of the men she was blackmailing happened to be on the City Council. So that theory didn't wash.

It was depressing. Here I was, driving home to New York. In defeat. In retreat. Back to square one.

And worse off than when I started. I'd come to Albany with a theory I thought made sense. Only it didn't make sense, and now I had no theory at all.

Naturally, I went over the case in my head all the way home. Not that it did me any good. All I knew was, to the best I could determine, just before she died Julie Steinmetz had made appointments to see at least two Albany City Councilmen.

And I had no idea why.

28

I don't like funerals. I skip them if at all possible. Given my druthers, I'd like to skip mine. Cause they're not for the dead, they're for the living. The relatives of the dead. And I have problems dealing with such people. I don't know what to do, I don't know what to say, I feel so awkward. The only thing I can think of to say is how sorry I am, which seems so stupid and so wrong. Yet nothing seems right. I just feel miserable and uncomfortable. And then I think, shit, well why shouldn't I feel bad at a funeral? But I don't think the bad I'm feeling is the bad you're supposed to feel. You're supposed to feel bad for the dear departed and the ones they left behind, not just uncomfortable for your own inadequacies. Of course, realizing that makes me feel even worse.

It's hard to function under such circumstances. I've gotten better at it, however, working for Richard. You see, some of Richard's clients are dead. That's because he handles accident cases, and sometimes the accidents are fatal. And I have to sign 'em up, just like any other client. Of course, I'm not dealing with them, I'm dealing with their families. Which, as I've said, makes me terribly uncomfortable. I feel like such a schmuck asking questions of a wife who's lost a husband, or a mother who's lost a child. But it's my job and I have to do it, so I do. And the only thing that makes it bearable at all is the knowledge that the reason that I'm there asking them questions in their time of grief is because they asked me to come.

No one asked me to come to Julie Steinmetz's funeral. But I did.

It was at the Riverside Memorial Chapel on Amsterdam Avenue. I drove over, found a parking space, went inside. A sign in the lobby said, Steinmetz, Second Floor. I went up and found it.

It was pretty much what I'd expected. Medium-size room with a casket. Closed, thank god. About half a dozen people were standing around talking. Well-dressed yuppie types. Most likely Julie's friends and acquaintances from the fashion industry.

At the far end of the room a plump, middle-aged woman, dressed in black, sat on a chair. She wore glasses. The eyes behind them seemed dull and unseeing. Her whole face was a mask of doom. At first glance she looked totally dispirited. But her lips were set in a firm line. Her jaw was set too. As if there was anger behind the grief.

The obituary in the New York *Times* had said Julie was survived by her mother. This woman had to be her. There was no mention of a father, so he was either dead or long departed. The woman was alone, isolated, unapproachable.

I felt like a total shit. But I had an obstruction of justice charge hanging over my head that just might get changed to murder.

I walked over.

"Mrs. Steinmetz?"

For a moment I thought she hadn't heard me. I didn't

have the balls to say it again, and I was on the point of turning and walking off, when the eyes flicked behind the glasses and turned to stare up at me.

"Yes?" she said.

I took a breath. "I'm Stanley Hastings," I said. "I knew Julie. I just wanted to tell you how sorry I am."

For a moment or two she just looked at me. Then she said, "Thank you. So you're one of Julie's friends." She shot a glance at the people at the other end of the room, then looked back at me. "Julie's high society friends," she said. "You know, aside from the funeral director, you're the first person who's spoken to me."

I could understand that. Sitting hunched in her chair with her jaw set, she'd looked like some malevolent gorgon. I wouldn't have spoken to her if I hadn't had to.

"I take it you're not from New York?"

"No. I'm from Albany."

The magic word. On the one hand I tried not to appear excited, but on the other hand I wasn't going to let it drop. "That's where Julie grew up?" I asked.

She frowned. "Why do you want to know?"

"I'm sorry," I said. "Just making conversation. It's an awkward time. Hard to know what to say."

She snorted. "Yes, of course," she said, irritably. "Isn't it hard on you? What's to become of me?"

The phrase 'who gives a shit?' came to mind. I could grant the woman her grief, but she was being downright nasty. And from what I'd seen so far, she was less upset about losing her daughter than she was about how she was being treated.

I was mushy enough to feel bad for her anyway. "You all alone?" I asked. "The newspaper didn't mention Julie's father."

"Dead five years now. First him, now her. It's very hard."

"She never mentioned a brother or sister. Was she your only child?"

"My only child. There's no one. No one."

Jesus Christ. I was ready to crackup and start screaming and begging for mercy. Given my natural reluctance to deal with the grieving, things couldn't have been going worse. I was living poison to this woman. Everything I said was just driving her deeper and deeper into abject despair. I had a feeling she must have wanted to get away from me as much as I wanted to get away from her.

Wrong again.

She looked up at me and said, "You going to the cemetery?"

I sure hadn't planned to. But that sure sounded like an invitation. "Yes," I said.

"How are you getting there?"

"I have my car outside." I paused, wondering if she was fishing for it. "Could I give you a ride?"

She was. She almost smiled. "That would be very nice. I was supposed to ride with the funeral director, but that's rather grim."

Grim. Good lord. What did she think *I* was? For that matter, what did she think *she* was? The woman had practically invented grim. But, I figured, the ride would give me a chance to pump her about her daughter. Particularly about her daughter's home life. The way I saw it, coming from Albany had earned Mrs. Steinmetz her ride to the cemetery.

I told Mrs. Steinmetz I'd be glad to take her, and excused myself from her oppressive company.

I walked over and introduced myself to Julie Steinmetz's circle of acquaintances. Ordinarily I'm shy at meeting people. But with Julie's mother watching me, I didn't want to appear to be a total stranger. I also wanted to pick up any gossip about Julie that might help me. So

I strode right in saying, "Hi, I'm Stanley Hastings," right and left, and shaking hands with everybody and saying what a terrible thing it was, and did you know her well? and what a terrible thing to have happened, weren't you surprised? and who could have possibly done such a thing?—and by the end of it they were all looking at me kind of funny. But all things considered, I think I played it pretty well. And while of course everyone there knew that they didn't know me, I'd have been willing to bet you each and every one of them figured me to be a friend of someone else.

I'd also be willing to bet you I didn't learn one damn thing useful. No one young man stood out as Julie's particular flame. No one stood out as Julie's particular friend at all. Aside from me, the mood was convivial, almost party-like. The people gave the impression they were just ready to move on to the next watering hole.

Which was of course the cemetery. Which turned out to be the Cypress Hills in Queens. I knew how to get there of course, having driven by it many times in my travels for Richard. This time I didn't have to think about it. I was in a funeral procession. Just line up and follow the hearse.

As funeral processions go, this one was rather limited. Of the revelers from the funeral parlor, at least half of them dropped out, apparently having an aversion to cemeteries, Queens, or both. That left the hearse, the car from the funeral parlor, a rental car with the remaining revelers, and me.

I shamelessly attempted to pump Mrs. Steinmetz on the way out. She was more than willing to talk, or rather, complain. I was doing my best to feel sympathetic for her under the circumstances, but even knowing she'd just lost a daughter, it was hard. Everything she said was laced with bitterness and self-pity. It was as if her daughter's death had been a personal affront, aimed solely at her. Still, she was willing to talk, and I was willing to listen.

Julie Steinmetz had grown up with her parents on a small farm on the outskirts of Albany. Years ago, Mr. Steinmetz had actually farmed the land, until rising costs had made it impossible to turn a profit, and like many other small farmers, he'd gone under—another personal affront, aimed directly at Mrs. Steinmetz. He'd then gone to work at a factory—I never did learn at what—where he remained till he died, yet another personal affront.

Julie Steinmetz was twenty-eight. She'd grown up on the farm, gone to high school in Albany, gone to Cornell, but dropped out after one year (another personal affront), and come home to live with mom and dad. She'd hung around Albany till she was twenty-three, largely, I gathered, socializing and enjoying the night life. Through some contact or other—I gathered from the tone of Mrs. Steinmetz's voice, a man—Julie'd become infused with the idea of going to Manhattan to become a model, and had taken off to do so. This coinciding with Mr. Steinmetz's death, had left Mrs. Steinmetz alone and, to hear her tell it, destitute, and seemed to be the chief source of her bitterness.

I sprang the names of the city councilmen on her, not identifying them as such, just as people Julie might have known. The name Fletcher didn't ring a bell. The name Keven Drexel was familiar to her. Mrs. Steinmetz couldn't be sure why. She thought it possible he was one of Julie's old boyfriends. I gathered Julie had always been rather uncommunicative about her boyfriends, and having met Mrs. Steinmetz, I could understand why.

We got to the cemetery about then, and in a mercifully short ceremony, Julie Steinmetz was laid to rest.

Mrs. Steinmetz and I got back in the car, pulled out, and headed back for New York.

"Where can I take you?" I asked.

"Port Authority. I have to catch the bus."

"Oh? What time?"

"It doesn't matter. They leave all day long." She shuddered. "What does it matter? What does it matter now? What am I going to do? What am I going to do?"

The woman dissolved into sobs.

Which destroyed me. I wouldn't know how to deal with a sobbing woman even if I weren't driving a car. But cruising along the twisty Interboro Parkway there was really nothing I could do.

I felt bad for her, of course. But I must say the "What am I to do?" sounded extreme. I didn't understand it really. I mean, it wasn't as if Julie had been living with her. The woman had been alone before. She had to deal with her loss, but not with a change of life style, if you know what I mean. I know that sounds heartless, but I was just trying to make some sense out the situation. I desperately needed something to make sense for me somehow. As usual, nothing did. So while I couldn't deal with the woman's grief on the one hand, on the other I couldn't follow her. "What am I to do?" Try and dissect what that meant.

I'm sure I would have had no luck on my own, but when she pulled herself together, Mrs. Steinmetz told me.

"Two hundred dollars a week," she said. "That's what Julie sent me. Every single week. Ever since she got established. Well, less at first, a hundred, but for the last three years it's been two.

"But no more. Gone. Finished.

"And no insurance. Nothing. A kind girl, but not smart. Not a planner, you know? Spent every cent she got. Nothing saved. Her apartment rented, not owned. No provisions. No insurance. Not even a will. Of course, she didn't expect to die."

So. A concrete fact. Not a particularly helpful one, but at least a fact. Julie Steinmetz's death reduced her mother's income by two hundred dollars a week.

"That's terrible," I said. "What will you do now?"

That was just what she wanted to hear. She jumped on it almost eagerly.

"That's just it," she said. "What *can* I do? I'm old. I can't work. I can't maintain the farm. The taxes and the upkeep. With two hundred a week it was tight. Without it, there's no way. No way."

She seemed ready to lapse into sobbing again. I wanted to head that off, so I said quickly, "So what'll you do, put it up for sale?"

That staved off the weeping all right. She shot me a venomous look.

"For sale?" she said. "Are you kidding me? It's been on the market for five years. Ever since my husband died. No one wants it. There's no profit in farming it, and it's no good for anything else. Just flat, treeless land. Worthless."

My head snapped up. I was suddenly tense and alert.

I guess I just read too many mysteries, but the minute she said the word, 'worthless,' newspaper headlines started flashing in my head. URANIUM DEPOSITS IN UPSTATE NEW YORK. OIL DISCOVERED ON ALBANY FARM.

I took a breath. The case was getting to me. This wasn't a mystery story. Worthless land was worthless land. Mrs. Steinmetz's problems were simply mundane, not the result of some sinister plot. My problem was I was stuck with an unsympathetic grieving mother and I was gonna have to fight midtown traffic to get her to Port Authority.

So I said, "So you've been trying to sell the farm for five years, but no one's interested?"

"Yes," she said. "I'll have to put it on the market again. Not that it will do any good."

"Again?" I said. "I thought it already was on the market."

"It was. Up until a month ago."

"What?" I said, once more tense and alert.

"It's been off the market since last month. Now I'll have to see the broker, register with them again."

"Wait a minute. I don't understand. You took it off the market. Why?"

"I don't know."

Jesus. "I'm sorry. What do you mean, you don't know?"

"Julie called me. Told me to take it off the market."

"Why?"

"She didn't say."

"Didn't you ask?"

"Of course I asked. She didn't tell me. She was breezy, mysterious, the way she always was. 'There, there, Mom, don't you worry about a thing. Just do as I say and it will be all right.' "

"Maybe she found a buyer."

"What?"

"Some rich New Yorker who wanted an upstate retreat."

She shook her head. "The place is falling apart. I try, but I got no help. And even then. The foundation's rotting away, you know? You couldn't renovate it. Have to tear it down and rebuild. And if you're gonna do that, you might as well just buy land. And if you're buying land, you don't buy flat, treeless land that's no good for growing its keep."

"She must have had a reason. Didn't you have any idea?"

She frowned, shook her head. "Only one thing I could think of."

"What's that?"

"New highway's going through."

"Oh?"

"Not through my land. If it was, at least they'd have to pay me for that. But right along the north field."

"Wouldn't that up the value?" I said. "Just the access? Why wouldn't some housing developer want to put up a subdivision?"

She waved it away. "Yeah. Sure. Ten or fifteen years from now, little good that'll do me. You don't build a flock of houses in the middle of nowhere. They'll subdivide all right, but they'll start closer into town. By the time they get out to my farm I'll be long gone."

"All right. Well, what about a gas station? Department store. Maybe even a whole shopping mall? If this is a major highway you're talking about—"

"Oh it is. Four lanes wide."

"But it's not a thruway? I mean it's not like you'd be caught between exits. If someone wanted to build a mall, there'd be access?"

She sighed. "Yeah. That's the dream. Someone plunks down a pile of money to build a shopping mall. I'm out of there like that. Get me a place down in Florida. Getting old, you know. It's the winters I can't take."

"Well, maybe that's it," I said. "Maybe that's what Julie had in mind."

She sighed. Shook her head. "Not a chance."

"Well, why not?"

"Couldn't happen. Not on my land."

"No? Why is that?"

She sighed again, frowned, and shook her head at what I realized was another in a long line of personal affronts.

"It isn't zoned commercial."

This time I knew my way around. I turned into the Empire State Plaza on the first pass, parked in the garage, wrote my car location in my notebook, took the elevator up to the North Concourse, came out the right tunnel, and walked down to City Hall.

The gray-haired clerk sprang up when I came in. She met me at the counter.

"I got all the New York papers," she said. "Every one. There wasn't a mention of the City Council."

"I know," I said.

"So what's the story?"

I smiled. "I think you have to re-examine your reverse logic. Just because someone tells you they're not a reporter, doesn't necessarily mean they're a reporter."

"You're not a reporter?"

"No."

"Well, you could have fooled me. What do you want?"

I couldn't resist. I pulled the ticket out of my pocket. "I got this parking ticket out by the monument, and I was wondering—"

Her jaw dropped open. "I don't believe it. After everything you said—"

I shoved the ticket back in my pocket and held up my hands. "Just kidding. This ticket is my own damn fault, and I'm gonna pay. I don't care about it and I'm not a reporter."

She looked at me suspiciously. "Well, maybe you *are* a reporter and you haven't gotten the whole story yet."

"That's an angle. What *is* the whole story?"

"What?"

"I have a few more questions."

"Oh?"

"There's a new highway going through."

Her eyes narrowed. "What about it?"

"That's what I came to ask you. What's the City Council got to do with it?"

"Nothing. It's the Department of Highways."

"Yes, but that's not quite true, is it? The City Council has nothing to do with the roadway, but the situation it creates with the land around it is another matter."

She frowned. "I beg your pardon?"

"As I understand it, the highway is running through land that is zoned residential. Aren't the councilmen voting on whether that land gets zoned commercial?"

"Council members," she said.

"What?"

"Council members. Not councilmen. There are four women on the council."

The sexist pig strikes again. "Right," I said. "Council members. Well, don't they vote on it?"

"Yes, of course. They vote on that next week."

Bingo. "Well, that's mighty interesting," I said. "I'd sure like to know about that."

"Why?"

"So I can print your denials, of course."

She frowned.

"That was another joke."

"Who are you?" she asked.

I shrugged. "Maybe I'm an inspector sent by the mayor's office to check up on things."

"Are you?"

"No. But if you want to play guessing games, that's as good as any. Look. What does it matter who I am? I'm a guy who wants to know about the government. Let's talk about the zoning thing, cause it's as good an example as anything."

"Now I *know* you're a reporter."

"If you say so. Look. Let's talk zoning. When the Council votes, what will they be voting on? I mean, is this a yes or no proposition? We either zone commercial or we don't?"

She shook her head. "No. It's an either/or proposition."

"Either/or?"

"That's right."

"Well, for the layman who doesn't understand, why don't you spell it out? Either or what?"

She took a breath. "Well, you have to understand. The public is resistant to change."

"I'll buy that."

"So, any time you're going to change a zoning ordinance, you'll have people in favor, people against. No matter what you do, you're gonna offend someone. You can't please 'em all."

"Fine. How does that apply to the situation?"

"The highway's going through and the land's to be rezoned. They won't rezone it all. That would create an outcry from the conservationists and the old-timers who want to preserve our historic values and all that. That's why it's an either/or proposition. The land in question is divided into two tracts. When the council meets, they'll vote to rezone one."

"And the other?"

"The other they won't."

30

After that, it was just legwork. I love saying that, because it's what a real detective would say. Or at least what a fictional detective would say—I've certainly read enough books with that phrase in 'em. And I know exactly what it means. It means the detective has finally cracked the case, and all that remains is the routine but time-consuming task of gathering the information, checking everything out, and confirming his theories.

This was certainly true in my case. I had the solution now. Julie Steinmetz, the dutiful and provident daughter, had seen a chance of relieving her mother's financial woes—and perhaps even of relieving herself of the necessity of forking over two hundred bucks a week in support payments—by the simple expedient of bribing the City Council to change a zoning ordinance. In doing so, she had incurred the wrath of someone who didn't want the zoning ordinance changed, and who had attempted to insure the fact that it wouldn't be by the simple expedient of having her killed. This person had gone to the elaborate precautions of arranging for a handy fall guy, in the hope of confusing the investigation so utterly that the police would never even start looking in the right direction. The fact that he had bothered to do so, meant that it was necessary. And if it was necessary, it meant his involvement in the case must be obvious if one only looked for it.

Which wasn't that hard. There were two tracts of land. If someone didn't want one zoned commercial, he must want the other. This was the type of deduction even I could handle. So as I say, it was just legwork.

It was also something I knew how to do. It was the sort of thing I did sometimes for Richard—trace down who owned a particular piece of property on which a client was injured, so Richard would know who to sue. I spent the day at the Department of Highways, the County Clerk's office, and the Department of Taxation. I had no problem getting what I wanted. All the information was a matter of public record—anyone can ask for it.

This is what I found: of the two tracts of land, tract A consisted of several small farms, among them that of Mrs. Steinmetz; tract B consisted of undeveloped land, eighty percent of which was owned by a single company. According to the Tax Assessor's Office, for the past ten years the taxes on that land had been paid by Farber Kennelworth Development.

A Manhattan firm.

I had one more thing to do before I left town. I didn't have to, I just wanted to.

A call to the restaurant where I'd tailed POP had confirmed that Keven Drexel had a dinner reservation for six o'clock. I timed it just right. He was sitting at the bar with the young blonde when I walked in. His face hardened when he saw me, and he took his arm from around the blonde and put his hands on the bar, clearly in preparation to stand up should the need arise.

I dispelled the need. I put up my hands, palms out, and said in my most conciliatory manner. "Please don't get up. This will only take a minute."

"No it won't," Drexel said "I've had quite enough of you. I have no comment, and I'm not answering any questions."

"I'm not here to ask you questions," I said. "I'm here because I owe you an apology."

That got him. Whatever he'd been expecting, it wasn't that. He frowned. "Apology?"

"That's right. For the other day. I was wrong. I was out of line. And I'm sorry."

"Oh?"

"Yeah. You didn't see anything in the paper about you taking a young woman to a motel, did you?"

"No."

"And you won't. It was a mistake. All my fault. That's why I want to apologize. For insinuating you went to a motel for a romantic interlude with Julie Steinmetz. I was wrong. You didn't do it."

Keven Drexel relaxed somewhat. He picked up his drink. Smiled at the blonde. "See, honey. I told you there was nothing to it."

"Right, Miss Carr," I said. "I want to apologize to you too. I hope I didn't cause you any worry by suggesting Mr. Drexel had gone to a motel to meet another woman. He didn't."

"Damn right, I didn't," Drexel said.

"Right," I said. "You didn't. You went there to take a bribe."

Drexel's glass stopped halfway to his lips.

"That's right," I said. "A bribe to influence your vote on the City Council." I turned to the blonde. "See, Miss Carr, there was nothing sexual involved. This was a straight case of graft."

Jean Carr looked at Keven Drexel. His mouth was open and his face had gone a pasty white. She looked back at me. Then back at him.

I smiled at Drexel. "Only thing is, you didn't get it. Julie Steinmetz was dead when you got there, so you didn't get the money. Tough luck. Must have been a hell of a disappointment."

Drexel wet his lips. He seemed to be trying to think of something to say. If so, he failed.

"So I'm sorry. About what I said. And I'm sorry you

didn't get your bribe. Too bad. It would have told you how to vote." I shrugged. "Now I guess you'll just have to vote your conscience."

I smiled at Drexel, nodded to the blonde, and walked out.

I staked out Farber Kennelworth Development at seven o'clock the next morning. I didn't really expect anyone to be coming to work at seven o'clock, but I wasn't taking any chances.

I was also pissed as hell. And if a short little man with a stringy red moustache happened to show up, I didn't want to miss him.

I figured it was a good bet. (Not my missing him, though that was a good bet too.) No, I figured it was a good bet he would show. Unless he was an actor hired as an unwitting dupe, or a hit man hired especially for the propose, the bogus Marvin Nickleson had to be connected with Farber Kennelworth Development. There was no other explanation. Everything fit too well. If that wasn't true, I might as well just pack it in. Cause that was my deduction, I was damn glad to have made it, I was in fact proud to have arrived at it, and if it didn't pan out I was going to feel like a kid who didn't get to go to the movie show. I might even throw a temper tantrum.

Which certainly would have puzzled the early morning

commuters. And by eight o'clock there were plenty of 'em.

I was on the sidewalk outside a building on Second Avenue not half a dozen blocks from the building where I was told Julie Steinmetz worked, but which was actually the building where Monica Dorlander worked. Though, actually, I *was* told that it was where Monica Dorlander worked, though Monica Dorlander wasn't Monica Dorlander. Though she was, she just wasn't Julie Steinmetz.

So I had come full cycle. Here I was, once again, standing on the sidewalk in the bitter cold, freezing my ass off, and just like Monica Dorlander or Julie Steinmetz or whatever, the bogus Marvin Nickleson didn't show up.

Which didn't surprise me. Because much as I thought he would, I also thought he wouldn't. Because that was the only thing that made sense. The bogus Marvin Nickleson had let me see his face. That had to mean he was counting on never seeing me again. And how could he count on never seeing me again if he worked not six blocks from the address he had sent me to stake out?

And yet he had to. I didn't know anything about Farber Kennelworth Development, but it seemed unlikely there was a guy named Farber Kennelworth. Probably there was a Mr. Farber and a Mr. Kennelworth. By rights, the bogus Marvin Nickleson had to be one of the two. It was the only thing that made sense.

So there I was with two conflicting theories, both of which were the only thing that made sense.

And by late morning, when I could assume even the most prestigious member of the firm could reasonably be expected to be there, he still hadn't shown up.

There was no other entrance to the building, I was sure of it. The Second Avenue entrance was it. It was a corner building, but there was no entrance on the side street. And the building didn't run all the way through the block. And there's no subway on Second Avenue, no chance of an underground entrance of that type. And there was no garage on the block that might have connected to the building in some way. And I'd been watching the front entrance all the time. No, there was no way the guy could have gotten by.

I worried that he had.

By eleven-thirty or thereabouts, since I still didn't have a watch, I decided, screw it, I'm going in.

I went in the lobby. I checked it out first. There was a small newsstand, some banks of elevators, and then the back wall. No entrances, no exits. No doors, locked or otherwise. Nothing.

I checked the directory. Farber Kennelworth Development was on the seventh floor.

I got in the elevator and checked the buttons. The bottom button was "L" for lobby. There was no "B" for basement. No lower level to take an elevator from. No, the entrance I'd been staking out was it.

I pushed seven. The doors closed and the elevator went up to the seventh floor. I got out, walked down the hallway, and found a solid wood door marked FARBER KENNELWORTH DEVELOPMENT.

I put my ear to the door. I could hear the sound of a typewriter within.

Well, what do I do now? Do I go in and see who's there? The secretary who's typing will immediately stop and say "May I help you?" And what do I say then? Do I claim a bogus appointment with Mr. Farber or Mr. Kennelworth? That will go over big if it's just a trade name, and there *is* no Farber or Kennelworth. But why wouldn't there be? How the hell should I know? Suppose there *is* a Mr. Farber and I ask for an appointment and she gives me one? Or I ask to see him and she asks me, "What about?" What do I say, "Development?" Would that be stupid, witty, or exactly right? No, "a property," that's what you say. I wanted to see him about a property. And then she asks my name and I give her a phony one, and then she asks me to take a seat, and then she shows me in to see the guy and it isn't him. What do I do then, say, "Sorry, Mr. Farber, I wanted to talk to Mr. Kennelworth"? That'd go over big. Or say, "Excuse me, Mr. Farber, but is your partner a dinky guy with a scraggly moustache?" That would work fine too. Jesus, and then he's gonna ask me about the property, and what do I say? Cause I don't know a thing about property. Except it comes in acres. That's it. I say I have an acre and a half. But would that be enough to interest him? Probably not. A hundred acres. "I got a hundred acres, Mr. Farber." What type of land, what's it been assessed at, what do I wanna do with it?

I got back in the elevator.

I went down to the lobby. There was a pay phone there. I went to it, punched in information, asked for the number of Farber Kennelworth Development.

I called the number.

A female voice answered the phone. "Farber Kennelworth Development."

"Mr. Farber, please."

"Who's calling, please?"

"Mr. Acres."

Asshole. Acres is what you're selling.

"One moment, please."

She put me on hold.

Idiot. Acres selling acres. Why couldn't you say Mr. Thompson? You could be Thompson selling acres. You can't be Acres selling thompson.

She clicked back on. "Mr. Acres?"

No, Mr. Thompson. "Yes."

"Mr. Farber is on another line. Would you care to hold?"

"No, I'll call back."

"Would you like to leave a number?"

"No, I'll call him later, thank you very much," I said and hung up.

All right. So far so good. There was a Farber. Did it follow that there also was a Kennelworth?

I dropped a quarter in the phone and punched in the number again.

The same female voice said, "Farber Kennelworth Development."

I disguised my voice slightly. "Mr. Kennelworth, please?"

"Who's calling, please?"

This time I was ready for it. "Mr. Thompson."

"I'm sorry, Mr. Thompson, I didn't recognize your voice. How are you?"

"I have a slight cold."

"I could tell. One moment, please."

So. There was a Kennelworth. There was also a Thompson, and Kennelworth would think I was him.

Seconds later a man's voice said, "Hi, Charlie?"

I hung up the phone.

So. There was a Kennelworth and a Farber. The voice of Mr. Kennelworth was not the voice of the bogus Marvin Nickleson. I hadn't heard the voice of Mr. Farber, but assuming he had managed to get into his office this morning without flying, he wasn't Marvin Nickleson either.

But now I had a new lead. Charlie Thompson. Who the hell was he? He knew Kennelworth. The secretary there certainly knew him. That should make him pretty important, shouldn't it?

Could *he* be Marvin Nickleson?

I called information, asked them if they had a Manhattan listing for a Charles Thompson. They had six of them—did I have the address? No, I did not. And who was to say this Charlie Thompson had to live in Manhattan? In all probability, he didn't. Which made tracking him down only slightly more unpromising than tracing five hundred POPs.

I hung up the phone and took stock of my situation. The way I saw it, it was gonna be a long day.

It was.

I hung out in the lobby most of the afternoon, trying to look like I belonged there. I don't know if I did that great a job or not, but at least nobody hassled me. Staking out an office building in the lobby is probably a no-no in the detective biz, but I just couldn't hack the sidewalk. I tried it right after the phone calls, and I was out there turning blue when a guy went by with a ghetto-blaster on which the weatherman was announcing a wind-chill factor of minus twenty-eight. What a guy with no gloves was doing carrying half a ton of radio in that cold was beyond me, unless maybe it was frozen to his hand. At any rate, that was enough for me. I spent the rest of the afternoon inside. And while no one hassled me, in my head I envisioned building security guards holding whispered conferences about the suspicious gentleman on the premises, and every now and then I couldn't help glancing out the door to see if the cops they'd summoned had arrived to pick me up.

Naturally, they never did, and the afternoon passed, and rush hour arrived. And elevators started coming down and people started streaming out, and then the lobby wasn't the place to be anymore, cause someone might get by me in the crowd, whereas outside I couldn't miss anyone coming out the door. So I hit the sidewalk again, and while it was still cold it wasn't that bad, because there was a constant stream of people coming out to watch, so I was occupied.

Till rush hour ended. And the people stopped coming out. At which point I was finally able to convince myself it was time to pack it up and go home.

Except for one thing. It occurred to me I should check the office of Farber Kennelworth Development to make sure no one was still there.

I headed for the elevators. Just as I got there one came down and a man got out. I'd never seen him before, but his coming down reminded me that stragglers were still coming down. And there were half a dozen elevators. If I went up in one, I could miss Marvin Nickleson coming down in another. But if I didn't go up, how was I gonna find out if the office was closed?

I started for the elevator. Stopped. Started. Stopped.

Shit.

I said it out loud. I do that now and then when I get frustrated. As I said, I sometimes talk to myself out loud, particularly in moments of stress. This was just one manifestation of it. I'll recognize some personal failing in myself, or I'll recall some past instance when I acted like an asshole, or some decision of mine which I have cause to regret, and I'll say, "Shit." Or if the personal failing is humiliating enough, or the past experience embarrassing enough, or the cause for regret deep enough, I'll say, "Fuck."

As I grow older and older, naturally these past experiences grow more and more numerous, and the instances of my recalling them grow more and more frequent, making the spaces between these instances grow shorter and shorter, and it occurs to me what is happening is I am gradually evolving into one of those pathetic old men you see walking down Broadway, compulsively muttering a constant stream of obscenities. I think there's a name for that. If I were a better writer, I'd know it.

Shit.

I got in the elevator, went up to the sixth floor. There was no one in the corridor, and no light from under the door of Farber Kennelworth Development. Unless the bogus Marvin Nickleson had gone down in an elevator while I had come up in mine, he hadn't been in today.

But Farber and Kennelworth had. So he wasn't them. Or they weren't him. Or whatever.

I took the subway home, which is always a bitch from the upper East Side, because you gotta go down to Grand Central, shuttle to Times Square, and then back up again.

And the homeless are patrolling the cars in force these days. You can't ride from one station to the next without hearing some person's tale of personal woe. It's as if they had it choreographed. The train will pull out of the station, the man who'd been working the car will disappear through the door at the front of the train, and the door at the rear of the car will slide open and the next performer will appear. "Good evening, ladies and gentlemen. I'm your personal bummer from 79th to 86th Street, here to remind you of the pain and misery and suffering in the world." And the guy knows he's working a hard house, and his only chance is the people who just got on, cause the people who've been on since 42nd Street have already had three or four tales of woe, and compassion has shut down and numbness has set in, and unless this guy's got a particularly good spiel, he's not gonna move 'em.

Needless to say, I was feeling like hell when I got home. Alice was on the computer again, natch, but for once I didn't care. I didn't feel like talking to her. I was so bummed out, I didn't feel like much of anything.

She stopped though, and said, "Hi."

"Hi," I said.

She shook her head. "I don't have to ask, do I? A total washout."

"Total."

"Hey, it's your first day, you know you're right, it's gonna work out."

"Sure."

I must have looked really gloomy, because Alice got up, put her hands on my shoulders and leaned against my chest. She was wearing a sweat suit. I find women in sweat suits incredibly sexy. Their bodies move around in them freely in particularly attractive ways.

"Hey," she said, "don't look so depressed. What do you need, a pep talk?"

A pep talk was not exactly what I had in mind. I hugged her a little tighter.

"Stanley," Alice said. "Tommie's still up."

Ah, the simple joys of parenthood. Tough on a man who still has trouble thinking of himself as a grownup.

Over Alice's shoulder I noticed some checks lying on the desk next to the computer.

"What's that?" I said.

Alice looked. "Oh, I was just entering those checks."

"Checks?"

"Yeah. Into the computer."

"What?"

Alice turned around and pointed to the screen. "It's 'Managing Your Money.' A program. I enter all the data from the checkbook into the computer. Then when we do our taxes, we don't have to add up the checkbook, the computer does it for us. Just call it up and print out all the totals and we're done."

That sounded so good there had to be a catch to it somewhere. "Oh?"

"Sure. Let me show you."

Alice picked up one of the checks. "All right. Look. I made ten bucks today for running off some form letters."

Alice bent over the keyboard. "So I type it in here in the proper blanks. Date. Amount. Name. Category. Then at tax time the computer calls it up. What do you think?"

I thought her ass looked great in that sweat suit.

"Terrific," I said. "So you made ten bucks today. That's

ten better than me. What's the other check?"

"Oh, that's a dividend."

Alice picked it up and began typing it in.

"Oh," I said.

More small potatoes. Some five or six years ago one of Alice's great uncles died and left her a hundred shares of National Fuel and Gas. As a result, four times a year we got a whopping thirty-one dollar and fifty cents dividend check. I can't say it changed our lifestyle much, though for a while I got some mileage out of facetiously referring to Alice as 'The Heiress.'

I'd dismissed the check and gone back to admiring the contours of the sweat suit when it hit me.

"Jesus Christ," I said.

Alice stopped typing and turned around. "What?"

"That check."

"What check?"

"The dividend check."

"What about it?"

"You know what it makes you?"

Alice frowned and looked at me as if I'd lost my mind. "Thirty bucks richer."

"Yeah, but what else?"

Alice looked totally exasperated. "I give up. What?"

"You're a stockholder."

33

The first time I met Leroy Stanhope Williams he had a cast on his leg. Leroy was one of the first clients I signed for Richard. He was also the only one I ever kept in touch with. That was because, aside from being an agreeable and intelligent person, Leroy had one outstanding characteristic that made him invaluable to a person in my profession. You see, Leroy was a thief.

I hate to say that, because it immediately conjures up petty images. And there was nothing petty about Leroy. He was a grand thief on a grand scale. He robbed only from the rich, and he gave only to himself. He stole mainly art objects. Leroy was a connoisseur and a collector. Unfortunately, coming from a background on the streets of Harlem, Leroy had no money. At least, no money of his own. And having developed a taste for fine art through an education which began in reform school and ended with a degree from NYU, Leroy had attempted to combine both worlds in order to change his life style. In this endeavor, he was entirely successful.

Leroy was a black man some five to ten years my junior,

with a high sloping forehead that gave him an intellectual look, and a speech pattern that did nothing to belie it. He dressed impeccably, tastefully, conservatively. He always looked like some foreign dignitary about to address the U.N.

Leroy had done me some favors in the past. The last one had almost gotten him killed. This one, I hoped, at worst would only get him arrested.

It was a quarter to five. Leroy and I were standing on the sidewalk outside the office building of Farber Kennelworth Development. I knew what time it was because Leroy had a watch, one that I'm sure cost more than my entire wardrobe. I didn't know what the wind-chill factor was because no one had walked by with a radio, but you don't need a weatherman to know which way the wind blows. Suffice it to say it was cold.

Leroy blew out some frosty air, clapped his gloved hands together, bounced up and down in a manner that managed to be agitated and dignified at the same time, and said, "Would you mind explaining it to me again, why we are standing here in the freezing cold when there is a warm lobby not ten feet away?"

"If the man I'm looking for comes out we don't have to do this."

"Why can't we wait for him in the lobby?"

"We might miss him in the lobby."

"You really expect him to show?"

"Quite frankly, it's a long shot."

"It's rather cold out for a long shot."

"I know. But if he were here and I missed him, I'd never forgive myself."

"That doesn't make any sense."

"Are you kidding? It's perfectly clear."

"It's perfectly clear, it just doesn't make sense."

"Why not?"

"You admit there's only the slimmest chance the man might show up at all."

"This is true."

"If we were to wait for him in the lobby, and if by the very slimmest chance this man might show up, there is then an even slimmer chance we might miss him. Is that correct?"

"I suppose so."

"And the reason we are holding out for this minuscule chance is that, were it to occur, in that unlikely event you should never be able to forgive yourself?"

"That's right."

"Hmmm," Leroy said. "But for that to happen, since you know what he looks like, it occurs to me the only way for you to miss him would be not to see him at all."

"Exactly."

"But if you didn't see him at all, you wouldn't know you'd missed him, would you?"

We waited in the lobby.

At five o'clock, people began to stream out. Of course, never having ventured beyond the doors of Farber Kennelworth Development, there was no way for me to recognize anyone who worked there. On the other hand, there was no way for them to recognize me.

With the exception of the bogus Marvin Nickleson. I tried to spot him in the crowd. Naturally, I couldn't. And though I was vigilant as hell, the thought occurred to me that Marvin Nickleson was a shrimp of a guy who could easily vanish in a crowd. And Leroy's fine logic notwithstanding, I couldn't shake the nagging fear that somehow he'd been there and I'd missed him.

After a while the elevators began coming down with only stragglers.

Leroy turned to me and said, "Well?"

"Well what?"

"What do you think? Are they closed?"

"I don't know."

"Well, what time was it when you went up and found them closed before?"

"I don't know. I haven't got a watch."

"That's unfortunate. Well, approximately then. Would you say it was approximately now?"

"More or less."

"Well. Shall we?"

I hesitated. I was reluctant to go up because, of course, while we went up in one elevator, Marvin Nickleson might be coming down in another. But I didn't feel like mentioning it to Leroy somehow.

"Let's go," I said.

We went up in the elevator and walked down the hallway to Farber Kennelworth Development. There was no sound from within and no light under the door.

The lock, however, looked formidable.

"Think you can handle it?" I asked.

Leroy gave me a withering look.

"Sorry. I withdraw the question. You want me to stand guard?"

"I would prefer it if you were to stand casually next to me as if we were two legitimate businessmen about to enter our office."

I did that. At least I tried. As an experiment sometime, try to act casual. I never felt so self-conscious in my life.

Leroy, however, had no problem. Humming softly, he fished two metal strips out of his pants pocket, inserted them in the lock as if they were a key, and seconds later the door clicked open.

"After you," Leroy said.

I pushed the door open and stepped inside. Leroy followed, closing the door behind him.

It was pitch dark. I pulled a flashlight out of my coat

pocket and snapped it on. I hunched over and kept my hand around the front, shielding the beam.

Leroy snapped the light switch on.

I wheeled around. “What are you doing?”

Leroy smiled. “You are an amateur. In the event someone were to walk down the hall and see the light on under the door, they would assume someone was working late. If they were to see the flickering beam of your flashlight, they would assume the office was being robbed.

“With the light on we are relatively safe. Nonetheless, I have no real wish to be here. Have you any further use of my services?”

“Only if the offices or files are locked.”

“Then let’s see.”

They weren’t. It was a small suite consisting of two offices, presumably those of Farber and Kennelworth, and the reception area. Neither of the offices were locked, nor were any of the desks or cabinets or files.

Leroy excused himself, pleading a desire not to reside in jail. He also added the suggestion that I be brief.

I tried, and I probably was, though it seemed an eternity to me.

I did the offices first. I found nothing there. The desks yielded an assortment of papers and notes, which might have been interesting, but it wasn’t what I was after and I didn’t want to take the time.

That left only the waiting room. There were two desks and the files. The files were a last resort. I’d tackle them if I had to, but there were twelve drawers full, and going through them was going to be a bitch. So I was rooting like hell for the desks.

The first one was a washout. The top drawer, yielding lipstick, tissues, and a movie magazine, told me this was the receptionist’s desk and it wasn’t going to be here. I jerked the other drawers open and proved myself right.

I took the other desk, jerked open drawers. Middle. Top right. Bottom right. Top left. Bottom left.

Bingo.

I reached in, pulled out a stack of account books. I grabbed the top book, opened it on the desk.

And someone knocked on the door.

I almost hit the ceiling.

Jesus Christ! Who is that? And what do I do now? Do I open the door? Or do I sit tight and pretend no one's here? How can I do that, they can tell the light's on? So what? So they forgot and left them on. Or maybe one of the bigwigs is working in the back office with the door closed and doesn't hear the knock. Yeah, that's it. Just sit tight.

For me inaction nearly always wins out over action. I sat tight. In fact, I barely breathed.

The knock wasn't repeated.

Instead came a sound that sent chills up my back.

The sound of a key being slid in the slot.

The lock clicked back.

The door opened.

A maid with a cleaning cart stood in the doorway.

I gawked at her. She looked surprised to see me. I couldn't blame her. There I was, standing there with my topcoat on, hunched over a pile of the company's account books, looking like a kid who got caught with his hand in the cookie jar.

"Oh," she said. "I didn't know anyone was here. You're working late."

"Yes," I muttered.

"I'm sorry," she said. "I thought they'd all left. I'll do the other office and come back. You gonna be long?"

"No."

"Well, don't you worry. I'll just do the other office first."

She backed out and closed the door.

Jesus Christ. What a victory. Ace private detective manages to bluff out cleaning lady—croaks out yes and no answers rather than confessing on the spot. What a guy.

If I had indeed bluffed her out. If she wasn't down the hall right now calling security. Come on you son of a bitch, get it and get out of there.

You wouldn't believe the job I did on those books. I would have put Evelyn Wood to shame.

It wasn't in the first, second, or third, but in the fourth it was right there on the first page. A list of all the stockholders of Farber Kennelworth Development.

The name Charles Thompson jumped off the page. However, he turned out to be a minor holder with only fifty shares. No, according to the company books, the major stockholder, with in fact a controlling interest in Farber Kennelworth Development, was a Carlton Kraswell of Trenton, New Jersey.

I hit Trenton at eight in the morning. I'd have liked to have been there earlier, but I'm only human and I slept through the alarm.

I came in on Route 33 and passed a sign that said ENTERING TRENTON. I was thankful for the sign, because otherwise I wouldn't have had a clue. It didn't look like a city much, just a street of small frame houses set close together. I followed the road aways until I came to a curve with an arrow that said, TO NEW YORK. That didn't look good, so I hung a U-turn, worked my way back a bit and hung a right.

I found myself on a village street with a few stores. There was a police car parked on the corner, so I stopped, got out, and gave the cop the address. He said, "Oh sure, that's in the Hiltonia section, up by Sullivan Way." He gave me directions to get there that I knew I could never follow, even writing them down. So I thanked him and asked him where I could get a map somewhere. He directed me to a 7-11 that sold 'em. Those directions included one light and one turn, and that I could handle and I got my map.

It's a good thing I did, because even with the map I got lost and made a wrong turn and wound up in the municipal district. A couple of turns later I saw a sign that said, GOVERNMENT CENTER, and I suddenly realized Trenton was a state capital too. So far as I knew, that had nothing to do with my investigation, but it struck me as an interesting coincidence that in the space of a week I'd been to two state capitals. It also struck me as evidence of how apolitical I am that I'd never been to either of them before, and didn't even know one of them existed.

I caught my bearings off the map, made only one more wrong turn, and found myself on Sullivan Way. I passed the Trenton Country Club. In the summer it probably looked like a million bucks, but now it was January, there was no snow on the ground, and everything looked bare and desolate.

Or maybe that's just how I felt. That I was a fool on a fool's errand, I was just wasting my time, and there was no way this was gonna pan out.

I came to a crossroad, checked my map and discovered I'd gone too far. I turned around and passed the country club again. It didn't look any better this time around. I passed the Trenton Psychiatric Hospital. I considered checking in for a refresher course on positive thinking.

I kept a sharp eye on the map, made the right turns, and suddenly there I was. It was a small residential community of perfectly nice houses and lawns. A nice place for nice people with nice families to live. A place no better, no worse that I could see, than that where Councilman Steve Fletcher had lived in Albany.

Carlton Kraswell's house was a modest two-story affair on a corner lot with a couple of trees and a swing in the yard and a car in the driveway. Which somehow seemed all wrong. I don't know why, I guess somehow I'd expected a mansion with an iron gate and Dobermans prowling the grounds. But here he was, just an ordinary respectable citizen like everybody else.

I began to have serious doubts. Or I should say, I continued to have serious doubts.

I backed my car up to a point where I could observe the front door of the house without being seen. Sat and waited.

I must say, the whole thing looked very unpromising. The only bright spot was the car in the driveway. For one thing it was a Mercedes. For another thing, it was there, indicating the owner was probably home.

But when would he come out, that was the question. Well, he might come out to get his paper. But there were no newspaper boxes by the road. That surprised me. I would have expected there to be a Trenton *Times* or *News* or what have you, with red or green or yellow metal boxes on poles at the foot of the drives. But there weren't. Nor were there mailboxes. These Trenton people got neither papers nor mail. So if Carlton Kraswell were indeed home, there was no reason for him to come out unless he wanted to go somewhere.

But he didn't. An hour went by. Nothing happened. I was beginning to manufacture hollow ruses by which to flush the Kraswell from his den. A phone call, first to see if he was home, and second to try to get him out of it. But what would I say? Maybe it didn't matter. Maybe the minute he said, "Hello," I'd recognize his voice. Am I that good at voices? Was his voice that distinctive a one? Had he *disguised* his voice when he posed as Marvin Nickleson? What would be the point of that? How the hell should I know?

No, you gotta have a ruse. A letter. A special delivery letter. "It's the post office, Mr. Kraswell, we have a special delivery letter for you." That would do it fine. If that's the way the post office works around here. If special delivery letters aren't actually delivered. But how could they be, with no mailboxes.

As if on cue, a mail truck rounded the corner, rumbled up the hill. It stopped in front of Kraswell's driveway. The mailman got out, walked up the drive to the house.

I couldn't believe it. The guy had a special delivery letter for Kraswell, just like I thought, and was going to ring Kraswell's bell.

He didn't. He took a bunch of letters from his bag, stuck 'em in a box on the wall by the door.

So. That was why there were no boxes by the road. These guys got delivery up the drive.

The mailman got back in his truck and drove off.

I sat and waited. Come on schmuck. The bait's in the trap. Go for it.

It was forty-five minutes later, and I was seriously considering the phone idea again when the front door opened. A man stepped out on the porch. He must have been sleeping late, because he was wearing a blue bathrobe. I looked at him, and somehow all my feeling of incompetence and futility melted away.

I smiled with immense satisfaction as the man I'd known as Marvin Nickleson riffled through the mail, snuffled once from the cold, and tugged at his scraggly moustache.

I wasn't going to tackle him alone. I know that blows my image as a private detective, but then again, what doesn't? And this was a guy who shot people. Or at least had them shot, if he hadn't actually pulled the trigger himself. Somehow I thought he had. I couldn't help thinking of the guy as an actor—after all, he'd played the part of Marvin Nickleson—and as an actor, I figured him for a one-man show.

At any rate, for me, getting shot is kind of a low priority. I mean, when I write down a list of things to do tomorrow, you'll never see getting shot on it. And seeing as how I didn't have a gun to shoot back with, tackling Carlton Kraswell alone didn't seem like such a hot idea. No, I was gonna need help.

I drove back to New York and hunted up MacAullif.

Who wasn't pleased to see me.

He grimaced, he rubbed his hand over his face, he rolled his eyes to the ceiling, and said, "Why me?"

"Come on, MacAullif—"

"No, *you* come on. Why do you have to bring me this?"

"I need help."

"You always need help. If it's not one thing, it's another."

"Hey, it's not like I'm asking you to square a parking ticket. This guy's a murderer."

"Of course he's a murderer. People who kill people usually are. You went looking for a killer, you found him. What do you want me to do, stand up and cheer?"

"I told you. I need help."

"Yeah, but why me?"

"I know you."

"That's hardly my fault. A guy who gets mixed up in murder investigations is gonna meet a few cops." MacAullif snatched up the phone, punched the intercom button. "Daniels, get the Willford file and get in here."

I stared at MacAullif. I couldn't believe it. I mean, I'd expected sarcasm and derision, but not an out-and-out refusal.

"You saying you won't help me?"

"That's right."

"Why not?"

MacAullif winced and shook his head. "Why not? The man asks me why not? All right, how's this?" MacAullif ticked off the points on his fingers. "One: it's not my case. Two: I solved my ax murder, but I got four more cases pending, and one's a triple homicide. Three: New Jersey's out of my jurisdiction. Four: you're a pain in the ass. You can't stay out of trouble, and every time things start getting a little sticky you come running in here looking for help. I run five hundred license plates for you, that's still not enough. Five: you got no proof. Six: you're a pain in the ass again. You want me to run down to New Jersey where I got no jurisdiction and arrest a guy for murder where you got no proof. Now if I listen to you long enough, you probably got some harebrained scheme for getting proof, but if I do that this department's gonna go to hell, I'm going to be in hot water, and it'll probably take five years off my life."

The door opened and Daniels, one of MacAullif's young detectives, came in carrying a file folder.

"Sir," he said.

"Ah, Daniels," MacAullif said, with elaborate sarcasm. "If you could just hang on a moment. I know you got that triple homicide to deal with, but first I gotta take care of this asshole's personal problems." MacAullif turned back to me. "Now, where was I? Six? Seven? Probably doesn't matter. I think you get the idea."

"So what am I supposed to do?"

MacAullif shook his head. "An idea gotta hit you over the head with a hammer? It's not my case. This upstate police chief—it's his case. You want the Jersey cops to move on this guy, any authority to do so's gotta come from him."

I frowned. "The guy is not too swift."

"Maybe not, but he's in charge."

"And he thinks I did it."

"I like him already. O.K. I told you what to do. Get the hell out of here."

I did. I got the hell out of there. And I thought about it. And I got my car and I headed for Poughkeepsie.

On the way up, I thought things over. All in all, it wasn't that bad. MacAullif was right, of course. It was Creely's case, and like it or not, I was gonna have to work with him.

Creely was a small town cop, and his facilities weren't that good, and as I told MacAullif, he wasn't that swift to begin with. Plus the fact he had me pegged for the killer.

That was on the minus side. On the plus side was the fact he *was* a small town cop and his facilities weren't that good, but despite that he had refused assistance and was trying to handle the case himself. Which put him in a hell of a position. Having told the state cops to fuck off, if he couldn't come up with something soon his ass was on the line. He might not want help solving the case, but the thing was, he *had* to solve it. By now that much must have dawned on him. And by now he must have found out that the evidence against me was *not* piling up as he had hoped, and that, coupled with Sergeant Clark's assurance that I had not committed the crime, must be giving him serious doubt. He was in a mess, and by now he must be feeling pretty desperate to get out of it. So he ought to be inclined to listen.

Or so I hoped.

I pulled up in front of the police station. The sign was hanging on the door, so I guess Creely still was chief. How long that remained true probably depended on whether he cracked the case.

I pushed the door open and walked in.

They were all there. Creely, Davis, and Chuck. For once, Creely wasn't chewing gum. That's because he was having lunch. He had a sandwich in one hand, and a can of Coke in the other. He was leaning back in his chair with his feet on the desk. Davis and Chuck were sitting around eating sandwiches too. They gave the impression of a bunch of guys after work hanging out and shooting the shit.

They all looked up when I walked in.

Creely grinned and shook his head. "Well, speak of the devil and here he is."

So. They'd been talking about me. Somehow that didn't bode well.

"Well, Mr. Hastings," Creely said. "You're a little early, aren't you? Your arraignment's not till next week."

"I know."

"So what are you doing here?"

I took a breath. "I came to tell you who killed Julie Steinmetz."

Creely waved it away. "Oh, we know that."

Shit. They had their own favorite candidate. Now I not only had to sell 'em on my theory, I had to talk 'em out of theirs. Unless, of course, their favorite candidate was still me.

"You do?" I said.

"Oh sure," Creely said. "Of course, we can't prove it. But we know who did it all right."

"Well, that must be pretty frustrating," I said. "I'm really sorry. Unless, of course, you still think it's me."

Creely grinned. "Oh," he said. "So that's why you're here. No, no. Don't give it another thought. We know it wasn't you."

"You do?"

"Oh, sure. Even without Sergeant Clark vouching for you, we know you didn't do it. You're not the type. And as your lawyer says, even if you were the type, you couldn't be that stupid." Creely shrugged. "But then on the other hand, if you really still think we might fancy you for this crime, maybe you *are* that stupid. But set your mind at rest. We know it wasn't you."

"Well, this may surprise you, but I'm kind of glad to hear it."

"Yeah, well don't go celebrating all over the place. We still got you for obstruction of justice. Which is exactly the sort of thing I *do* peg you for, and the charge just might stick."

"Fine, but that's not what I'm here for."

"Right, right," Creely said. "You're here to tell us who killed Julie Steinmetz." Creely waved his Coke at Davis and Chuck. "Pay attention, boys. I'm sure this is going to be good." Creely shook his head. "You fucking amateurs are such a pain in the ass, you know it? I can't ignore your theory or I'll catch heat for it, and now I'll have to waste a lot of time running down a bunch of false clues."

Jesus Christ. I was tempted to walk out. If Creely didn't think I was the murderer, who gave a damn what he thought?

Except for that obstruction of justice charge. And the fact I couldn't bear to think of letting that prick Carlton Kraswell get away.

"All right," Creely said. "Go ahead. Tell us your theory."

"Gee fellas," I said. "I feel kind of out of my league here. Why don't you just tell me who did it, and then I won't have to embarrass myself by being wrong."

Creely frowned. "Well now, you have to understand. We haven't got a shred of evidence. Nothing. Zip, So we're talking strictly off the record here. If you quote me on this I'll deny it." He jerked his thumb at Davis and Chuck. "So will they."

"I understand," I said. "I wouldn't quote you to a soul. I'm in enough trouble already."

"That's for sure."

"So tell me. Who did it?"

Creely took a bite of his sandwich, chewed it, cocked his head. "Well," he said, "the way we dope it out, it's gotta be Carlton Kraswell of Trenton, New Jersey."

I stared at Creely. "What?"

"Yeah, that's the way we see it."

"Carlton Kraswell of Trenton, New Jersey?"

"Best we can tell."

I sank down into a chair. "Son of a bitch."

Creely grinned. "That surprise you?"

"It sure does."

"Oh yeah? Who did *you* think it was?"

"Carlton Kraswell of Trenton, New Jersey."

"Well, you shouldn't be so surprised. You happen to be right." Creely cocked his head at Davis and Chuck. "You get the feeling this guy ain't used to being right?"

I shook my head. Looked at Creely. "Would you mind telling me how you figure that?"

Creely shrugged. "I would assume the same way that you do. When Davis was arresting you, a car pulled into the driveway of the motel, backed right out again. Naturally, Davis caught the license number. POP-422. We ran the plates. Found out it was registered to Keven Drexel, of the Albany City Council. Julie Steinmetz was originally from Albany, which made a connection likely. So we immediately checked on the City Council to see if they had any matters pending in which Julie Steinmetz might have an interest. Her mother owns a farm up there, the new highway's going through, and the land's to be rezoned. If her mother makes out, other people don't. The people who don't are a Manhattan firm that owns the land, and the stockholder with the controlling interest in the company is Mr. Carlton Kraswell of Trenton, New Jersey."

I rubbed my head. I felt as if I were in a daze. "Would you mind if I asked you something?" I said.

"What's that?"

"How long have you known this?"

Creely shrugged. "Oh, for a while. Not the whole thing, of course. But the general idea. Let's see now, you were arrested on Friday, right? We ran the plates right away, got the lead to Keven Drexel on the City Council. But we couldn't check it out then. We were a little busy, what with you, and the bullet, and the body, and the state cops and all that. And then we were into the weekend. We didn't want to move on the City Council then, because we didn't want to make any waves. At least, not till we were sure of our ground. We let it go till Monday, when the City Hall'd be open, and we could check it out in the normal course of business.

"Meanwhile, we checked out the background. Found out we could link Julie Steinmetz with Keven Drexel from when she used to live there. They'd actually dated for a while. And, of course, we knew about her mother living there on the farm.

"Monday we checked with the City Council, found out about the highway going through, the zoning ordinance, the whole bit.

"The rest was just legwork."

It should have amused me to hear him say that. Somehow it didn't. "Tell me something," I said. "When you checked on the City Council—did you let 'em know what you were after?"

"Shit no," Creely said. "When you're messing with something political, it's a hot potato, you don't want to make any waves. Politicians are skittish, excitable, a pain in the ass. You handle 'em with kid gloves. You let 'em know what you're after, you never get what you want. And the first thing you know, someone with political pull's calling someone with enough clout to put pressure on you to back off. Then you got a real mess."

Creely shook his head. He jerked his thumb. "No, I sent Davis and Nothnagel up there in plain clothes and had them feed 'em a line. What'd you tell 'em, Davis?"

Davis took a pull on his soda. "Oh, some bullshit story. We posed as out-of-town reporters looking into a parking violation scandal."

My eyes widened. "Oh, good lord."

"What's the matter?"

"Nothing." I rubbed my head.

"Hey," Davis said. "I know it sounds stupid as hell, but it worked. The simple stuff usually does. I swear the woman never knew what we were after."

"I'm sure she didn't," I said.

"So," Creely said, "that gave us all we needed to know about the City Council. After that, we checked out the other members. Even found a guy who matches your description of the man in the check-hat. Guy by the name of Steve Fletcher."

"I see," I said. "Tell me something—these councilmen, Drexel and Fletcher—did you talk to them?"

Creely wrinkled up his nose. "Christ no. What would be

the point? They wouldn't tell us nothing, and then if it turned out they were involved, the fat would be in the fire. No, that would be stupid as hell."

"It certainly would," I said.

"Naw," Creely said. "We just poked around real quiet-like and dug out the dirt.

"Here's what we got. It turns out there's another city councilman—a Harvey Lipscomb—ever hear of him?"

"No, I haven't."

"Yeah, well other people have. The guy's got a bit of a reputation. For having his hand out, you know? You want to bribe a city councilman in Albany, Lipscomb's the man to see. So naturally we start checking up on him.

"Now at the same time we've been working from the other end, finding out who owns the property this zoning ordinance is gonna affect. We'd come up with Carlton Kraswell. When we start checking up on him it gets interesting, cause Kraswell has ties in Albany, and if we go back enough years we find we can link Kraswell with Lipscomb."

Creely had finished his lunch. He unwrapped a stick of gum and fed it into his mouth, chomped it up. "Which gave us the picture. Julie Steinmetz tried to feather her mother's nest by bribing city councilmen to change a zoning ordinance. Naturally, the first person she approached was Lipscomb. Which was too bad for her. Because Lipscomb was in bed with Kraswell, who happened to be on the other side. And who had probably already bribed him to vote the other way.

"Of course, Lipscomb wouldn't tell Julie Steinmetz this. And being bought on the other side wouldn't bother him none, either. He'd just take her money anyway, and assure her she had his vote. Then report that back to Kraswell. Probably even sell him the information.

"At which point Kraswell would go bananas. Start taking inventory. How many councilmen did he have, how many did she have, could the ones she was buying be bought back, stuff like that. What he found out wasn't reassuring. Julie Steinmetz was an attractive young woman, not above using sex to get what she wanted. He might be able to outbid her, but he couldn't outfuck her, you know what I mean?

"Well, it has to drive him crazy. The guy's sitting on all this worthless property that could be a gold mine if it weren't for some dumb cunt standing in the way.

"So he has to kill her.

"And he has to cover his tracks. So he finds some credulous P.I. stupid enough to buy his story, and frames him for the murder, figuring that way we'd never get a lead to him at all. Which might have worked, if it weren't for Davis here spotting that car pulling in."

Creely scratched his head. "Anyway, that's how we figure it. What do you think?"

I wasn't quite sure what I thought. But I sure knew how I felt. I felt, as usual, like a total asshole. I remembered what MacAullif had told me about my judgment not being so good. Well, I must say, in this case I thought he was wrong. But he wasn't, was he? I'd completely discounted the possibility of Creely solving the case. In fact, the idea had never even entered my mind. But he *had* solved it. And he'd solved it without running five hundred license plates, playing "Zelda," attending a funeral, hassling two city councilmen, and having his wife inherit a stock. He'd solved it quickly and easily, because his man Davis was a professional, who'd naturally gotten the *entire* license plate number of the car that pulled into the motel, whereas I was an amateur who could only see POP.

But that wasn't what made me an asshole. What made me an asshole, I realized, was that I had dismissed Creely from consideration, not because he looked and acted like a caricature from a movie, not because he peppered his speech with colorful epithets, not because he lied to Richard about reading me my rights, not because he struck me somehow as an unconscious parody of himself, but simply because he was an upstate cop from a small town. And without realizing it, I, in my infinite and unfounded arrogance, had fancied myself the street-smart city slicker, and Creely the hick from the sticks.

Which was devastating. I was not only an idiot, a moron, and a fool, I was also a snob and a bigot.

On the one hand, it was hard to take. On the other hand, I'm getting so used to being wrong, my personal failings should no longer surprise me.

And there was a silver lining. Creely's solving the case had exonerated me. And confirmed my own theories. Yeah, that was the way to look at it.

I turned to Creely. "So now what?"

Creely shrugged. "Aw, well, that's why we were discussing you."

"Oh?"

"Yeah, as I said, we can't prove anything."

"Yeah, well I can. This guy Kraswell happens to be the guy who told me he was Marvin Nickleson."

"You sure?"

"Absolutely. I went to Trenton and saw him myself."

Creely looked concerned. "You didn't talk to him, did you?"

"Huh-uh. I just took a look to make sure it was the same guy."

"And it was?"

"Absolutely. No question."

"And he didn't see you?"

"No."

"You sure?"

"Yeah, I'm sure."

"Good. That could have really blown it."

"Blown what?"

"Well, that's what we were talking about. Like I said, we got no proof."

I put up my hands. "Wait a minute. We're talking in circles here. I'm not following this. I just told you I can I.D. the guy."

Creely waved it away. "Right, right, as the guy who hired you to follow Julie Steinmetz. He'll say he didn't. It will be your word against his."

"Yeah, but—"

"But what? You haven't thought this out, have you? You see the guy, you say, 'hey, that's the guy,' you think that's all there is to it. You gotta think like a cop. And when you think like a cop, you gotta think like a prosecutor. Cause when we give him the evidence, he's gonna look at it and say, 'how the fuck am I gonna try this?' And you gotta have the answer." Creely shook his head. "I hand a prosecutor this case, the cocksucker's gonna chew my ass.

"And who could blame him? I mean, how'd you like to be the guy trying this case? Look what we got. We can show Julie Steinmetz was killed with a .32 caliber automatic—the bullets matched up, by the way—but it's a cold piece, stolen, no record. No way to link it up with Kraswell. We can show Julie Steinmetz had reason to want the City Council to vote one way, and Kraswell had reason to want it to vote the other way. I say we can show that, but I should say *maybe* we can show that, because you know damn well Kraswell's gonna have some slick attorney fighting like hell to keep it out. But say we can show that. That alone doesn't link him to the crime. What does? You. We gotta put you on the stand, let you tell your story."

Creely rolled his eyes. "Jesus Christ, the prosecutor's gonna love *that.* I mean, assuming you can tell the story straight without sounding like a total moron—and that's a big if—well then, Kraswell's attorney's gonna cross-examine you. That's a scene I'd almost like to see, if I didn't happen to be on the other side. When he starts in on the Monica Dorlanders and Marvin Nicklesons, you're gonna look like an idiot, the press is gonna be in hysterics, and the jury's gonna be so damn confused they won't know which end is up.

"Then the guy's gonna be able to show the murder weapon was found in your car. At that point, if there's one person on the jury that believes you, I miss my bet."

Creely shook his head. "If it goes like that, I doubt if Kraswell ever has to take the stand at all. But if he does, he simply says he doesn't know what you're talking about and he never saw you before in his life. And the smug son of a bitch is probably smooth enough to get away with it."

Creely threw up his hands. "And there you are. Your honor, I rest my case. Would you like to send the jury out of the room to confer, or you wanna just let 'em say 'not guilty' now?"

I took a breath. "So what you gonna do?"

"Well," Creely said, "that's why we were discussing you."

"Me?"

"Yeah, you. Cause you're the one who met this guy. You now confirm he was the guy. If we believe you, he's guilty, and we do believe you."

"So?"

"So we need to prove it."

"Why do I get the feeling we're talking in circles again?"

Creely chuckled and shook his head. "Well, we are now, aren't we? I know why that is. Cause I'm leading up to something, and I don't expect you to be particularly pleased."

I'm afraid I laughed.

"What's so funny?"

"Is there *anything* about this case that should make me particularly pleased?"

"You should be pleased you're not charged with murder."

"There is that. All right, what do you want?"

"I want to nail Kraswell. To do it I need your help."

"And I'm not going to like it?"

"I think it would be safe to say that."

"So what's the pitch?"

"All right," Creely said. "We can't nail Kraswell by any ordinary means. We have to pull a scam on him."

"What kind of a scam?"

"We gotta set him up, and you're the one who's gotta do it. To do it, you're gonna have to play a part. You ever done any acting?"

"I used to be an actor."

"Oh, really? That'll help." Creely cocked his head. "This part may be a bit of a stretch for you, though."

"Oh yeah? What do I have to play."

"An inept detective."

37

I staked out Kraswell's house at seven in the morning, just like Creely told me to. I wasn't wearing a wire—I wanted to, but Creely wouldn't go for it. My idea was to talk to Kraswell wearing a wire and get him to make a damaging admission. Creely's idea was I didn't have the brains to pull it off. Which really didn't seem fair. I mean, after all, I'd found the guy, hadn't I? And I'd trapped a killer once before wearing a wire, and that had gone all right. And in this case it should have been even easier. Because I had to be the last person in the world Kraswell wanted to see. If I walked up to him, he'd have to say something, and whatever it was, it was bound to be damn interesting. It seemed to me there was no way it couldn't work.

Only Creely wouldn't go for it. And as MacAullif said, Creely was in charge. So there I was, stymied. Creely and I batted it around for a while, and neither one of us was particularly happy, but the end result was we finally made a deal.

We didn't agree to it there and then, and I didn't come to it all by myself either. First I went and consulted with

Richard, and then I went and consulted with my wife, and we all talked it over and batted it back and forth, and finally we came up with a deal. Then I went back and laid it on Creely, and he wasn't that happy about it, but he wasn't that unhappy either, which was about how I felt, and the long and the short of it was we made a deal and I wound up staking out Kraswell's house at seven in the morning, according to Creely's plan.

Creely's plan was simple and straightforward. I was to put Kraswell under surveillance and follow him everywhere he went until he spotted me doing it. At that point I was to report to Creely that I had been made. Then I was to continue following Kraswell until he managed to elude my surveillance and began backtracking me.

Which Creely was sure he'd do. Because, Creely figured, by playing it that way, Kraswell would take me for a meddling private detective, working on his own to solve the case ahead of the bumbling cops. That, coupled with the fact that I was the only one who could identify him as the man who had posed as Marvin Nickleson, would convince Kraswell that the only way he could be really safe was by eliminating me. He would then attempt to do so, and Creely would catch him at it. And having tried to murder me, Kraswell would have a slightly harder time selling the jury on the fact he'd never seen me before in his life.

That was Creely's plan, and for obvious reasons I didn't like it, but I'd agreed to it, so here I was, staking out Kraswell's house, just as I'd done before. And as before, there was no sign of life but for the car in the drive.

Along about eight o'clock people started coming out of other houses, getting in their cars and driving off. But not Kraswell. Some of the people were eyeing me kind of funny as they drove by, and I wondered what would happen if one of them called the cops. Creely was working with the Jersey cops, of course, or we couldn't have done this at all, but he was dealing with the big boys in homicide. A radio patrol cop wouldn't have a clue. And if one showed up to check me out, it was gonna be a mess. And if Kraswell spotted him doing it, the game would be up. In that case, it wasn't my plan, it was Creely's plan, so it would be his fault. But that would be small consolation what with a murderer going free, and me stuck on the hook for obstruction of justice. So I sure hoped a patrol car wouldn't show up.

None did.

But then neither did Kraswell. Ten o'clock, eleven o'clock, still no sign.

He was out at eleven-fifteen.

It was a nice sunny day and it had warmed up considerably, probably somewhere in the forties, and Kraswell looked dapper and spiffy with a light topcoat open over his three-piece suit. He got in the Mercedes and pulled out. I gave him a little lead and pulled out after him.

I'd had a long discussion with Creely about letting Kraswell spot me. I figured I could do it easily by just following a little too close. Creely wouldn't hear of it. Said anything that obvious would tip Kraswell off. Creely felt my surveillance of Kraswell should be absolutely normal and routine. That I should, in fact, do my best *not* to let him know he was being followed. If I did that, Creely said, he'd spot me all right.

At first I thought Creely was just being sarcastic. When it turned out he was dead serious, it didn't do much for my ego.

But that's the way I'd agreed to play it, so that's what I did. I stayed far enough behind that Kraswell shouldn't get suspicious, but close enough that I shouldn't lose him. I followed him through a series of turns, wondering where the hell we were going.

We were going to the supermarket.

Kraswell pulled into a big parking lot in front of an A&P, parked the Mercedes, and went in.

Well, hot damn. Do I follow him in? What's normal routine on this one?

I thought it over, and figured in the course of normal routine I wouldn't give a damn what Kraswell did in the supermarket and I'd wait for him outside, so that's what I did.

He was out in twenty minutes with a couple of bags of groceries. He loaded them into the Mercedes and drove off.

I followed him home. He parked the Mercedes, took out the groceries, and went into his house.

I resumed my position on the corner.

I had a few choice thoughts about the effectiveness of Creely's plan.

Kraswell was out again by twelve-thirty. I followed him through a series of turns onto Route 29, and got off again somewhere downtown. A few more turns and Kraswell pulled into a municipal garage. I gave him half a minute head start and pulled in too. I twisted around and around and spotted Kraswell catching a parking space on level three. I whizzed on by and got my own spot on level four. I left the car and sprinted down the ramp just in time to see Kraswell disappear into a stairwell at the far corner of the garage. I hotfooted it over there and followed him down the stairs.

I came out into daylight, looked around and saw him walking down the street half a block away. I followed him, not too close, not too far. Jesus Christ, what the hell is routine, anyway? What a hell of an assignment. Act normal. That's like act casual. Can't be done. What the hell is normal, and how the hell do you simulate that?

Kraswell walked up a block and turned left on State Street, which sounded promising.

It was. After a few blocks the street widened, and we

came upon massive stone structures that could only be government buildings. In fact, the first one had a sign out in front of it that said, STATE HOUSE. I was disappointed at first when Kraswell walked right by it, but when I got a little closer I saw the sign actually read, STATE HOUSE RENOVATIONS IN PROGRESS: LEGISLATURE MEETS IN ANNEX. The next big stone building said, ANNEX, and Kraswell went in there.

I did too, from a normally discreet distance, which was a bit hard to determine since it was a U-shaped building—or since it wasn't curved I should say a double-L-shaped building—with the entrance set way back from the street so you had to walk into it between the double-Ls. Which left you trapped there, in case the guy you were tailing happened to turn around.

Kraswell didn't. He just went right in the front door. I quickened my pace and got there just in time to see him walk through the small lobby and step into an elevator.

All right. That decision I could handle. Under normal routine surveillance, I didn't take that elevator.

I stood there looking stupid and watching the elevator indicator, which stopped on three. Which might or might not have meant anything, cause it could have been Kraswell getting off or it could have been someone else getting on. But what the hell, I figured routine surveillance might be to check it out. When the next elevator arrived I took it up to three and found myself in a long hallway with a lot of closed doors and no sign of Kraswell, nothing to choose from.

I took the elevator back down, went out and staked out the State House Annex from across the street.

Kraswell was out in about fifteen minutes with a well-dressed, portly gentleman, probably, I figured, uncharitably, a senator or assemblyman Kraswell wished to bribe. They came out and walked back down the street the way

Kraswell had come. I tailed them from across the street and half a block behind. That seemed as normal as I could get, not knowing what normal really was.

They walked a few blocks, went into a small restaurant, and proceeded to have lunch. I stayed outside getting hungry and waiting for them to come out, perfectly normal there.

They split up after lunch and Kraswell headed back for the garage. I tagged along. Kraswell took the stair. I followed a flight behind. I took the last flight of steps two at a time, ran to my car, started the engine, nosed down the ramp, and waited for the Mercedes to pull out ahead of me. It did and I followed, always one floor behind. I waited up the ramp until Kraswell paid his ticket, and I saw which way he turned. He pulled out and I pulled up fast, paid my ticket, and took off after him. I caught him in three blocks, dropped back to a safe distance behind.

We took Route 29 again, followed a by-now familiar route through a couple of turns and home.

Kraswell parked the Mercedes in the drive, locked it, opened his door and went inside.

And that was it. After that he stayed put. He didn't go out, and no one went in.

By the time five o'clock rolled around, absolutely nothing else had happened. That was the time Creely had told me to pack it in, so I started the car, pulled out, and drove around till I found a pay phone. I took out my notebook, looked up the number Creely'd given me, and punched it in.

Two rings and a voice said, "Yeah?"

"Stanley Hastings, reporting in."

The voice said, "Just a minute," and I was on hold.

It was closer to two minutes. Then a voice said, "Hastings? How'd it go?"

"Creely?"

"Yeah."

"What are you doing here?"

"What, you think I got some case more important than this? What's the story?"

"It's a washout."

"He didn't go out?"

"Yeah. He went out twice. Once to the supermarket and once to the State Capitol."

"And what did he do?"

"First time he bought groceries. Second time he had lunch with someone."

"Who?"

"I don't know. Guy in a suit. Probably a senator or assemblyman or something. Met him at the State House, they went out for lunch. After that he went home and stayed put."

"O.K. Good work."

"Good work, hell. It's a washout."

"Why is it a washout?"

"Cause he didn't spot me."

"You sure of that?"

"Absolutely. And he's not gonna, either. You got to let me crowd him."

"No way. Don't even think that."

"If I don't this is never gonna work."

"You're wrong. This the *only* way it's gonna work. You try it your way, you blow it. You blow it for you, you blow it for me. You blow it for me, I'm history. So you don't try it, you got that?"

I took a breath. "Yeah."

"Fine. You did good. He didn't spot you today, you hang it up, you try again tomorrow. Don't worry so much. You're doing good."

The phone clicked dead.

I looked at it a moment before hanging up. Doing good,

was I? I wondered what it felt like to do bad.

I hung up the phone, got back in the car. Creely'd had me make a reservation at a downtown hotel, just in case. I'd been hoping I wouldn't have to use it, but I guess I should have known better. I drove over there, registered, and went up to my room, which was as drab and cheerless as I'd expected.

I called Alice and told her what had happened, or rather what hadn't. She was sympathetic and supportive as could be, but somehow it didn't help. I was really bummed out.

I went down to the lobby, had an overpriced and undistinguished meal in the hotel dining room, bought a paper to check out the movies, didn't see anything I felt like going to enough to hassle with finding out where they were, went back up to my room and watched TV.

When eleven o'clock rolled around I found out Trenton's local news wasn't any more inspiring than Poughkeepsie's. I stayed awake through Johnny Carson's monologue, then switched the set off and went to sleep.

I woke up to the sound of a key sliding into the lock.

38

This was it. Suddenly, unexpectedly, from out of left field, it was happening here and now. Creely was right and I was wrong, and his plan had worked after all, and I was an incompetent detective ("The Number One Answer!"), and despite my best efforts, Carlton Kraswell had spotted me anyway, and backtracked me to the hotel, and here he was coming in the door, and the plan had worked, only I'd told the cops it hadn't and called them off, and now they were nowhere around, and here was Carlton Kraswell coming in to kill me.

As I said, I don't wake up well under the best of circumstances. I tend to be groggy and confused, and have trouble getting my bearings. With a murderer coming in the door, the problem escalates. Holy shit, what do I do now?

Well, Carlton Kraswell was a shrimp and I'm nearly six feet tall, but I can't fight to save my life, which is what we're talking about here, and I'm unarmed and the son of a bitch was bound to have a gun, and guns reduce me to jelly.

Round One to Kraswell.

I'm wide awake, skip the coffee, I'll just get up without it. I'm sure a shot of adrenaline will do.

The sound of the key turning in the lock provided that.

I slid out of bed. I was sleeping in my underwear. Momma says always wear clean underwear, you never know when you're gonna get hit by a truck. Or shot. Actually, my mom never said anything like that, but that's the way the old saw goes. Or was it clean socks?

Who cares? Schmuck. What you gonna do?

No place to run, no place to hide.

Except the bathroom. I darted for it on little cat feet. Sprang inside.

Just as the door swung open.

Shit. Too late. He knows you're there. So what? You think he wouldn't find you in the bathroom?

I slammed the door. Is there a lock? Can't see, it's dark, should I risk a light?

No. No lock. But my hand, groping for it, touched the knob.

Which started to turn.

I grabbed it, hung on for dear life.

There. I'm bigger, I'm stronger, he can't turn it.

Wrong again. False premise. It's easier to turn a doorknob than it is to hold it still.

The knob was turning. This way, that way, a little more, back and forth—

Click!

He'd done it. And now he was heaving his weight, what there was of it, against the door. I pushed back, but Jesus Christ, the door is moving! That little shrimp must really want to kill me bad.

I heaved back, put my whole weight into it, gained an inch or two back.

Paranoid-Flash-Number-907: what if he starts shooting through the door?

He didn't. He just heaved furiously with a burst that gained a little ground, and I heaved back and he heaved again, and I gave a giant lunge with all my weight and the door slammed shut.

I grabbed for the knob again.

But it didn't turn.

Instead there was a knock on the door.

A knock? ("Knock knock." "Who's there?" "Carlton." "Carlton who?" "Carlton Kumta-kilya.")

A voice said, "Hastings. Open up." A familiar voice. A voice affecting a high-pitched Southern drawl.

I opened the door.

The lights were on. Chief Creely was standing there. Two Jersey cops were holding a handcuffed Carlton Kraswell.

I turned to Creely. "How the hell'd you get here?"

Creely grinned. "You kidding? You think I'd take your word for anything? You tell me he didn't spot you, it's odds-on he did. Lucky for us he didn't spot the two cops that were tailing him too."

"You had cops on him all the time?"

"Yeah."

"You didn't tell me that."

"No. You'd have looked for them." He jerked his thumb at Kraswell. "Probably tipped him off to them too."

I looked at Kraswell. "He have a gun?"

"Oh yeah." Creely jerked his thumb again, and one of the cops held up a plastic evidence bag. "Didn't think he'd take on a big bad dude like you with his bare hands, did you? Naw, he was armed and we got him dead to rights."

"Then we have our deal?"

"Well, I could penalize you for telling us the guy wasn't wise, but basically I'm just a nice guy."

Creely turned to the Jersey cops. "O.K., boys, before you

run him in, we give this joker five minutes in return for his almost getting killed."

One of the cops said, "That's irregular as all hell."

"Ain't it now?" Creely said. "But on the other hand, who gives a shit?" He jerked his thumb at Kraswell. "This joker's got the right to remain silent, but that don't mean he can't listen." He turned to me. "All right. You're on."

This was it. My big scene. I was gonna have to play it in my underwear, but what the hell, you gotta work with what you got.

I grabbed my briefcase, threw it on the bed, and popped it open. I reached in and pulled out a stack of papers, computer printouts I'd had Alice make me. I took them, marched up to Carlton Kraswell, and stuck my finger in his face.

"You're busted for murder. But that's the least of your troubles." I thrust the papers at him. "You know what this is? It's a bill for my services. You hired me to do a job for you, I did it, and now you're gonna pay. I talked to my lawyer about it, and he says there's no question. All the work I've done in this case was a direct result of representations made by you. Now those representations happen to be false, but that does not relieve you of responsibility, or in any way alter the validity of our oral contract. You're responsible for everything, up to and including my being here today. These bills come to a total of four thousand, four hundred and twenty-seven dollars and thirty-two cents. The reason there's so many is, I billed you individually, so I could break 'em down into lots of less than fifteen hundred dollars each, which means I can take you to small claims court. Which means I can make you pay 'em without even having to hire a lawyer. Though if it came to that, my attorney would be happy to oblige. But he says there's no question—four thousand, four hundred and twenty-seven dollars and thirty-two cents, and you're gonna have to pay.

"Which is kind of interesting, don't you think? Cause you're probably the first murderer in history who ever hired a private detective to help catch him. You can think about that while you're in jail."

I turned to Creely. "Chief, this is a great pleasure. Allow me to introduce you to Carlton Kraswell, alias Marvin Nickleson." I turned, gestured to Kraswell, smiled and said, with considerable satisfaction, "My client."

That more or less wrapped things up. The cops took Kraswell into custody and we all moseyed down to the police station and the Jersey cops charged Kraswell with the attempted murder of me, and Creely charged Kraswell with the murder of Julie Steinmetz, and Kraswell called his attorney, who turned out to be as slick and slippery a shyster as one would have expected, and he showed up and started screaming entrapment and frame-up and police corruption, and Creely started talking about instituting extradition proceedings, and the lawyer started talking about fighting them, and the Jersey cops started talking about which crime took precedence, and Kraswell, who'd been advised by his attorney to remain silent, just sat there tugging at his moustache, and aside from him, all of them seemed happy as clams because it was just business as usual and they were getting on with it.

Somewhere in all that the cops took my statement and after that I was free to go, and before I knew it there I was, driving up the New Jersey Turnpike through the early morning rush hour traffic just like some damn commuter and just as if the whole thing had never happened.

But it *had* happened, every bit of it. And by and large, I had to admit I was pretty pleased with the way it had turned out.

Which bothered me. Being pleased with it, I mean. Cause the thing is, I realized what I was pleased about.

I suppose I could be proud of my accomplishments. After all, it had been my first real client, my first professional case. And I'd been lied to, cheated and framed. And despite that, I'd managed to plow through the bullshit, sort out the facts, deduce what had happened, and find the killer. Maybe not as quickly and easily as the professionals had, but I'd still done it. Which had to be encouraging to a man in my position. Which had to give me reason for being pleased.

But that wasn't it, and I knew it. No, by and large, I had to admit, the thing that pleased me most about the whole affair was the prospect of having Carlton Kraswell pay me my fee.

Which bothered me a lot.

You have to understand, I'm a product of the sixties. And if you grew up in the sixties, you've got a lot of problems in this day and age. For one thing, you're getting old. For another thing, you got a legacy from your childhood that's sometimes hard to live with. For example, it's embarrassing to be part of a generation that screamed, "Make Love, Not War," only to find out twenty years later with the advent of AIDS, that making love may kill more people than making war ever did. And it's hard to emerge from that psychedelic culture into the modern world of crack and death, and find yourself with kids of your own, for whom you're fighting a valiant struggle to try to teach them to Just Say No. Different times, different values.

Yeah, values, that's what it's all about.

Value.

Money.

When I went to college, none of us studied business administration. Few of us went to med or law school, either. Liberal arts, that was where it was at. Fine arts. And no crass commercialism, either. Art for art's sake. No, I'm not a money-grubbing industrialist. I'm an actor, a poet, a prophet, a writer, a sage.

Plans for the future? What future? I don't trust anyone over thirty, so I'm never gonna *be* over thirty, right? The Peter Pan generation. I won't grow up.

Rude awakenings.

Yeah, you get older and things change, and you find you have more and more regrets. And you wonder how many of them are just because you're getting old. And then you start to question your own motives and values and feelings.

Like my zinging Keven Drexel in the bar. That was, I must admit, a wholly gratuitous exercise that had absolutely nothing to do with my investigation. And I have to ask myself, did I do it because the smug son of a bitch was a sleazy bribe-taking scum who deserved the comeuppance, or did I do it merely because I'm a middle-aged family man who can't buy sanitary napkins without blushing, and he's a handsome young stud, and I couldn't resist popping him one in front of his flashy blonde?

And then there's Alice. I think of Alice and I feel bad too, cause I realize I've done an injustice there. Because Alice's work on the computer is important to her, and I should take an interest. And looking at it rationally, I know that selling computer programs at seventy-five bucks a pop is just pie in the sky, and isn't going to get us rich any more than printing résumés at ten cents a page, and it's wrong for me to be more interested in one because it sounds more lucrative than the other. And even if it was, that shouldn't matter, I should be supporting her in any case. And yet for all that, here I am, a crass, capitalistic moron, whose interest picked up immensely when she mentioned seventy-five bucks.

And it bothers me that I ride the subway and am annoyed by homeless beggars, and then get home to find my wife has received a dividend check. And what bothers me is the fact that it doesn't bother me, that I accept these things as a matter of course. And I have to ask myself, Jesus Christ, how far has this hippie from the sixties come?

And I don't really know. The word liberal doesn't embarrass me the way it embarrassed Dukakis, but as I get older and try to raise my family and make it in the outside world, I have to stop and look around every now and then and wonder just how hypocritical I am. I think I still have the same values that I had back then, back in the Age of Innocence, the age of peace marches and brotherhood, the age of Beatles and Dylan, the age of youth. It's just the money thing that gets in the way.

So it bothers me, the satisfaction I get out of the Marvin Nickleson/Carlton Kraswell thing. Out of having had my first real paying client. And the thing is, despite how badly the whole thing went, despite being lied to, set up, framed, arrested, cheated, squeezed and mooched, I have a feeling if another chance came along for me to make two hundred bucks a day plus expenses, I'd probably jump at it.

And it bothers me that I feel that way. And I question my motives and I question my values, and I try to justify my feelings, and all in all I have to admit, no matter how hard I try to rationalize, the fact is I can't do it. In point of fact, I have no excuse.

But I have bad teeth.